T0028920

THE
SALT-BLACK
TREE

BOOKS BY LILITH SAINTCROW

THE DEAD GOD'S HEART

Spring's Arcana
The Salt-Black Tree

DANTE VALENTINE

Working for the Devil
Dead Man Rising
The Devil's Right Hand
Saint City Sinners
To Hell and Back
Dante Valentine: The Complete Series

JILL KISMET

Night Shift
Hunter's Prayer
Redemption Alley
Flesh Circus
Heaven's Spite
Angel Town

BANNON & CLARE

The Iron Wyrm Affair
The Red Plague Affair
The Ripper Affair

GALLOW & RAGGED

Trailer Park Fae
Roadside Magic
Wasteland King

Afterwar
Cormorant Run

THE SALT-BLACK TREE

LILITH SAINTCROW

TOR

TOR PUBLISHING GROUP

NEW YORK

This is a work of fiction. All of the characters, organizations, and events portrayed in this novel are either products of the author's imagination or are used fictitiously.

THE SALT-BLACK TREE

Copyright © 2023 by Lilith Saintcrow

All rights reserved.

Map by Jon Lansberg

A Tor Book
Published by Tom Doherty Associates / Tor Publishing Group
120 Broadway
New York, NY 10271

www.tor-forge.com

Tor® is a registered trademark of Macmillan Publishing Group, LLC.

The Library of Congress Cataloging-in-Publication Data is available upon request.

ISBN 978-1-250-79156-6 (trade paperback)
ISBN 978-1-250-79155-9 (hardcover)
ISBN 978-1-250-79158-0 (ebook)

Our books may be purchased in bulk for promotional, educational, or business use. Please contact your local bookseller or the Macmillan Corporate and Premium Sales Department at 1-800-221-7945, extension 5442, or by email at MacmillanSpecialMarkets@macmillan.com.

First Edition: 2023

Printed in the United States of America

0 9 8 7 6 5 4 3 2 1

For Claire and Lucienne,
who believed more than enough

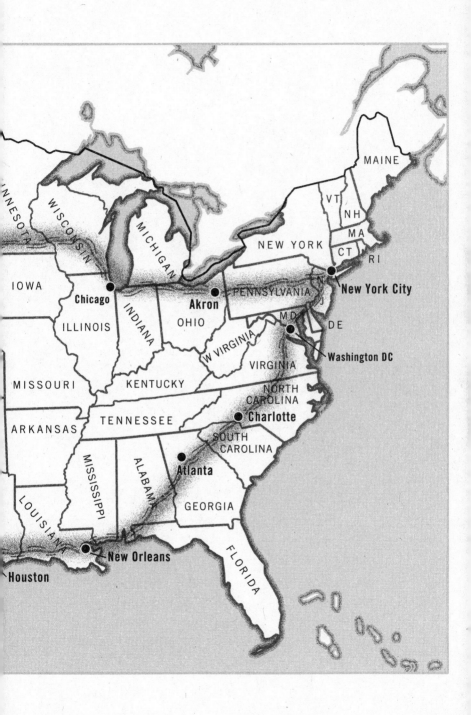

NOTE

The reader is presumed to have read Book One of this duology; otherwise, certain matters may be completely opaque.

It should also be mentioned that the divinities described herein travel the human world much differently than humans do, and may or may not have an independent existence since they are, after all, shapechangers like every other endless, eternal thing—mortal souls included.

Belief is strange, is it not? And very powerful . . .

. . . we live by mythologies.

—Anaïs Nin

THE
CHARIOT

ENTIRELY DIFFERENT

The ride back to Ranger's was a bone-jarring gallop, the black horse slipping and sliding, melting into a motorcycle at odd moments, throwing itself across small streams once the desert faded and they were back in rolling winter prairie again. The sun was a low bloody coin disappearing behind distant bruise-shadows of western mountains, and Nat Drozdova was fully occupied clinging to reins or clutching handlebars, her shoulders aching every time the big beast veered. Sparks struck from its iron-clawed shoes sent up tiny acrid puffs—very possibly brimstone, though she'd never smelled it before—and she was sure it was doubling back once or twice, running alongside a deep, swift, cold stream chuckling with sharp menace.

Just waiting for her grip to loosen. Just waiting for her to fall.

Sheets of icy water thrown up on either side, her tailbone bruised as the beast landed stiff-legged, bolts of pain zipping up her back, her teeth clicking painfully together over and over again—even the worst bus ride was a cakewalk compared to this. No fluid union, no sense of connected togetherness, just an endless rattling, jarring, thumping as her head bobbled and she clamped her knees to elastic, heaving sides.

Finally, the song of hooves rang on concrete instead of dirt and rock; Nat was almost tossed from the saddle as the horse shook himself angrily, shrinking into a motorcycle again. His whinny became a scream of defiance, but Nat's fingers had cramp-tangled in the reins and her knees, while numb, still stuck like glue to his sides. He rattled over washboard road at a punishing pace, pavement breaking away on either side in great frost-heaved chunks; nobody had driven here for a very long time.

Icy wind roared, stinging her face, and instead of too hot and sweaty in a magical desert, she was now miserably cold. The motorcycle-horse screamed, shaking his head again as his mane whipped, stinging her hands, but Nat held on.

There was no other choice.

Finally there was a long rubber-smoking howl as he swelled into horse-shape once more, a jolting as if the entire motorcycle would shake itself to pieces as it shifted back, and a billow of nasty black smoke. The world shuddered to a stop and Nat let out a surprised cry, saved only from a girlish scream by the fact that there was no air left in her lungs to fuel it. Westering orange sunlight escaping under a long low band of snow-bearing clouds filled her eyes, and there was a shout.

"*Hi* there, you bastard!" It was Ranger in his fringed dun rancher's jacket; the Black man darted close and grabbed at the horse's bridle. "Ain't no way to treat a lady, you just *mind* yourself now."

Oh, thank goodness. I'm back. Nat couldn't make her fingers unclench. The reins swelled and stiffened into handlebars once more; the engine's choppy growl smoothed out and died with a resentful rumble. Fitful warmth returned, her entire body ached, and she couldn't *wait* to have her boots on solid ground again.

But she was no thief, and had forced this thing—whatever it was—to bring her back. As bad as the ride had been, she suspected accepting its offer to show her "shortcuts" would be even worse.

"Get her off," Ranger snapped. "Oh, you sumbitch, thought you'd take the long way home, did you? None of that now."

Another tooth-snapping sound cut cold air; Nat flinched.

Every girl loves horses, yes, but this thing was only horse-*like*. The shape didn't make it as advertised; whatever was trapped in its galloping, restless body wouldn't have hesitated to shake her free in the middle of a river, or while it galloped across the shimmering surface of a winter pond.

And then, those teeth—not the blunt herbivore-seeming ones, but the other set—would close around whatever mouthful it could grab. Or so her imagination informed her, and Nat Drozdova was very sure whatever she could imagine was far less awful than the truth.

For once.

Ranger made a swift movement, his brown fist pistoning out, a bright golden flashgleam lingering over knuckles. There was a crunch, and the horse's growl cut off cleanly. "I said *mind*," the cowboy continued, mildly enough, but his dove-gray hat was slightly awry, his hazel eyes blazed, and if he ever looked at *her* like that, Nat's heart might well stop. "And get her off there, horsethief!"

"Don't shout at me, *kovboyski*." Dmitri Konets sounded just the same, and Nat's fingers finally creaked open enough to slide free of solid, chilly metal handlebars. The gangster's hair was a wild mess instead of slicked back, his black eyes burned with carnivorous glee, and even though he might very well murder her sometime in the very near future he was still familiar, and Nat was almost glad to see him. "Eh, *zaika moya*, have fun? Should've let me drive."

"Th-th-that w-w-wasn't . . ." Her teeth chattered, chopping every word into bits. *That wasn't part of the deal.*

"I know." He dragged her free of the motorcycle, his lean tanned hands strangely gentle; Ranger had the handlebars now and pulled the resisting hunk of glossy black metal, silver springs, wheels, and still-grumbling engine towards the barn. The porch light of Ranger's trim blue ranch-style house was on, a golden beacon, and more incandescent light spilled through the half-open barn doors. The cold was even worse now that they'd stopped, which shouldn't have been possible; the warmth in Nat's core fought a frigid blanket.

"Breathe." Dmitri held her up, coiled strength belied by his leanness; Nat's legs wouldn't quite work. "That's it, nice and easy. Take drink."

There was a chill metallic tap at her chin; the gangster tipped a mouthful from a dull silver hip flask past her lips. Nat spluttered; the liquid burned like vodka and most of it went straight down her throat without so much as a hello, a nova exploding inside her ribs. The heat was amazing, tropical, and very welcome; she decided she liked temperate zones better than desert or this winter prairie bullshit. Going from winter to summer and back again couldn't be good for your immune system.

Did divinities get colds? Did they need flu shots? There were so many questions, and nobody she could trust to answer them.

Nat went limp, every bone inside her aching flesh quivering at a slightly different rate. Her forehead rested against Dima's shoulder; the flask vanished, and he dug for something else in his pockets. His arm was a steel bar holding her upright, and that unhealthy, unsteady heat blazed from his jacket and jeans like a gasoline-greased pile of burning tires sending great gouts of black smoke heavenward.

"There," he crooned, with lunatic calm. "Hush now, little *zaika-zaya, krasotka moya*." He was stiff-tense as if ready for a punch or some other violence, but Nat was too tired—and too glad to be stationary—to care much. "Eh, Cowboy? They gathering again."

"I know." Ranger sounded grim. "Where the hell did you run to, horse?"

"*Silly girl,*" the horse replied, its voice full of shrapnel and burning oil. He made a low, shuddering, grinding moan, a motorcycle's various metal joints resisting. "*I offered her shortcuts. Stupid, silly girl.*"

"For the love of . . ." Ranger sighed. There was a creak, another sharp thump—sounded like he'd punched metal. "That girl ain't no horsethief. You and your mischief; I swear I'm half ready to remake you."

"*Go ahead*." The beast was completely unrepentant. "*You'll never have a faster horse*."

Ranger muttered a blistering obscenity, and for once didn't follow it up with a *pardon my French*. "Curses work both ways."

Whatever Dima had forced down her throat worked wonders, or maybe Nat was stronger than she thought. In any case, she found her legs would finally work again, pain receded like the tide going out on a pebbled beach, and she pushed ineffectually at the gangster's disconcertingly broad chest. "I'm all r-r-right." Even the teeth-chattering was going down.

A dark line showed high on Dmitri's left cheek. It looked like a knife-cut, but there was no blood, just flesh swiftly sealing itself back together. The sun's bleary red eye slipped behind distant, serrated mountains, and a crackling-cold wind brushed over Ranger's house. There was an uneasy mutter from the barn, animals moving; Nat shuddered.

What else did he have in there, next to the big black motorcycle-horse? She found she didn't want to know; there was a limit to even *her* curiosity. Go figure, adulthood was 40 percent figuring things out for yourself, with another 40 percent of avoiding knowledge that might drive you crazy.

Not that she had far to go to reach that state. The remaining 20 percent of being grown-up was probably taxes and approaching mortality, though the idea of Uncle Sam pursuing Dmitri Konets for not filing a return was bleakly hilarious.

Was there an Uncle Sam? She'd probably find out, if this kept up.

"You came back." Dmitri tucked his chin slightly, peering into her face. A flush of effort pinkened his cheeks, and his black suit was a bit rumpled. Had he and Ranger got into a fight?

I don't care. Nat supposed she looked a little worse for wear, too. *I just want to go home.*

But that wasn't quite accurate, Nat discovered. The thought of going back to her mother's little yellow house, halfway across the continent on South Aurora Avenue in Brooklyn, was even more unappetizing than riding Ranger's predatory magical horse.

Nat's backpack, warm and heavy, finally settled against her shoulders like it was relieved to be off the carnival ride as well. It was the closest thing to "home" she had now, smaller and far more bedraggled than a snail's spiraling domicile.

"I don't w-want to be a h-h-horsethief," Nat managed. Her throat was so dry the words were husks of themselves, left propped and forgotten in a field while a faded scarecrow leered from a listing pole.

Dima's faint flush drained away, and his jaw hardened. "No other way to get what you want, *Drozdova*. Not when rich bastards sit on it."

Oh, so you're a real Robin Hood. Go figure, twenty seconds in his presence again and she was already irritated. The sharp unsteady feeling was a tonic, filling her with fresh strength, and her legs felt more like her own usual bodily possessions now instead of just insensate noodles. "I'm h-happy to s-see you too."

Ranger reappeared, swinging the barn door closed; Dmitri stepped away from Nat like she was carrying something fatally communicable. She swayed, but the steady fire in her chest poured strength through the rest of her. The sense of deep, inalienable energy filled her again, and she wondered if she looked burningly vital, impossibly *real*, like the two men.

The two *divinities.*

"Sorry about that." Ranger's iron-toed cowboy boots ground icy gravel as he hurried towards her; he could probably crack a boulder by kicking it. "You did right well, Nat. He just takes some gettin' used to, that beast."

So I gathered. And even if she liked the cowboy, even if he said he liked her more than her mother, he still hadn't warned her that the horse—or whatever it was, trapped in a shapeshifting body—was very strong, not to mention wholly murderous. "It's all right." There was nothing else to say.

The Black man's fringed jacket was torn, too, and Nat was abruptly tired of men and their squabbles. Even if she didn't agree with Mom on everything, Maria Drozdova's frequent assertion that males were saved only from being more dangerous by their unending stupidity held a great deal of water.

"No, it ain't." Ranger glanced over her shoulder, his sculpted mouth tightening. "Y'all better go. I'll do what I can, horsethief."

"I could call you something worse," Dima muttered, and jabbed his left hand at the glossy black muscle car crouched leonine before the ranch house's stairs. His right, Nat saw with a sinking sensation, was full of that same dull-black gun he'd had before, except with no long silhouette of a silencer. "Come, *zaika*. Into car we go."

Wait a second. "I—what *happened*?" Nat shuddered; the bright white vapor of her breath shivered and plummeted, thin ice breaking on hard ground with a soft musical noise. "What the hell?"

"Oh, naw." Ranger shrugged, a loose easy motion, and stretched his neck, tilting his head from one side to the other. His lean, capable right hand rested on a revolver butt, slung hip-low on his broad leather belt; the matching gun on his other side gleamed secretively from its well-worn holster. "Hell's entirely different, ma'am, pardon my French. You go on now. Come back and visit anytime."

Yeah, not so sure I want to, now. Nat summoned a polite, weary shadow of a smile, and tacked unevenly for the black car. Dmitri walked backward, placing each foot with a cat's finicky delicacy, and Ranger's boots made soft stealthy sounds as he set off in a different direction.

Towards the road, not his house. Maybe they hadn't been

fighting each other at all. The wind was knifelike, her breath froze as it left her mouth, and though Nat had quickly grown used to not feeling the weather, she shivered.

"*Potoropis*." Dmitri peered past her, his black eyes narrowed and his lip lifting slightly. Strong white teeth gleamed, and though his snarl wasn't directed at her, it still sent a shudder down her back. "Quickly, *devotchka*. Not many left, but always more come."

Well, that's not terrifying or anything. Nat's boots were almost too heavy to lift; her backpack now weighed a ton. Even the stealthy, hidden glow of the Cup and the black-bladed Knife in its depths wasn't comforting. "More what?" *The starving things, of course. Great. Fantastic.*

"You didn't tell her?" Ranger laughed, every scrap of warmth gone and his voice cold as the gangster's. "'Course not, why am I surprised? Get gone, I'll keep your trail clear as I can."

Dima swore, lifting the gun. Its muzzle pointed past Nat, carefully not *at* her, but she still hurried, not liking how big and bottomless the hole at the end seemed.

Like the Well, only without the quicksilver glitter in its throat.

She skirted the black car; its engine throbbed into life and she flinched, letting out a small hurt sound. Suddenly its interior seemed like an old friend she couldn't wait to meet again, but she paused at the open passenger door, the dome light sending a distorted golden rectangle onto the pavement, touching the edge of the porch's wooden stairs.

There was very little twilight on the prairie in winter; day ended like a descending guillotine blade out here. Glimmering stars, peeking through dusk's veil, were snuffed behind a lowering sky pregnant with fresh snow. Nat tasted the penny-metal of approaching precipitation, and a tiny, cold flake kissed her cheek.

Dark shapes, gleaming slightly, clustered a fair ways from Ranger; behind them, the driveway warped like the glimmer over hot pavement on a blinding summer day. Nat's breath froze again, thin ice falling down the front of her peacoat; she stared, almost unable to believe her own eyes for the hundredth—or thousandth—time since walking into the Morrer-Pessel Tower to negotiate for her mother's life.

She will eat you, Drozdova. After you bring her what she wants, so she can bargain with Baba Yaga to allow the theft of a native-born child.

She wanted to call what the metal horse had said a lie. She wanted to call all of this a hallucination, a cruel practical joke, a forgiving insanity.

Anything other than truth.

The shadowy things tumbled over each other, sharp cheesecloth-veils of utter negation swallowing even the faint ambient glow of winter night in the Dakotas. A few more tiny white spatters of snow drifted down, and Nat was suddenly very sure an iron-haired woman was bending over a glossy desk top high in a Manhattan skyscraper's penthouse, her red-painted mouth pursed as her coal-hot gaze somehow pierced the intervening distance and came to rest upon a girl she called *granddaughter.*

So Baba was watching. The image was so clear, so crisp, Nat could take no refuge in tattered, comfortable disbelief.

"Get in the *car,*" Dima snarled. There was a sharp report and a brilliant flash. One of the muffled, razor-edged shapes imploded; Nat could swear she saw the bullet as it streaked free, an improbable gleam.

Silver. Well, that doesn't surprise me.

Nat clambered into the car; its hood ornament, a beast caught somewhere between snarling wolf and slump-shouldered bear, glittered angrily. She slammed the door, her teeth chattering afresh even though whatever he'd given her to drink still burned behind her breastbone and the vivid bright warmth of divinity poured strength through her, a steady reassuring glow.

Did her mother feel a corresponding weakness each time that flood filled her daughter's body? Did it hurt?

More flashes, and faraway popping noises. Nat twisted and craned, trying to look out every window at once; the driver's door opened and Dmitri dropped into his seat. He didn't bother reaching for his seatbelt, just twisted the wheel-yoke and popped the brake; the black car jolted and shot forward, but not along the driveway.

He steered them for the far side of Ranger's house, and Nat found her lips moving silently.

Of all the useless things to do, she was *praying*.

LARGELY IMAGINARY

It was a far smoother ride than the motorcycle-horse. Faint vibrations poured through the black car's body; Dmitri's pupils held drifting red sparks and his lips skinned back from sharp pearly teeth as trees flickered by on either side and the wheels bounced. There was a snap and a crunch; barbwire snaked aside, sliced cleanly as if snipped by bolt cutters. Nat got her knees onto the passenger seat and twisted, working herself around so she could stare out the back window.

Nothing there but a winter night. But still, the cold pressed against the car's thin shell, prying and poking.

"Sit down," Dima snapped. "Put seatbelt on, *devotchka*."

You first. Nat stayed where she was, her mouth dry and heart pounding so hard static filled her head. Her palms were slightly damp too, and a prickle of moisture along her lower back was proof that divinities could indeed sweat under stress. "What th-th-the *hell* . . ."

"*Those who eat.*" His hands white-knuckled on the racing yoke—of course his vehicle wouldn't have a proper wheel, that would be entirely too prosaic for him—the gangster stared into the darkness. Nat snapped a glance over her shoulder, out the windshield, hoping to see something familiar or sane, but the headlights had turned from bright scorch-white to a low filthy yellow glow.

Like muffled lanterns, she thought, robbing pursuers of an easy target.

"You said they didn't . . ." She grabbed at the seat-back as the car made a straining, fishlike turn; it lifted over a hidden gully, skimming gently on pure air, and nausea bit at her stomach because it was just like being in Koschei the sorcerer's flying van.

"No trouble to full-grown, *zaika*, but they scavengers." For once Dmitri didn't light a cigarette; his eyes narrowed. "And you not done baking yet."

Great. That's just great. Nat clung to the seat's back, awkward and ridiculous, staring wildly out the rear window as if she could somehow stave off approaching doom just by watching it. "When were you going to tell me they were so close?"

"Oh, you worried? I told you, Dima keep you nice and safe. Egg under little hen." His teeth gleamed afresh, his profile sharp as the motorcycle-horse's while it tore, bucking and twisting, across open country. The engine's humming dropped into a deeper register, and though it was impossible, they seemed to be going even faster. "Sit *down*. And tell me where we go."

Where are we going? Sure. Yeah. But she already knew, Nat realized. Maybe she only had to be scared out of her wits before the signal came through clearly, or maybe she'd seen it in the Well's shimmery depths.

Along with her own birth. What had happened afterward was a nightmare, and she didn't want to think about it.

She managed to struggle free of her backpack without hitting him in the shoulder *or* head, and finally, breathing heavily, she collapsed in the now-familiar passenger seat, tremors pouring through her. Her shoulders, her knees, her bones, her very veins still remembered the horse's gallop.

She suspected they would for a long, long while. Maybe even the rest of her life.

How long would that be?

She will eat you, Drozdova. After you bring her what she wants.

Dmitri exhaled sharply, cut the wheel hard left, and there was another popping *ping* as the car sheared through more barb-wire fence. One of the weathered, silvery support posts was torn free and bulleted away, vanishing into darkness; the car touched down on a two-lane paved road running arrow-straight. Tires bit again, a hum rising from contact with concrete, and the windshield glittered with frost-stars. Slowly melting snowflakes spattered clear, bright glass.

The flakes were growing bigger, whirling through the head-lamps' yellow cloud. It had to warm up to snow, right? But Nat was cold deep down, in a place no heater could ever reach. Not even the magical cherry-tree desert's scorch could thaw her there.

"Well?" Dmitri's eyes were dark again, no little red sparkles. He dug in his breast pocket, and for a moment she was utterly, deadly certain he would produce that gun once more, and point it at her this time. "Where we going now?"

He fished out a battered red cigarette pack decorated with gold foil, tapping one up with quick, practiced motions. An orange flicker bloomed, no need for his silver lighter; he held the fuming stick in one hand while rolling his window down slightly, and the sound of the wind was an old friend.

"West." Nat's throat was parched as the desert. "And south." She wasn't hungry; she hadn't been hungry in what felt like days. Terror, like divinity, was a great appetite suppressant.

She didn't need to pee, either. It was a miracle.

"You gonna narrow that down for Dima?" He took a drag; the smoke's burning eye winked as if they were all in on the joke.

"Maybe." As much as she distrusted him, Nat was still glad to be back in a situation she halfway knew something about. Funny, how all it took was a more immediate danger to make her feel almost charitable towards a bigger, but relatively further-away one. "You gonna narrow down how close they came to catching us?"

"Catching *you*, little *devotchka*." His smile didn't change, but he touched something on the dash and the headlights were back to pure halogen brilliance. "They know to leave Konets alone."

Great. "Because I'm not a full . . . not a real divinity yet." Score one for Nat Drozdova, she was getting used to this.

Well, maybe her score was only a fraction at this point, or an infinitesimal decimal. There was no such thing as becoming fully accustomed to finding out your dying mother was a goddess who had stolen another divinity's heart, that you could ride a shapechanging horse through a magical desert, or that hungry sharp-frigid shadows were pursuing you across the continent.

She didn't even know what *day* it was.

"But you getting there." Dima's smile was once again full of lunatic good cheer. "Only a matter of time, now."

Nat hugged her backpack. The Cup burned inside her high-school bag, a warm secret like the cats showing her the best place to hide in an abandoned house. If she took the unicorn mug out now to show the gangster, what would he do? It wasn't a bloody, glittering gem with a cardiac muscle's steady pulse, but he was, after all, who he was.

A god of thieves.

"Only a matter of time," Dmitri repeated meditatively, when she didn't speak. "Where we goin', *devotchka moya*? Say the word, Dima take you there."

I can show you shortcuts. Just whisper in my ear.

Nat shuddered, a hard wringing motion. Once she was far enough away, would Mom recover? If Drozdova's daughter crossed an international line, would either of them . . . change? Or would Nat get sick, cancer striking her down? Borders and countries were largely imaginary; it wasn't the lesson they wanted you to take from geography class, but what was taught and what was learned were very different things.

She will eat you, Drozdova.

It had to be a lie. *Had* to be. "California," Nat heard herself say. A tired, defeated little word, but the car's interior warmed for a bare moment, touched with summery gold. "Where else?"

"Where else indeed." He gave her a sly sideways glance; Nat was suddenly very sure he knew she had something valuable in her backpack, and was simply biding his time.

What else would she lose, on this feverish, fucked-up road trip? A prairie road stretched under them, snow whirling in feathery horsetails across its gray back as the wind intensified; she had no idea which direction the headlights were pointing. Sooner or later, they'd reach an interchange, a freeway, a town. A city.

Anywhere was all right, as long as those shadowy things weren't there. How fast was enough to escape them?

Dmitri finally stirred again. "You should rest." Resentfully, as if reading her mind or annoyed that she was dragging those *things* behind her, though neither was her fault. Par for the course. "Close your eyes. We drive for a while."

"Okay." Her toes were no longer numb, and Nat could even feel her fingers. Her teeth didn't chatter, though it certainly felt like they wanted to, and she could still taste high brassy terror like sucking on a penny—some of the kids in high school swore that was an easy way to fool a breathalyzer test. Nat had her doubts. "Maybe we could stop for snacks? When it's daylight?"

He turned his chin, his black gaze leaving the pavement for a long terrifying while to rest upon her. "*Da.*" The car chuckled; the road was so straight he could probably take his hands away and the vehicle would handle steering on its own. "Anything you like, *devotchka.*"

More snow clotted the windshield. The wipers started.

There were a lot of cities between here and California, maybe even hotels like the Elysium where she could find other divinities. It shouldn't be a huge problem to slip away from the gangster, and if she traveled far enough, fast enough, she could possibly stay one step ahead of the horrible, drifting, hungry shadow-things too.

They were a terrifying unknown, and Dima Konets the devil she knew. She saw no reason to stick around for *either* of them to get what they wanted.

Nat Drozdova had taken a big black horse to the Western Well under a cherry tree, and ridden him back as well.

What else could she do? It was, she decided, as she slumped trembling in the comforting, cradling passenger seat of a fast, shiny black car, well past time to find out.

Especially if the big motorcycle-horse was, as she tried not to suspect, telling the truth.

WORSE IN THE WORLD

A winter night moved westward, its white-furred coat swirling. The wind, hurling itself across rolling prairie, sensed Wyoming's endless grass sea and urged its snow-hooves faster. A low-slung black car, its silver hood ornament swollen-shouldered now and its eyes bearing glitters like diamond chips to match the glare of headlights, ate up the road miles while the snowstorm sharpened its claws, descending upon a tide of shadowy scavengers, scattering them in every direction.

California, little Drozdova said, and after an afternoon of vicious combat Dima was in a fine mood. The only thing better would have been lifting a small article the damn cowboy wouldn't miss for a while, but for once Konets was willing to forego the pleasure. He smoked slowly, drawing the incense-fume deep into his lungs while two fingers rested on the steering yoke's figure-eight, the road's dips and slight rises passing underneath tires that, while not flaming, glowed with an edge of dull lava-red.

The cloying deathbreath tang of mortality was fading rapidly from the girl in the passenger seat. They could drive a little faster now, though he wouldn't take her through the thiefways. Those grim, shadowed places with their low crimson glow weren't for the likes of her, Konets knew.

Not unless there was no other choice.

Instead of mortal camouflage, Nat Drozdova now smelled of

crushed grass, warm freshness, and a thin white ribbon of jasmine. The edge of horse and exhaust from Ranger's fastest, most feared mount added to the perfume, as well as a veneer of desert spice and the flat iron scent of a deep well with liquid gleaming at the bottom—a drink fit to gripe a mortal dying of thirst, or anyone else stupid enough to take a mouthful.

She hugged that schoolgirl backpack like it was her only possession in the wide, wide world. Perhaps it was, though of course one of their kind could travel as lightly as they wished.

And of course as she strengthened, Maria Drozdova waned. That was another reason not to take his personal roads through the country he had adopted at such a high, glittering, bloody price, his secret ways through the warp and weft of the world. Every divinity had their own means and methods of travel; Maria should have taught her child how to access spring's soft green country.

He didn't think she had, though.

Finally, as they glided through the dark, cutting across the leading edge of a snowstorm's fury, his *zaika*'s shivers eased. So did her deathgrip on the black backpack. There was something in there, but it didn't throb or cry out to him with a particular clamoring voice. No, it just made his palms itch and his fingers tingle, so he took another deep drag, letting the calming bite of smoke fill his throat—and the rest of him.

Now Maria's plan was much clearer. Not only had she hidden a bloody fist-sized gem somewhere only she or her daughter could reach, but she had also sown arcana in certain locations. A fresh new native-born incarnation would manifest their own, of course, but not until she reached full strength. Having the old ones hidden in continental taproots—where the concentration of numinous force would mask and preserve even items of great power, places even Konets might not be able to steal from without a great deal of painstaking effort—would slow the incarnation process a great deal, and now that he'd spent some time with a little *devotchka* raised to believe she was a mortal rube instead of a divinity, Dima was forced to admit the bare truth of what everyone suspected.

Maria Drozdova had indeed been planning a very particular kind of theft. Trading what she'd initially stolen to Baba was one way to make the old woman overlook the brazen, carnivorous act—not the only way, but one that stood a good chance of working.

Dmitri Konets had planned some complex, long-running games in his time, but this was something else. "You want smoke?"

As soon as he said it, he regretted opening his mouth. The girl shook her head, staring out the windshield like she expected the mouthless hungry things to appear in front of them, inky cutouts against headlight shine.

She had no faith in him at *all*. It shouldn't have stung, for after all a thief was a thief, and he should know.

"No." It sounded like her throat was dry; little Drozdova coughed slightly. The cordial he'd forced between her unwilling lips would have made a mortal thief lucky for years, granting health and strength far beyond their ken; to a fellow divinity, it was like a mouthful of Dima's own blood willingly shed. A powerful draft indeed, and her oblivious to its potency, let alone implications. "Dmitri?"

He made a short, irritated noise.

"Thank you." Now she looked at him, her face bathed in dashboard glow. "For . . . for fighting them off."

The freeway hummed below, the wind howled on either side—oh, it was a hungry, hungry night, and though *those who eat* were fearsome things what rode the snow-brooms was even worse. Hair unbound, greenish-pale raddled body bare, trailing darkness and ice in her wake, Winter roamed the prairie.

Even the mouthless shadows would flee her approach.

Baba called the girl *granddaughter;* little wonder she liked tender little Nat better than her mother. Dima was forced to admit he agreed with the old beldam about something, a bitter realization indeed. "I told old lady I keep you safe and sound." He checked the rearview, unnecessarily—any mortal out tonight would be lumbering behind a snowplow or feeling their way from one mile marker to the next.

"Because you want your heart back." There was a catch in the words. Even a brave little girl had her limits.

"Don't worry, *zaika moya.*" Dima quelled the urge to shift in the driver's seat. His eyes narrowed slightly, and when he exhaled, heavy perfumed smoke crept towards the cracked-open window before being sucked out into the slipstream. He could be polite, he decided. She might still dislike the pleasant, drugging fumes. "We have long way to go. Try to rest."

"Oh, sure. Because riding a murderous not-horse and finding out shadow-monsters are real is so restful." Irritation flashed in her tone, a breath of ozone warning on a mild spring day. "Is there anything that *doesn't* want to eat me?"

Oh, you don't like being beautiful, little girl? Women, never satisfied with anything. "At the moment, Dima is more interested in burger." They could probably reach Nell Bonney's place with little trouble, and she was always open on nights like this. "You like fries? I know a place—"

"I shouldn't have asked you." A disdainful turning away, all that sunny regard gone—well, the weather changed quick in springtime. Both here and in the old country.

"*Those who eat* take everything they can, *devotchka.* Like Ranger's little horsey, like everyone else." *Like your dear mamma,* he wanted to add, but she wouldn't believe even the strictest truth if it dropped from his lips. Nobody trusted a thief, even one with a habit of telling some truth.

Honesty was the best misdirection of all. It often pleased him to wield it like one of his little friends, gleaming blades and bone or black handles distracting the prey before the blades bit deep, remaining pristine no matter how much gore was splashed.

Snow stacked at the edge of the windshield wipers' arcs, frozen white mini-peaks toppled as the wind veered or the car bounced. The engine-beast hummed, happy to be running again though it disliked not using its full speed.

"Friendly wants your heart, too." Little Drozdova surprised him once more; she sounded amazingly steady, all things considered. "How often do divinities eat each other?"

"How often there a plane crash? Safer than driving, but rubes afraid to get on the fuckin' plane." Dima considered manifesting a bottle of mortal alcohol in the car; the only thing he had right now was his flask. At least the smoke kept her scent corralled.

Walking into Baba's office, she'd smelled entirely like prey. Now his little *devotchka* was stronger, blooming bright and sure, petals stretching but not fully unfurled. His mouth still watered, and he suspected it would for a long while yet.

Hunger was an old friend, in all its different shades and forms. It could also be a tool, wielded sharp and swift; what else induced the rubes to his worship? They wanted, and he provided a way.

"But my . . ." She paused. "But *Maria* didn't eat yours. Even though she knew this country would make her sick."

Bright little girl. Was she putting together the pieces? *She's my mother*, Nat had hissed at him. *Can you just not?*

Or was she beginning to believe his hinting? Dima couldn't quite decide whether he liked the prospect. "Dead God's Heart not gonna do your dear mamma any good, *zaika moya*. Like cow eating lamb instead of grass."

"But Friendly's different." Another shy, sipping, distrustful glance, as if she expected him to snap at her. "Because he's a cop and you're . . ."

"Robber? We play that game, *da*." Deadly serious, like all amusements.

"Why didn't de Winter eat me? Or Maria?"

"Oh, no." He had to laugh, a fox-bark freighted with heavy scented smoke. Explaining how water was wet and the sky blue normally irritated him, but they had a long drive before them, and at least she wasn't ignoring nasty old Dima. "Baba eat you, she have to hive off a new Springtime. Learned her lesson in the old country, having to change shape with the weather instead of when she like to." His ears tingled, catching the subtlest of shifts—twice now, *Maria* instead of *Mom*.

Perhaps the little girl *had* figured out a thing or two. Loyalty bred blindness; so did its opposite. Much better to stick to business, and stealing, of course, was best of all.

"Hive off." Nat shuddered again, a delicate movement. The car took no notice, a hard shell around tiny, tender cargo. Some of his nephews transported goods, and no doubt skimmed a little off the top as everyone had to in order to survive. "That sounds unpleasant."

"Lot worse in the world, *devotchka*." Another truth nobody would ever thank Konets for. They blamed him, as if he was the disease instead of a mere symptom.

"Yeah." She settled her backpack more comfortably. Whatever was inside made his hands itch all the way to his wrists. "I'm beginning to find that out."

You have seen nothing yet, my little doll. But there was no point in saying as much. He decided they could go a bit faster, and the car's thrumming dropped a few notes. "Nice things too. You like cheeseburger? I know good place, it's on the way."

The rubes would not quite see his car at this speed. They would sense his passage—a chill on the nape, an angry subsonic buzz—and the more sensitive among them might hear distant smoke-roughened laughter, or perform some atavistic, propitiating action without knowing why. Knocking on wood, lighting a candle, throwing salt over a shoulder, or simply pulling over and waiting until the cold current bulging under the skin of the world subsided were all time-honored ways of avoiding notice.

Or attracting it. Sometimes an entire mortal gathering would turn silent while a divinity passed, a herd sensing predatory proximity.

"Like your brother's biker bar?" The girl's tone was dry as Dima's sensitive fingertips. She was probably raising an eyebrow like Baba herself.

The Drozdova was doing very well indeed. A thief could feel grudging respect for bravery from one not of their kin; it wasn't against any rule.

"Oh, no. This a purely social call." More laughter bubbled under Dmitri's breastbone, along with a faint gurgling. He wasn't precisely hungry, not for physical sustenance.

But maybe he should show her a pleasure or two. After all, Baba was attending to their pursuers tonight, and if you were passing by Deadwood, it was silly not to stop for a bite.

ARCANA

Trapped in a metal cabin traveling at unspeakable speed through a South Dakota snowstorm, bouncing gently as if the tires weren't touching pavement, wasn't even the weirdest thing that had happened to her in the past few days.

In retrospect, Nat could see all this was probably inevitable. What normal kid was greeted by talking cats, not to mention the birds, dogs, and even the high piping voices of rats intoning *good morning, little Drozdova*? What normal child found a circle of softly singing mushrooms under a tree's skirts in an overgrown bit of playground; what normal mother smelled like ozone when she was angry or had a front gate that opened on its own as she drew close? Of course everyone considered their own upbringing ho-hum and humdrum no matter how haunting or horrific, until they grew up a bit and could compare notes.

Of course Nat Drozdova would end up here. Of-fucking-*course*.

Dmitri looked very pleased, all things considered, and the cut on his cheek now just a thin, shrinking line. Nat was just busy thanking her stars she didn't get carsick. Of course, the sisters at school would have said she should thank God, the Virgin, and maybe some saints to top it all off—wouldn't want anyone to feel left out.

Why had Mom sent her to *Catholic* school? Did nuns keep the hungry shadows away?

Dmitri kept smoking, puffing like a steam engine; every time Nat's shoulders relaxed slightly and she closed her eyes, absorbing the heat blasting from the car's vents, the images from the Well returned and she jolted back into stinging alertness.

There was no possibility of direct answers. Leo had dirt in his mouth, Mom wasn't exactly honest by any stretch of the imagination, Baba de Winter had her own agenda, Ranger had put her on that murderous motorcycle-horse, and despite any short-term kindness he displayed the gangster in the driver's seat was going to kill her if he could get his hands on what Mom had stolen. She didn't know enough about other divinities to guess who would help her or who wanted to eat her, and none of her work friends . . . good God, she didn't even have a job now.

Wait—are *there any good gods?* There was Nurse Candy, but she was back in New York. And even she asked about the Heart first.

Casually, of course. But she'd still asked.

It all added up to Nat being confused, utterly alone, and not quite sure of her own sanity. As usual, and as always. She stared at the snowy road, headlights glaring through curtains of shifting snow. No lights in the oncoming lane, and no ruby brake-glow before them either.

Who would be stupid—or desperate—enough to drive tonight? Only a god of gangsters, apparently. The storm whirled on either side, white flakes vanishing into darkness. If she opened the door and tumbled out, would she survive the fall?

Was it worth the attempt? Were those mouthless black-paper cutouts draped with floating cheesecloth-veils lurking in the ditches, or out in the fields beyond the ubiquitous three strands of barbwire keeping the highway channeled like an obedient canal?

Stick on the straight and narrow, some of the sisters at school had said more than once. *Strait is the gate.*

Well, if this was the primrose path to hell, it was nowhere near as pleasant as advertised.

A gust of snow smacked the windshield. For a moment, the image of a face—burning dark eyes, a long sharp nose, thin-lipped mouth, and a pointed chin—stared at Nat before Dmitri hissed and the wiper on the passenger side scraped it away.

The sibilant out-breath resolved into words. "See?" The gangster took another deep pull off his glow-tipped cigarette. "Baba watching. Very, very interested in my little *devotchka*."

Great. Nat wished she could pull her jean-clad knees up and hug them. Making herself as small as possible seemed like a wonderful idea at the moment. "Is that a good thing?"

"Could be." Did he have to sound so blasted cheerful? "Tonight she keeps the hungry things away. Ranger probably out too, doing what he can. Drozdova has a few friends in the world."

What a great piece of news. If I can trust you saying it.

That probably wasn't fair. Dmitri was honest about wanting to kill her, and had even attempted, in his weird way, to give Nat a lesson in using a divinity's . . . powers.

Next I'll get a cape and spandex. It was exotic to think of having some kind of power, let alone freezing a street's worth of cars in a weird time-bubble, or turning on a jukebox just by staring and wishing.

What else could she do? Why hadn't Mom taught her *anything*?

"I want to know something," Nat heard herself say. Asking a gangster with violently poor impulse control who had a vested interest in murdering her probably wasn't a good move.

Still, what—and who—else did she have?

"Mh." He stared at the road, his fingertips on the yoke, barely even pretending to steer. For all that, the car's voice changed, its thrum settling a few notes deeper still. "Dima thinks you want to know a whole lot, *devotchka*. We got time."

Maybe he even meant to sound comforting. Nat's hands weren't quite shaking, but they were cold even with the car's heater doing its best.

At least it didn't smell like sand and spice. If she said *take me back to the Well*, would he know what she was talking about? Probably.

So she unzipped the top of her faithful schoolbag, dug in its interior—maybe she should have packed more than a change of clothes, a spiral-bound notebook, all her remaining cash, plus some toiletries—and extracted the unicorn mug.

It gleamed softly in the shadowed interior, its gilt taking on the mellow radiance of actual gold. It was probably a trick of the dimness, but it still looked realer-than-real. Like the Well itself, the tree, the big black horse—or like Dima, like Mom before she got sick, like Baba de Winter.

Was Nat looking that vital, that alive, that *real* too? Would she just have to stay the maximum distance from Mom so she didn't drain off the power, the divinity?

Put that way, it didn't sound so bad.

"You gonna ask what that is?" Dmitri blew twin jets of smoke through his nose; the vapor curled dragonlike before slithering towards the window and vanishing out into howling snowstorm. "Man oh man, your mama really told you nothing. Makes you wonder, don't it."

No, I don't wonder. There was knowing other people lied like it was breathing, which Nat had always figured was just the way the world worked. Then there was keeping quiet about talking cats, singing mushrooms, and all the other crazy stuff she'd seen since childhood, which was self-defense. There was lying to other people, which was what the sisters at school called a sin but if it was the only way to survive, why would any reasonable person refrain?

Then there was lying to yourself. Another thing people did with apparent ease, but did *she* want to?

"You're probably going to try to steal it, huh." Nat weighed the mug, wondering at its glow, its pleasing heft, its sense of utter and unassailable rightness. Its weight sent deep happy warmth up her arms, and golden coruscations trembled just under her skin, breaking free with pleasant tingles.

Was she going to turn into a holy nightlight, like a plastic Mary with a bulb behind? Her mother didn't glow at random moments, even when her quick, volcanic temper was triggered.

"Maybe." Dmitri didn't glance at what she was holding, but maybe he didn't need to. "That's a grail."

Get the fuck out. "Like the Holy Grail?" A deep swimming sense of unreality poured through Nat. The mug cast dappled reflections on the roof, and if it bothered the gangster to have a bright light in the car while driving at night, he made no sign. "But that's . . . I mean, Jesus . . ." *Oh boy. Oh holy what the fuck.*

"That cross-hanging mama's boy love to get his hands on it, I bet. Little drink from that give even a rube something nice. But I tell you this, *devotchka,* nobody but me allowed to steal from you." He nodded, the corners of his mouth turning down and his eyes sparking like the motorcycle-horse's for a moment. A bright point of crimson, visible and just as quickly extinguished, leaving a faint tracer in its wake. "Nobody but Konets, and you can take that to bank."

Gee, that's awful nice. "It was my mother's, right?"

"Smells like you. Yours now." He sucked on the cigarette again, then tossed its pinched, spent end through the slightly open window. How he could smell anything with the amount of smoking he did was beyond her. The orange-glowing dot vanished into the night, and another soft load of snow smacked across the windshield a moment later. His grin widened, teeth glinting. "Your mama buried it somewhere rubes and even most of *us* can't get to, just to keep it away from you. Every one of us got our arcana, *zaika moya,* like my sharp shiny friends. The Drozdova got a Cup, a Knife, and something she keep secret."

The Knife was in Nat's backpack too, in a wooden box with almost-invisible joins. *Something she keep secret*—well, Maria

Drozdova kept all *kinds* of secrets, and so did her daughter. In that one small way, they were alike. "Is your car an arcana?"

"No, this beast my chariot, see?" Dmitri dug in his breast pocket, pulling out yet another crumpled cigarette pack. This one was white with red lettering she couldn't quite make out. He shook up a coffin-nail with his left hand and paused, frowning at the road before them. "Your mama had a nice one. Old days, the cats used to pull it. Now, though . . . Got to admit, I wondered why you weren't drivin'."

Mom's old black car, faithfully nursed along by Leo, would fly apart at freeway speeds. Even with the snow coming down in sheets the highway in front of them was relatively clear, feathery dry white whipping across it like the broom behind her mother's kitchen door, kept for clearing the back porch. Maria insisted all sweeping be done a certain way, hard and fast until Nat's arms ached.

She stared at the mug's glow, running a fingertip along its rim. "Her car's pretty old."

The first unicorn mug—bought with scrupulously saved chore money from the pittance Leo argued Mom into granting her daughter—had broken while being washed, or so Maria said. Dishes broke, it was no big deal.

Nat had still cried. The loss was still sharp, in the way only old childhood hurts could be. Now she wondered.

About all sorts of things.

"But *you* not old." The gangster lifted the pack to his mouth, pulled out the cigarette standing to attention, and stuffed the white-and-red box back into his jacket without looking. "Getting stronger all the time."

I hope so. Was he actually trying to be helpful? It sounded like it, but of course, that was probably a trap. "Thank you. For telling me."

"*Pozhaluysta.* Now put thing away, *vesna moya.* I'm driving."

She plunged the mug back into her bag, rewrapping it by touch—the last thing she needed was Dmitri seeing her single pair of clean panties. She hugged her bag close while they drove, and the silence between them was new. It wasn't exactly pleasant, but it wasn't combative or charged, either. It was just . . . quiet.

Which was great, because she had thinking to do, even if she'd rather not. Still, her hands were finally warming up and she sagged in the seat, staring at the brushed-clean pavement under the headlights, anemic yellow dashes in the middle of the highway melting into a single line because they were traveling faster than anyone normal—any *mortal*—could on a night like this.

MORE THAN ONE PATH

Half a continent away from her stupid, stumbling daughter, a divinity lay in the borderland between dream and waking, listening to snow-choked silence outside the Laurelgrove Hospice's disinfectant-reeking hallways. This city took pride in never sleeping, but even the far-off mutter of traffic was muted under a blanket of soft, killing white.

It was a winter very like the old country's, and Maria Drozdova suspected a certain grandmother was piqued.

The hospice room was ugly, its functional bed uncomfortable. The nurses were slatterns and the shouting, jovial doctors not even worthy of a literary skewering, let alone a physical one. The pink upholstery, the stench of Lysol and bleach, the lack of proper black bread or good soup, the absence of sweet hot coffee and the buzzing of fluorescents—oh, it could have been a version of mortal hell, and even the armfuls of dying flowers brought in by reluctant visitors or the straggling, half-dead houseplants at the nursing stations could not soften its hideousness.

Many had made the mistake of thinking Winter's tender green granddaughter could be trapped or insulted. More often than not the beautiful Drozdova laughed, miring pursuers or other transgressors in thick black mud. Sometimes she settled upon a handy, sun-dried boulder to watch, gaze alight and pretty chin resting on one soft hand, while they struggled and sank. Some begged for mercy, others railed furiously. Thrashing only sped the process; some of the trapped slowed, attempting to treat a divinity's displeasure as mere quicksand and reach solid ground.

Finally, the glutinous semiearth closed over their heads, and she feasted upon their despair and suffocation.

It was a novelty for her own body to become a sucking hole, one Maria despised even as it fascinated. The deep, tearing pain in her chest—what the mortal doctors, with their utter lack of imagination or sensitivity, called a cancer—provided snippets of sharp inimical strength at random intervals, burning even as she grasped them. Even her stubborn refusal to give in had its limits, though she had not reached them yet.

The plastic tube in her throat was an annoyance; she had raged at Leo until twilight unconsciousness swallowed her, then surfaced to find herself stuffed like a solstice goose. Fortunately, the more her body transformed to a merely mortal shell, the more efficacious were the mortal treatments; they were unwitting allies, and as soon as she regained her proper place she would reward them according to their deserts.

A tiny gleam, thread-thin, showed between her eyelids; her lashes were scant and graying now like the rest of her hair. Not too long ago, a wrench like a tooth pulled from its socket told her the maggot-child had retrieved a second arcana—it had been so long since Maria held her beautiful golden cup, tracing its jewels with a loving fingertip, calling forth whatever she desired from its depths. She longed to do so again, and longed to unleash the Knife upon those who had used her temporary misfortune to insult or pettifog her.

First, she had decided, would be her once-husband. Did he not understand her fading meant his own? He had betrayed her for the parasite wrenched free of her bowels, the selfish, grasping child who had the temerity to drain her mother's strength. Then Maria could attend to the rest at her leisure.

The shadows thickened, their edges turning sharp. One of

Maria's paper-skinned hands, lying discarded on a rough hospital blanket, twitched. No, the scavengers would not approach her yet. First they would eat the vulnerable new incarnation, the tender green shoot.

Two mortal decades had dragged by as she carefully pruned the child, watering only enough to allow some growth, forcing the stem into a tortured shape, waiting for the proper time. The slinking, sniveling little brat couldn't even bloom correctly, but it didn't matter.

Maria had more than one plan. If the pale, polluted copy failed to outrun *those who eat*, some numinous force would return to her original—enough to stave off the scavengers until Baba, eager to reacquire what her darling Masha had stolen, could be persuaded to trade some surety for the Dead God's Heart. Even with all three arcana in her grubby grasp, the child still had to endure the final trial. Ruthlessly compressed and ridiculed enough to stay tractable, creeping, frightened Natchenka was unready for the burden of divinity.

And she loved her mother, like a good little American girl should.

At certain intervals those chubby little arms about her neck had almost moved Maria to a variety of tenderness. The tearstained little face, the tiny bits of school art brought home and offered with shy hopefulness, the meek, bovine obedience were all part of the plan, and showing just enough affection to keep the clinging vine dependent had even been easy, sometimes.

Yes, if one path did not lead to the Drozdova's renewal, another would. Patience was difficult, but Spring knew the value of waiting; what she did not allow to germinate Summer could not ripen and Harvest could not reap. If Baba let both Maria and her daughter become a banquet for carrion, the Heart might well be lost forever, and neither the icy grandmother nor Konets would risk *that*.

Just like in Leo's beloved chess—or in any other game,

frankly—the entire operation rested upon arranging things so every path led inevitably to victory. The little American maggot would call it cheating, but power was power and respected the rules only enough to arrange for its own continuance. A wolf-pack was not cruel because it trapped a sheep in an unwinnable cul-de-sac; it was merely the way of the world.

So Maria Drozdova dozed and half-dreamed, carefully husbanding her failing strength. No gust of snowy wind smacked her window, no rodent lingered in a shadowed corner with a bright inquisitive alien gleam in its beady eyes. Baba was not watching her at the moment, and while the shadows thickened, they did not descend. The cold stayed outside with the weather, mortal heating enough to keep the room reasonably balmy.

She had waited a little over two mortal decades, a mere eye-blink for one of her kind. She could wait a little more.

The end, after all, was assured.

FED AND SHELTERED

The highway joined up to a freeway heading south, signs flashing by almost too quickly to decipher. Hills rose steadily on either side, the prairie breaking into bits and heaving upward. Trees tossed, combing the wind in arms both evergreen and naked.

Time did funny things during magical snowstorms, or maybe it just behaved strangely after a day spent digging divinity arcana out of ancient wells and riding a horse who was also a motorcycle before finishing up with a gun battle against carnivorous, mouthless shadows. It didn't feel like long before the car slowed, the engine's insistent pulse quieting. An exit's curve reared before them, the car took a deep breath, and orange citylight smeared the sky. The snow gentled, flakes swelling as the night's breath warmed a fraction, and the wind's howl diminished.

But only fractionally. It still looked damn cold out there.

Dmitri was still smoking, but not at the same rate. A cigarette hung from his lip, its tip glowing dangerously, and he hummed a wandering tune under the engine's noise. Just when he'd started doing that Nat couldn't quite remember, and she hoped it wasn't a prelude to more unpleasantness.

Maybe she'd even dozed a little, though she wasn't quite tired. Emotionally exhausted, sure, but even the backache from sitting in a bucket seat for hours was strangely absent. And she wasn't desperate to find a restroom, either.

"I thought we weren't stopping until daylight."

He nodded, and no burnt bits drifted from his cigarette tip. It must be nice, not needing an ashtray. "We stop for snacks anywhere you want, yes."

"Those things might still be—"

"They got bigger problems tonight." Instead of just steering with two fingers, he had one whole hand curled loosely around the right half of the steering yoke, lazily making tiny adjustments to their course. "You like french fries? Milkshake? Coke?"

What the hell? She wasn't hungry, but it probably didn't matter. The gangster had something in mind, and arguing or trying to change it would get Nat nowhere.

At least, not yet. "I'm fine," she hedged. "But if you've got to stop—"

"For fucksake." He gave her an irritated sidelong glance. "You don't want nice dress, you don't want shiny present, you don't want dinner? What kind of girl are you, huh?"

The kind that knows not to take anything from you, thanks. "A rube, Dima." A sharp jolt of irritation went through her, probably leftovers from a day packed with several different flavors of terror, not to mention a bone-jolting ride and an emotional thermo-nuke. "A silly little rube girl. Didn't you know?"

The gangster snorted, the cigarette's tip twitching as it brightened. "Oh, you so much more than that." His free hand rose and he jabbed two fingers at the windshield. The snow whirled briefly aside, cringing under an invisible lash.

Feathery snow-brooms brushed the pavement clear for a short distance before them. The passenger-side mirror, speckled with melting ice, showed nothing resembling a trail behind them; maybe the snow just healed over their passage.

Like a scab.

A massive round sign—either built to look like a cross-section of a giant tree or a leftover from the time when old growth still covered plenty of America—blared a painted yellow WELCOME

TO DEADWOOD. The black car slowed still further, its engine's laughter suddenly conspiratorial, and when Dmitri whipped the steering wheel to the left Nat was almost ready for the jolt. The tires bumped, that same funny internal twitch Nat was learning heralded stepping into a divinity's space, and a small ice-frosted parking lot swallowed them.

At the far end, warm electric glow escaped restaurant windows. The brick-and-timber building bore more than a faint resemblance to an old-timey saloon, but the doors were glass instead of swinging wood. WAGON WHEEL, the sign proclaimed proudly, COME ON IN!

Neon buzzed in one of the windows, a red smear that could have said OPEN. Nat's eyes watered as she tried to focus. The gangster all but stood on the brakes, rubber squealed, and when all motion halted the car was nestled between two neatly painted white stripes, angle-parked right next to a handicap spot.

Maybe even a god of gangsters wouldn't pull into one of those, risking a divine parking ticket. Nat's arms ached, clutching her backpack. "You're a terrible driver." The words popped out of her mouth, surprising her, and Dima's short barking laugh did, too.

He sounded truly amused. "Never been in accident yet, *devotchka*. Sit still, let me get door."

Because you're such a gentleman. Right. She shook her head, reaching for the handle, and his hand closed around her left shoulder, fingers not quite biting in.

"Why you do that?" The edge of a snarl rode the words, but didn't quite break the surface. "I *said*, let me get door."

"I'm not going to run away." *At least, not yet.* Her throat was so dry she'd even take some Mountain Dew at this point. "Especially in a blizzard."

"Like that matter. Let me get door. Safer, you understand?" His grasp eased when she let her hand fall into her lap. "Good. See? Dima can be friendly."

"Sure you can." It probably wasn't the brightest idea in the world to antagonize him, but Nat had been pushed around enough. Besides, Ranger said she didn't have to put up with *all* Dima's bullshit, and even if the cowboy hadn't thought to warn her about his murderous mount, she appreciated the vote of confidence. "When you want something."

"Everyone want something." Having dispensed that little bit of wisdom, the gangster let go of her, and not only opened her car door but the restaurant's, ushering her in as if it was date night.

The snowy cold wasn't bad, just pine-scented and bracing. Still, Nat was glad of Leo's old peacoat. Her legs were still a little gooshy, so stepping into the restaurant's bright golden warmth was a welcome relief. It smelled of grilled meat, baking bread, coffee—all good things, without the underlay of bleach and stickiness shouting *food service*. In fact, the mix of aromas was more like a home kitchen, and a cheery soprano, "Sit on anywhere, be with you in a hot bit," rang out.

Tables and red-clad booths marched in neat rows. Everything was crimson gingham and bare wood, the floor polished planks and the kitchen behind a steel counter slightly less than shoulder-high. Steam hissed as something hit a grill, and Nat couldn't quite see into the cooking area past a glare of hanging chrome heatlamps. The paneled walls were festooned with grainy black-and-white photos in plain metal frames between bits of what she could only call Western kitsch—stuffed deer heads, dust-scorched antique signs from long-closed general stores and saloons, rusting farm implements, shelves crowded with knickknacks and gewgaws as well as small taxidermy animals.

The stuffed roadkill was a bit much, their glass eyes bright with interest, but Dima didn't give her time to absorb the surroundings. He ushered her to a long marble-topped soda-fountain counter, and a flicker of movement behind it was a statuesque woman in a green-and-red calico frock, blue eyes inquisitive as the motionless wildlife's. A faded bonnet, matching her dress, was tied under her chin, shading that bright gaze. Her skirt swung as she halted next to the glaring-indistinct window to the kitchen. "*Two plates!*" she bellowed into the brightness, and was answered by a furious clattering. "Come on in, y'all, and sit down. My oh my, the Drozdova comin' here—shoulda let me know, I'd've put on a spread, asked the local dignitaries, got a band to play—"

"Just passing through." Dima indicated a red vinyl barstool, its chrome pillar glinting; Nat clambered aboard. "How are you, Nell?"

"Oh, busy as hell, just as always." The woman's bright blue gaze didn't alter; Nat had the sense she was being weighed. It was depressingly familiar, and she settled her backpack on her lap. Hugging it—and the warm, forgiving glow of the Cup inside—felt a lot safer.

It was probably imaginary protection, but at this point she'd take it. She'd take just about anything, frankly.

Dmitri no doubt had some sort of agenda, just like at the biker bar. Maybe this was another relative? The gangster settled on the stool next to her. This part of the restaurant did look an awful lot like a soda fountain, though Nat had only seen those in movies. The woman looked like she'd ridden in a covered wagon, and she had the same buzzing sense of vitality, of *more-there*-ness.

A divinity, working in a restaurant? Or maybe this was like Ranger's roadhouse. Nat stared at gold-veined white marble, blinking furiously. At least in the car she could pretend to be watching the scenery, and the scraping, tingling sense of danger as well as steady motion kept the tears away.

As long as you kept moving, you didn't have to think about your problems, or about black horses saying horrifyingly plausible things about your own mother. Who might have been brusque and dismissive, but at least she'd fed Nat, put a roof over her head, and bought school clothes—complaining all the while, of course, because it was expensive to raise a child, but . . .

A fresh sizzling came from the blank glare hiding the kitchen. The smell of grilled meat intensified, as if Leo were searing steaks in a cast-iron skillet.

Cows got fed and sheltered too, didn't they? Right before the hammer descended and their carcasses were hung up for carving.

It was a terrible thought.

She will eat you, Drozdova. After you bring her what she wants, so she can bargain with Baba Yaga to allow the theft of a native-born child.

The nagging sense of a missing puzzle piece had vanished. The horse's words explained everything quite neatly, a razor taking the shortest logical route.

"Good heavens." The calico-clad woman halted on the other side of the counter, setting down two thick brown china mugs with flared bottoms. The rich good smell of coffee from fresh-ground beans rose on tiny threads of steam. "Y'all look miserable, miss. Is it the weather, or the company? Truth be told, I'm a bit surprised to see you ridin' around with *him*."

You and everyone else. "He wants something," Nat said, dully. She took a deep breath, and tried for what she hoped was a pleasant, social smile. "You're a divinity, right? It's nice to meet you."

"Ain't you polite." The woman's cheeks were apple-red, and her tanned, capable hands dove below the counter's surface, coming up full of bright antique silverware. "I'm Nell, Nell Bonney. Used to be Shamhat, back in the day. Civilizin's my game, though it never seems to take—if there's one thing humans're good at, it's finding new ways to be jackasses. Anyway, I keep a house here and there."

Old country? "So you're from somewhere else too?"

"We're all travelers, kiddo." A tendril of red hair slipped free of Nell's bonnet; she blew it out of her face with a quick irritated huff and in a trice had place settings in front of both Nat and Dmitri. The gangster settled his elbows on the counter and stared kitchenward, very pointedly ignoring both women.

But he wasn't smoking, and no trace of sneering good humor lingered around his mouth. If he was like this more often, he could even be considered handsome, or at least striking.

All his grinning and threatening drained any attractiveness away. Maybe that's why he did it.

"You're from New York way," Nell continued. "Did you happen to see my big sister out there? Goes by Candy nowadays."

Nurse Candy? "I did meet her." Nat wished the barstool was a little lower. Her feet dangled like a kid's, and her boots probably still had traces of magical sand on them despite wiping on the mat by the door. "She, uh, did some first aid on me."

"Nice to see she ain't forgotten it." Nell's grin held a gap between her front teeth and all the warmth in the world. "Her kind goes out first, and mine once it's halfway respectable. We fight— what family doesn't, you know—but in the end, it's always the same."

Did she try to eat you? "Oh." She couldn't find a single thing to say; Nat hugged her backpack tighter.

Nell's steady motion halted. She darted a venomous glance at Dmitri, who was still eyeing the kitchen-glare like he expected it to spit a cascade of dollar bills.

Maybe it would. Nat was suddenly, overwhelmingly tired of divinities, powers, arcana, and everything else. Going back to the little yellow house on South Aurora, heading upstairs, and curling up in the forgiving darkness of her bedroom closet seemed like the best idea in the *world*.

Unfortunately, that small dark place, stale with the smell of clothes waiting to be worn and shoes a growing girl could squeeze maybe a few more toe-sore days out of, wasn't the best refuge. Even in its very back corner the voices penetrated—Mom and Uncle Leo fighting, always over something Nat had done, or failed to do, or one of Maria's punishments. He was always attempting some kind of intercession, and more often than not wrung one free.

Uncle. Wasn't that a laugh. The prepaid cell in the bag she was clutching could call him, but what was there to say?

Nat Drozdova was utterly, irrevocably alone.

"What have you done to her?" Nell's fists rested on her hips, and she glared at the gangster. At least her eyes were a few shades darker than Maria Drozdova's, otherwise Nat might have flinched. "Konets, I swear, if you've—"

"I *protect* her," he retorted, hotly. "Little doll just saw *those who eat* for first time. I thought she might like burger, fries. Maybe even milkshake."

"Those who . . ." Nell examined Nat again, top to toe. "Oh, hell. No wonder you're pale. Chocolate, I think. Fixes everything. Have a little coffee, sweetheart. It'll help."

Nothing will help this. Nat kept trying to smile, but her mouth wobbled. "I'm sorry," she managed, through the lump in her throat. "Is . . . is there a restroom? Please?"

She didn't need to pee, but if she sat here much longer she might burst into inglorious, messy, childish sobs.

"Over there, under the moose." Nell pointed; there was indeed a giant stuffed moose head over a pair of swinging saloon doors. "Here." Her hand flashed again, producing—hey, presto, neatest trick of the week—a crisp white handkerchief. "Go on, take that with you. On the house."

"Eh, *devotchka.*" Dmitri spun on his barstool, eyeing her suspiciously. Tiny moisture-jewels dotted his dark hair, and his boot-toes glittered sharply. "No back door that way. Remember what—"

"Leave me alone." It was a wonder the words didn't choke her. Nat couldn't make an arm unfold enough to take the hankie, even though it was probably a huge honor or something, considering the other woman was a divinity. "Just leave me the fuck *alone,* Konets." She blundered off the stool, landed with a jolt, and headed for the restroom, the entire bright, cheery place distorting around her. Or maybe it was just the welling tears which made the environs seem wavering and indistinct.

She made it down a short hall lined with framed photos—black and white or sepia-toned, people in frontier dress staring straight-faced into cameras, a tiny breeze fingering her damp forehead. It was uncomfortably warm, her coat no longer a blessing, and she prickled all over. Between the freezing and the heat, contraction and expansion, she was about to shatter like overstressed glass.

It would almost be a relief.

TASTY FARE

I 've half a mind to throw you into the kitchen," Nell hissed, tucking the white cotton square back in one of her capacious skirt-pockets. "Just what are you playing at, Konets?"

His own irritation was a bright sharp blade. No wonder his uncles and nephews stole what they could; trying to be a nice fellow got you nowhere. "I thought she would like a burger, Miz Bonney." He made every word nice and precise, and kept his hands in plain view.

It didn't do to get the Homemaker excited. The calico was sweet and old-fashioned, but it hid an entire arsenal.

"She'll get what she needs. That's what this House is for." Nell's hat lengthened its brim, shadowing her face; only the tip of her nose showed. "You're hoping to sweet-talk Maria Drozdova's daughter into—"

"I do nothing to that girl." Dmitri's fingers tensed, marble cold and slick against his palms. It would be unpleasant to tear this place apart brick by plank, but if this snide bonneted bitch pushed much further, he would show both her and the Drozdova a thing or two. "In any case, it's none of your business, *Nelly*. Her mother stole from me, and will steal from little doll too. If I let her."

The kitchen's clatter paused for a moment, the air turning crystalline. Once, women of Nell's kind had bumped across prairie in covered wagons or arrived on steam-belching trains, determined to bring respectability to a "wild" frontier. Before that, her kind wore dangling chatelaines at their belt and ran households large and small, swishing skirts printed with finger-marks from tiny grasping hands. Back when the rubes were new she'd worn yet another face—the gatherers with pointed digging sticks who brought in most of the tribe's calories and began la-boriously babbling to rube children during mealtimes, language and food molding both offspring and males. *Play nice, take turns, share,* afterward it turned into *plant, reap, build, store, conserve, protect, maintain.*

As the rubes evolved so did she, and the dictum became simple: *Use your manners.* Or, boiled down to its essence, *obey.*

Her elder forms still lingered among the indigenous, gutter-ing candles caught in a cold draft of genocide. The tribes had venerated those who kept the fire built, the baskets well woven, and the clothing tidy; survival left them no choice.

When the Europeans arrived on this far shore they brought a Puritan woman with blue eyes and a set, firm mouth, her hands hard with work and her linens always neatly folded while she looked askance at any woman suspected of witchery.

Sometimes she even had benevolent phases, the Bonney. But the other side lurked just underneath, in cold, murderous res-ervation schools where her elder form's power was relentlessly worn away, replaced by Nell's own peculiar ideas of what consti-tuted "civilized." Sooner or later, a new form of Shamhat would always come along, modernizing and organizing, cleaning and cooking, teaching and training.

It was inevitable.

"Maria's still alive?" The blue gleams under the bonnet now held a distinct resemblance to gasflame. "But I thought . . ."

"Still alive." Dima's lips pulled back; it wasn't quite a smile, just a baring of teeth. "But probably not so pretty, now. Perhaps I can get milkshake?"

"Men. Dragged around by their bellies, when it's not their . . ."

Nell turned away, her lips pursed and calico skirt swirling. On summer days rubes would pack this place, spending tourist dollars on tchotchkes and eating down-home cooking; their pleasure would feed her in turn. The entire town, once a sinkhole of filth and murder, had been dragged relentlessly into a prim, profitable future.

It wasn't the worst that could happen, Dima knew. After all, it meant rich pickings, if he bothered to take them.

A tiny silver bell tinkled sweetly; Nell grabbed a snowy towel to wrap around her left hand. The first plate, heavy white ceramic dotted with blue forget-me-nots, slid out of the kitchen's inferno. Dima wondered, as he had the half-dozen other times he'd stopped for a bite, just what was behind that screen of light dispensing such tasty fare.

Maybe the Bonney also wondered about some of *his* little secrets. Curiosity wasn't solely for rubes; there was a light-fingered divinity with bulbous eyes whose job was to peep in every corner, unable to look away or leave anything as it was found.

Compulsion could grip the Eternal, too.

The plate thumped down before him with a nice heavy sound. The burger was two thick patties with pink blood in the middle, seared to perfection outside, on a toasted, garlic-buttered brioche bun. Lettuce, tomatoes, red onion, bacon, waxy overprocessed American "cheese"—oh, there were good things about giving your heart to Baba so this new land didn't take your birthright. The trouble with Maschka was wanting the cake *and* eating it; even a thief knew some few things had to be paid for in full.

And the fries! Thick-cut, golden, crisp on the outside and fluffy-white within, with a dish of mayonnaise and another of ketchup, both for dipping. A huge dill pickle spear, as crunchy as any hard-fried thing, and a sprig of parsley for cleaning the breath—though who would want to, Dima didn't know. In the old country ground meat was mixed with bread and fried, but here the luxury of pure meat was available. It was even *cheap*.

"Ah," he breathed, and didn't miss the slight change in Nell's eye-gleams. She was willing to be complimented for all her hard work, and sometimes even preened like a satisfied young bird at the praise. "Worth driving across country for, *miledi*."

"Should put something dreadful in it." Nell's tone was only moderately sharp, as she was only moderately mollified. "The girl's frightened, Konets. If you've done something you shouldn't—"

"I have been perfect gentleman." And this was what he got for it. His ears prickled, straining for his *devotchka*'s step in the hallway. She was probably crying in a toilet stall. Girls needed that sort of thing, and it would turn the snow outside to freezing rain. The poor rubes wouldn't know what hit them; they'd call it a weather event. "I am helping, even. Mascha raised her mortal, Bonney."

He didn't quite know why he said it. Perhaps because Nell was still watching him, the towel hanging from her left hand like a white rope, and he didn't quite like the way it twitched.

"Raised her . . ." Nell sucked in a deep breath, her ire at Dima forgotten now that there was another, much larger transgression to focus on. "Oh, no. That's not proper at all."

"Even hid her arcana in deep places." Dima finally lifted his hands, his fingers tingling as they wriggled with delight. A good burger had to be handled in proper fashion to keep its architecture stable. "Kept the girl from making her own. And guess what she pay Baba to look other way, huh?"

"I should have known you're no altruist." Nell's bonnet-brim didn't quite shrink, but the darkness underneath wasn't so deep. The tip of her nose emerged a little farther, and a slice of her tanned chin. "I'm not convinced you're going to remain gentlemanly either. Maybe I should have one or two of the Regulators keep an eye on her. Just to be safe."

Oh, those bastards with their tin stars didn't worry him at all. "You sure you want to lose them?" He scooped up the well-stacked tower of meat, vegetable, and bread, his jaw tingling with anticipation. If there were rubes present he might not have been able to get a proper bite, but bad weather and lateness of the hour meant this place was deserted.

Just one of the benefits of traveling in this particular way. His teeth sheared toasted brioche and lettuce, crunched through piquant onion, met melting tomato with sunlight still caught in its red flesh, pierced slightly waxen almost-cheese, then found meat. He let out a happy sound, and a shiver of pleasure slid down his spine.

Another silvery bell rang, its tone much deeper. Nell shook her head, swinging the towel as she ambled for the end of the counter, and Dima chewed slowly, his eyes half-closing. When his *devotchka* reappeared, he'd be able to see what the Bonney's cook thought she'd like, and the prospect was almost as pleasant as the tingle in his hands from brand-new arcana stowed temptingly close.

He was halfway through his meal before he realized what the second chiming noise meant, and that he had been a fool.

IN ON THE JOKE

The small pink-tiled ladies' room was a relief, even though it had a huge mirror over the sink Nat did her best not to look at. It was very clean, the lighting was soft instead of surgical, and though she didn't need the facilities Nat could still swing the heavy pink-painted wooden door of the single stall closed and lean against its comforting solidity, breathing in huge shuddering waves while hot salt water trickled down her cheeks.

Warm air soughed through a ceiling vent, no trace of dust or cobweb sticking to its shiny metal grille. The commode was an expensive hands-free model, probably waiting impatiently to do its job.

Why did divinities even have toilets? Was it just stage-dressing?

She had to brace her backpack against the stall wall to dig inside. The prepaid cell had migrated into the folds of her spare black T-shirt; it squirted through her fingers and she bit back an exasperated, shuddering sigh. Of course nothing could be simple, ever.

Flipping the phone open and turning it on was easy; waiting for it to power up while her breathing refused to slow down and her eyes watered so hard the entire stall blur-warped wasn't. She had to get the small digital screen almost to her nose before she saw she did, indeed, have three bars.

It was one piece of good luck. The prepaid plan was nation-wide, too. That was another.

Nat dialed. There was nothing to say, it was a waste of minutes and therefore cash, but she wanted—no, she *needed* to hear his voice. Someone who wouldn't sneer, wouldn't yell, wouldn't slide a verbal knife in.

You and your silly ideas, Natchenka . . . Well, let's hope you turn out pretty, because you're not bright . . . Stop lying, Natchenka, cats don't speak here . . . I will march you to that house at midnight . . .

All the terrible things Maria Drozdova had ever said circled her daughter like black birds. Nat could almost hear the feather-rustling, almost sense the sharp beaks; she held her breath and finished the string of numbers, whisper-recited them from the display just to be sure, and pressed the send button.

Her hand trembled; she clamped the phone to her ear. *Just ask how he's doing. Say you miss him. Maybe he's even worrying.*

A soft three-bar tone. "*I'm sorry,*" the phone chirped. "*You have reached a number that has been disconnected or is no longer in service. Please hang up and try again.*"

What the fuck? Nat checked the display. The number was correct, and it was the landline, unchanging and memorized since she was eight. She hung up, dialed once more, reciting each number again in a soft whisper just to be sure.

The same triple chime. "*I'm sorry. You have reached a number that has been disconnected or—*"

She tried again, third time the charm and everything, but all she got was the same bland message.

"No," someone in the pink restroom whispered, a broken, heartsick little syllable. "No, no no. No."

It was one thing to know there was nothing to say, to suspect Leo didn't really want to hear from her anyway because loving Mom left no room for anyone else. It was another thing to think that maybe he was relieved she was gone and the number was changed because . . .

The little yellow house sat behind a rotting picket fence, slumping with exhaustion. The garden, once a golden-haired Drozdova's pride and joy, was now a wilderness of dead snow-covered sticks; the brick chimney was busy quietly crumbling in increments. The big picture window in the parlor was broken, a sawtooth leer of jagged shards; the front door squeaked quietly as a cold wind pushed at its chipped, peeling paint.

The sudden mental image, clear and overwhelming, hit her like a punch to the gut. The phone dropped from her nerveless fingers, skittering across well-mopped tile, its display face still glowing green as a brief blare of tinny static burst from its innards. Nat sagged, trembling, against the wooden door, its bar lock giving a slight groan.

She wanted to say something, maybe *oh God* or *please* or *why are you doing this to me?* But her mouth was dry, and tasted of crumbling loam.

Dirt in my mouth. Except she hadn't eaten anything since Ranger's cornbread that morning—and wasn't it weird how the entire universe could change in a day, everything true suddenly gone and the entire collection of whirling bullshit constituting so-called "normality" staggering away like a singing drunk down a city sidewalk?

She pawed at the lock and spilled out of the stall, her black backpack's unzipped top flapping as she tacked unevenly for the sink. The mirror, nice and clean when she walked in, was now fogged. The entire bathroom groaned and pinged, sudden warmth forcing expansion upon drywall, lumber, metal, ceramic tile.

What the hell is going on? This wasn't a lake of fire stuffed with dead, screaming sinners like the nuns lingered over describing or rotating priests thundered about in mandatory chapel, but maybe Nat rated a personally tailored afterlife since she had, after all, committed the mortal, inescapable sin of being born and ruining her mother's life.

The faucet still worked. She rinsed her hands mechanically with cold water, splashed her face, and ignored the handy silver container of paper towels bolted to the wall. Dripping onto her peacoat and shivering despite the heat, she stared at the mirror's clouded eye.

If she wiped away heavy condensation, what would she see?

She couldn't get the image out of her head. Her house—no.

Her *mother's* house. Was Mama still alive? She could call the hospice to check, Nat supposed, and looked for the phone.

The floor was empty. Even when Nat folded carefully down, her hair held conscientiously aside as she peered in every conceivable corner, there was nothing but squeaky-clean tile, even behind the toilet's white porcelain column. The damn thing flushed while she was peering around its base, too, startling her so badly she straightened and almost reeled into the wall.

Oh, for fuck's sake. Nat lunged for her backpack, snatching the straps before it could disappear too. Her own voice startled her.

"I need to get out of here." Husky and slow, she sounded like a woman waking after a bad nightmare. *That's not entirely inaccurate.* "And away from him," she added.

A muffled, silvery chiming broke the thick, muggy silence. It sounded like someone had rung a bell in the hall outside—not just any bell, but the one clamped to the handlebars of the pink bicycle Leo had found as a rusted wreck and lovingly restored to apple-pie order for little Nat Drozdova.

He wouldn't just change the landline number, would he? Not unless Mom told him to, for some incomprehensible reason or another. When Nat was young, her mother's swiftly veering moods were terrifying; later, they were just like the weather. You simply hunched your shoulders and scuttled for your next destination, letting the squall split the sky overhead, hoping the lightning wouldn't strike you down this time.

Dmitri was probably waiting impatiently for her return. Maybe the bell was someone else needing to use the restroom.

Nell's place had been deserted, but someone caught in bad weather would see the big golden window, the neon OPEN sign, and wander in. Customers always descended in waves, wheeling and dipping like flocks of pigeons or starlings.

Nat pushed her hair back with damp fingers, zipping her trusty backpack and hitching it onto her shoulder. A clear droplet traced down the mirror, gathering strength from the heavy coat of mist, and even the bathroom's corners were looking a little damp.

Was that me? It wasn't out of the question, weird shit had collected around her ever since she could remember and the trend was only accelerating.

Everyone acted like they knew her, and knew what the hell was really going on. It was too much to hope that they'd let her in on the joke. It was like being in school again, the other kids laughing behind cupped hands, pointing at Nat the weirdo, Natty the freak, Nat the witch-girl.

I wish I was. Nat pushed violently at the door, bursting through. The same strange internal *thump* that meant entering a divinity's space thumped her solar plexus and she halted in confusion, a soft warm breeze caressing her wet cheeks, tickling her chin.

The door swung shut, a heavy moaning creak from over-stressed hinges. She whirled, but it had already closed with a heavy, final *snap* and was nowhere to be seen.

Nat Drozdova found herself next to a massive white fountain at the juncture of concrete walkways cutting through well-watered lawn. Past a long expanse of clipped green grass a massive white building soared, its domes—two smaller ones flanking a larger central curve—glowing with floodlights.

No snow. No prairie, no scrub-clad or timbered hills. No mountains, but high hills in the distance veined with bright traces of streetlamps. A smog-tinged city night enfolded her, sirens rising in the distance over a rumblemutter of traffic. Her eyes stung briefly, adjusting to bright floodlights. It was night, but the big white building was lit with a pitiless glow.

Nausea hit, hard and fast. Nat bent over, and retched so hard she almost turned inside out.

She couldn't even produce bile. When the stomach-clenching faded, she straightened, wiping at her sour mouth.

"What . . ." All the breath left her, because she recognized the massive white building from movies. It was an observatory, and it was all the way across the continent from New York. "Oh, hell."

She was in Los Angeles.

THAT EASY

The Laurelgrove still bore traces of Art Deco; remnants of former glory lingered in its pressed-tin ceiling and balky radiators. Hospice rooms with windows were more expensive but naturally a loving daughter wanted her mother to have the best, so pale snowlight fell through thin glass, touching the graying head of a man sitting, stolid and patient, on a pink-cushioned bench. Work-gnarled hands rested easily on jean-clad knees, and his chin was tucked almost to his chest.

Machines beeped and exhaled. Tubes carried liquids and oxygen to an ailing body; Maria Drozdova lay under a sheet and two thin hospital blankets.

Once beautiful enough to stop a prince's heart across a crowded ballroom, she was now a scarecrow with tarnished gray straw for hair. Her nose had risen, her cheekbones standing out sharply; lines radiated from the corners of her bloodshot blue eyes and thin, bitter-drawn mouth. Her black silk bed jacket embroidered with red roses was still neatly buttoned, the ruin of her hair covered by a pink kerchief tied by Leo's careful fingers as she stared at him, a faint spark struggling to light in her pupils.

The tube in her throat meant she couldn't speak, though a man who had lived with her as long as Leo had could certainly decipher a glance.

If he wanted to.

The nurses largely ignored him, and any doctor who glanced

in Leo's direction quickly looked away, even outside visiting hours. The elderly man's chest expanded and collapsed in time with Maria's labored breaths, and he seemed content to sit and watch.

A slate-colored afternoon settled over the city, ice congealing on every surface. The sky was too hard for snow; a frigid wind came from the north, whipping both sea and river into high white peaks. Plowed drifts froze into granite-hard hillscapes, and skyscrapers shivered under a dual assault of knife-edged air and accumulating ice.

There had not been a winter like this for more than twenty years, the newscasters all agreed. But it was warm in Maria Drozdova's hospice room, and the machines kept steady time.

A weary afternoon came to an early dusk. Pedestrians shivered and vehicles slid on slick, though salt-sanded, roads. A moving shadow dropped from the clouds, winging hard on the edge of a burst of wind more frigid than its fellows; the bird's eyes gleamed with bleak good humor.

Leo appeared to doze, a gleam showing under his eyelashes at intervals. When a hard-feathered burst rattled against the window he did not open his eyes, nor did he twitch.

He had been expecting this.

The machine monitoring Maria Drozdova's pulse quickened its rhythm. The room was silent, except for the new arrival—a glossy black bird, somewhere between a raven and a vulture, mantling as it perched on the bed's metal foot rail. It turned its head, its beak opened slightly, but it did not caw or shriek. Instead, it simply regarded Maria, whose skinny knob-knuckled hands twitched.

Two nurses passed the slightly open door to the hall. Maria's hands moved again, but she lacked the strength to reach for the button that would summon aid.

In any case, there was nothing mere mortals could do.

When the hall was silent again, another, softer feather-burst of sound filled the room. A chill touched every surface, rattling the IV pole and sending a burst of static through the electronics.

When it passed, Baba de Winter unfolded from the shadows at Maria's bedside. The beldame was just as thin as old Drozdova, but sheer cold vitality filled Grandmother's dark eyes; the iron chopsticks thrust through her vigorous gray mane bore tinges of wet red at their tips. A black layer-lace dress clasped her wasted form, fraying threads at hem and wrists hanging in trailing jellyfish fingers, waving gently. Some even lifted questing heads, blindly scenting prey.

"Oh, my dearest daughter," Baba said, quietly. "Look at you now."

Maria's bloodshot blue eyes widened, rolling like a terrified horse's. They darted a glance at Leo, whose lids had lifted; he regarded the beldame with bright interest and very little fear.

What mortal did not feel trepidation, facing her? But Leo Mishkin was not entirely what Dima Konets would call a "rube." He was no divinity either, though every artist laboring over a creation would have been proud of this one's endurance.

Still, he was a tired old man, and those know relief when they behold it.

The old Drozdova's pulse quickened, but her breathing—held to the steady pace of a respirator—could not. Her thinning, chapped lips writhed against the insectile thing clamped to her face, and as she shifted her bed jacket made dead cricket whispers against solicitously plumped pillows.

Baba bent close, and Mascha's weak movements intensified. A faint flare of red pinpricked her pupils. Her gaze kept flickering to Leo's, perhaps entreating him to speak.

But Grandmother Winter simply touched the edge of a pillow, smoothing harsh, much-bleached cotton. Her fingernails, resined deep heartsblood with exquisite care, scratched lightly, a cat's pinprick caress.

"Shhhh." Baba smiled, her lips now matching her nails. "You

didn't think it would be that easy, did you? After all, you stole from me too."

Maria's blocked throat vibrated with a small, despairing sound; her gaze fastened pleadingly upon her paramour. She could not speak anymore, let alone explain, bargain, or bully. He knew what she would want him to say, how she would want him to phrase it. Oh, yes, Leo knew the old Drozdova's overall plan, though perhaps not all its byways and hidden contingencies, and she counted on him to argue for her, or to pull the thing in her throat free so she could plead before this judge.

The beldame laughed. There was another soft feathery sound, a pop of collapsing air, and she was gone. Leo's breath puffed in the lingering cold, and he settled himself more firmly on the bench. Maria could keep a man from speaking, yes. She could keep him from warning a honey-haired little girl, keep him from using the vibration of voice on quivering air to express affection—but she could not force him to open his lips.

And a quasi-mortal man was beneath Baba's notice. The beldame would not question him.

)(

At least, for now.

GOOD HUNTING

The Griffith Observatory was a beautiful damn building, much more impressive in real life than in movies or pictures. A white spike like a bony finger loomed over her—at first she thought it was a fountain, but it was just a decorative feature, a copper plaque at its base indistinct in the darkness.

She couldn't decide whether this place was comforting or creepy deserted at night—after all, that was when you were supposed to see the stars, right? Except with a city's nightglow staining the sky, there probably wasn't much in the way of celestial pinholes to watch, and if she had to deal with a crowd of regular people eyeing her weirdness and sudden arrival, she might start screaming and never stop. Could a divinity be locked up in an asylum?

She didn't want to find out, and the perpetual threat from her teenage years—*look out, the men in the little white coats might come and take you away*—still grasped her nape with firm cool fingers, demanding she keep her head down, her behavior acceptable, and her weirdness from flying above the radar.

Nat, her chin almost touching her chest and her hands cupping her wool-clad elbows, peered through stray blondish curls at the observatory. She looked very much like Leo in that moment, though she would never know it; she was too busy gawking. She could almost see James Dean lounging against one of the white walls, his collar turned up and his pompadour gleaming—and *there* was a question, had he achieved divinity status? If Jay was still throwing parties in New York, maybe the rebel without a cause was still slouching and suffering through this city.

But Dean had died in a car crash. Or had he just sort of . . . become something else? Maybe he'd died but then somehow, impossibly, come back like Elvis was rumored to?

It wouldn't take a lot for her to start believing in nutbar conspiracy theories or UFO sightings, at this point.

The night was breathtakingly soft after the freeze of South Dakota, and full of the tang of smog married to something floral as well as a citrusy, woody topnote. A thread of jasmine pulled it all together, and Nat, alternately staring at the observatory or at a vast field of city lights visible behind its majestic bulk, couldn't decide between enduring car rides with Dmitri and this method of travel, whatever it was. Her stomach rolled before subsiding with a nasty, breathless twinge.

He's going to be angry. Of course the gangster would think she'd done this specifically to double-cross him, but Nat didn't have the faintest idea just what had occurred.

It was literally the story of her life.

The breeze ruffled her loosened hair, a warm, forgiving touch. So far California was a very nice place indeed—nobody yelling at her, making snotty little comments, or sneering with mockery. A disbelieving laugh rose in her throat; Nat clapped a hand over her mouth as if Mom had a headache and any noise was unbearable, unthinkable, unforgivable.

The image of the little yellow house, forlorn and crumbling, rose inside her head again. Maybe she was having some kind of hallucinatory breakdown.

Did divinities go mad? She had so many *questions*. Not that Mom had ever been big on answering even small, commonplace queries. Leo was better, but there wasn't much he could have said.

Not with dirt in his mouth.

Candy's short hurried whispers, Ranger's drawled asides, and Dmitri's offhand remarks were all Nat had to go on. She could start applying the scientific method, testing and retesting—all while collecting the arcana and eluding those terrible cold mouthless things. It was a tall order, and the urge to just sink down on the pavement and let the whole insane, malevolent world go on without her was overwhelming.

Night wind rattled tall bushes—oleanders, she thought, and rhododendrons—and tugged at her hair since her green knit cap was now tucked in a pocket. Nat hugged herself harder, watching the city lights. As soon as her stomach settled fully a quiet, inarguable sense of rightness dilated inside her—ever since she'd looked into the Well, the signal was coming through loud and clear.

There was something in this city she needed to find. It would lead her to the next piece, and the next, and once she had what she'd set out to get . . . what then?

She will eat you, Drozdova.

Her immediate panicked insistence that it had to be a lie had faded into used, sopping tissue stretched over a wide, yawning abyss. Nat hunched her shoulders, defensively. "It might even be a relief."

The words stung. After all, how else did you pay for the sin of being born? At least nobody was around to hear her talking to herself.

Crazy Natty. Witch-girl.

She turned in a complete circle, scanning for an exit; the parking lot was a good place to start. The surf-sound of traffic, while ubiquitous, wasn't very close. The thing she wanted wasn't in the big white domed building—that odd inner certainty was very clear—so she had no idea why she'd been dumped here, of all places.

It wasn't bad, she decided. Just puzzling. How in the hell had she done this? Dima said there were different ways of traveling.

He was going to be *furious*.

Well, she was just going to have to avoid him too. It was a pity she couldn't simply teleport wherever she wanted, but she probably shouldn't do it again until she had some idea of how it actually worked. The nausea was bad enough, but the risk of leaving a few internal organs behind like she was on a malfunctioning *Star Trek* episode was, for all she knew, more than zero.

If those cold, mouthless shadows came after her again, though, she might have to reconsider in a hurry.

Nat hitched her backpack a little higher. Her boots made soft, companionable sounds; the white parking lines had been freshly repainted and glowed under inadequate lamps. Pretty soon she was going to have to carry her coat.

The world wants to obey, Dmitri said. *Just ask.*

Well, like Leo always muttered when child-Nat was frustrated with her bicycle, she wouldn't get anywhere without practice. Thinking of him made her heart hurt. Had Mom told him to change the house number, or was that image—broken windows, rotting walls, listing picket fence, dead-frozen garden—actually true, a type of celestial security camera? Had Mom been the only thing keeping the house together?

That was impossible, the house was fine for months with just Leo and Nat living there. Even the finicky, perpetually blooming orchids had been fine.

She reached the parking lot and hesitated, staring over a vast empty expanse dotted with inadequate lamps.

"Good evening, Drozdova."

Nat flinched, casting around wildly. The owner of the purring, piping voice was a tuxedo cat, black ears perked and white chest gleaming. She had pristine pale socks, too, and sat on the red-painted NO PARKING curb, tail curled neatly around her feet.

So the cats spoke here, too.

"Oh," Nat managed, her heart pounding in her throat. "Hello."

The tuxedo blinked slowly, affectionately. Nat edged closer, careful not to loom, then crouched and extended her fingers. A careful, thorough investigation, tiny puffs of breath touching her skin, and the cat let out a pleased meow. "Much stronger now. It's very good."

Is it? "Is my mother . . ." Nat couldn't make herself say the word; it lodged in her throat like a bit of hard candy swallowed before its time. "Is she all right?"

"Still alive, but fading fast." Another slow blink, the cat very pleased to see her indeed. "It is the way of things."

I wish someone would have told me. Her backpack almost slid free; Nat sighed. "I might not make it in time." It was a terrible, terrifying thought.

If Mom did die before Nat got to the Heart . . . no.

No. She couldn't think about that. Even contemplating her own possible consumption was better than the image of Mom in the hospice bed, deflated and motionless, eyes closed and her terrible stinging mouth silent forever.

"In time? For what?" The cat's head tilted, inquisitive and interested at once. "You could scratch behind my ear, you know. I wouldn't mind."

Nat's cheeks felt strange. She realized she was smiling—though how she could at a time like this was beyond her, probably more proof that she was a bad daughter and even worse at this divinity stuff—and duck-walked a little closer, then smoothed her fingertips over the tuxedo's head. Finding the right spot behind the ear wasn't a challenge, nor was applying just the right amount of pressure—the small creature did all the work, all Nat had to do was be gentle. Anemic bushes rooted in dry dirt rattled as the breeze freshened, and a strengthening breath of jasmine rode moving air.

"I'm looking for something here. I don't know quite what." Her legs ached a little, but all in all, she felt remarkably good considering the past few days.

Was it Christmas yet? She'd lost all track of time, and it was warm enough for spring here. But a California winter probably qualified as summer elsewhere.

I don't know if I'll ever see spring again. The quiet, forlorn thought vanished without any fuss. Cramming unpleasant things into mental hiding spots was all but reflexive for Maria Drozdova's daughter.

The unsettling implication that one day they might burst free of all confinement followed suit.

"I suggest the Elysium." The tuxedo's tail-tip twitched; the cat leaned into Nat's touch with surprising strength. A rumble lingered under its tone, the purr almost too large for its slim, slinky body. "Beverly Hills, naturally."

So there's a divinity hotel here too; it's a whole-ass franchise. Good to know. "That's an excellent idea," Nat agreed. The hungry shadows couldn't get into those, Dima had said as much. "You've been protecting me all this time, haven't you. All of you."

"Pfft." The cat's eyelids dropped to half-mast. "You're the Drozdova." Just like a human might say *water's wet,* or *politicians lie.* "Our compact is ancient, and you mean good hunting." Her lip lifted, teeth gleaming very much like Dmitri's. "We remember. We'll remember long after the silly humans are gone, too."

That's comforting, I suppose. "Did you . . ." *Don't lie, Natchenka. Cats don't talk in this country.* "Did you ever talk to my mother?"

"I never met her." The cat didn't quite sound dismissive, just bored.

Well, that was what Nat got for asking an overly broad question. "The cats here in this country, I mean. Not you personally."

"Ah. No." The tuxedo flowed under her fingertips, letting Nat's touch wander down her neck, brush her shoulder, and scrub along flexible ribs. "Right there . . . yes, that's a good spot. Why would we?" she continued, meditatively. "*You* are the Drozdova. Native-born, and all that. A little harder, please."

Nat complied. "I don't suppose you like him, either. Dmitri."

A tiny chirruping sound melded out of the purr, the feline

equivalent of a laugh. "Oh, we understand him. He's a hunter too, after all."

I can see that. Nat found the spot at the base of the cat's tail and rubbed at exactly the right pressure. The tuxedo balanced on the concrete edge, a thousand tiny adjustments keeping her perfectly poised, her back arching with satisfaction.

Mom had never allowed a pet, despite all Nat's pleading. Was she afraid they'd talk, and Nat might learn . . . what?

A kid would trust a parent over their own lying eyes and ears. Nat had for most of her life. It happened all the time—adults knew best, they were the gods of small universes within the home walls. What choice did a child have but to be convinced?

It was enough to make you wonder if the rubes Dima was always scoffing at were the same. Kids believed in Santa Claus, the Easter Bunny, and in parental love. Grown-ups believed in paying insurance premiums, going to church, and getting laid.

The difference was, children couldn't choose. They had to take everything on faith.

"I'm scared," Nat whispered. It felt good to say it out loud, but also terrifying. Showing any weakness was a great way to get kicked right in the teeth.

But the cats, while maddeningly opaque and not overly concerned with answering superfluous questions, weren't cruel—but maybe they weren't simply because Nat wasn't a mouse or a bird.

Felines did play with their food, after all. Dima probably did too.

"Yes," the tuxedo agreed. "I suppose you are."

Did my mother want to eat me? The words stuck in her throat.

The tuxedo apparently had other business tonight, because she hopped lithely from the curb and half-turned, looking over her shoulder. Her eyes were wide and lambent, green-gold with reflected streetlamp light. "I suggest you call a taxi, too." Amusement glittered in her gaze, and her black tail lashed once, twice. "It's easier than walking."

"I don't even know how I got here." Nat stood, slowly.

"Through a door." The cat made another amused sound. "Nell Bonney's house has what you need, after all. Be careful, Drozdova."

I'd love to. I just can't figure out how. "Thank you. Have a nice evening."

The cat stepped sideways, melding into shadows, and was gone. The parking lot was just as deserted; if there was a security guard she was going to have to do some quick thinking and even quicker talking, or just run like hell and hope for escape. Nat exhaled hard, settled her backpack, and looked around for options.

Call a taxi. Well, she didn't have a phone anymore, but Nat didn't think it mattered, and she was right. A faint sound, drawing nearer, was the throb of a well-maintained engine.

She also didn't think it was Dima's big black car.

A pair of lemon-yellow headlights flowed smoothly through the parking lot. They belonged to a bright yellow taxi— not just *any* taxi, either, but the acme of all paid conveyances. It had old-fashioned bubble-bulging wheel wells, a stripe of black-and-white checkerboard down either side, and a lighted rectangle on its roof proudly shouting its availability. The entire car hummed with bright vivid reality as it swerved aside, banking in a tight arc and stopping on a dime right in front of the curb where Nat stood, the front passenger window rolling down.

The driver wasn't quite a surprise, either. A lean male shape in jeans and a faded green army jacket leaned across the front bench seat, an unlit cigar protruding from a hard-set mouth. "You lookin' at me?" he barked, but the brusqueness was merely professional instead of angry. His head bulged oddly, but as Nat bent to peer into the shadowy interior she realized it was a bright green Sikh turban.

A red air freshener shaped like a pine tree hung from the rearview, swinging gently; a hula girl with a swaying plastic-grass skirt was stuck to the dash.

Don't get in cars with strange men was a good rule to live by, but Nat had bigger problems. "Hello." Her throat was dry again, and the word was a little squeaky. "I need to go to the Elysium. But I don't have much money—"

"Don't insult me," the driver barked. "Honor to drive you,

ma'am. Get in, and don't dilly-dally. The Wailing Lady's out tonight, and she ain't nothin' to mess with."

Wailing Lady? That sounds appropriately terrifying. Nat reached for the front passenger door, thought better of it when the driver's cigar lit with an angry red gleam, and stepped to the rear. It opened with a heavy satisfying sound, and while the seat was covered in tough canvas, it didn't smell too bad. Especially with the windows down.

He barely waited for her to pull the door closed before the engine revved and the taxi lunged into motion like it had never intended to stay still. It wasn't like Dima's muscle car; no, the yellow automobile squealed through the entrance to the parking lot without touching a heavy, similarly bright-yellow boom lowered to keep strangers out. Nat flinched, sure there was going to be a horrific accident, but rubber smoked, the back end slewed, and the taxi took a hairpin curve practically standing on two tires.

New York taxis were aggressive, but nothing like this—and Nat could rarely afford them *or* rideshares. The yellow cab jolted and shimmied like a roller coaster, taking canyon curves with ruthless efficiency, veering into whatever lane it pleased. Which was fine on the deserted observatory road, but as the streetlights thickened other headlights appeared, not to mention brake lights, and Nat couldn't decide whether to squeeze her eyes shut, stare in horror, or start cussing.

She flinched, a horn blared, and the driver let loose a string of cheerful high-volume obscenities, almost poetic in their flow and vigor.

"—sonfabitchin' *road*!" he finished, and drew in a stentorian breath as he wrenched the wheel aside and they slalomed down a long hill, flashing past tentacles of urbanization. His turban had changed to a faded red baseball cap, and his cigar to a Swisher Sweet in a yellow plastic holder. A roulette smear of storefronts, houses, apartment buildings, palm trees, street signs, pedestrians, other cars, fruit stands, ignored stoplights, and brightly lit billboards whooshed past as a warm flood of orange-scented exhaust-laden wind whistled through the half-open window.

Nat's stomach flipped, she clutched at her backpack, a bright spike of pain went through her skull, and the cab slewed through a series of impossible turns, one after another, ending with a long smoking smear of rubber and a cheery, "The Elysium, ma'am, and how didja like the ride?"

Oh, shit. For the second time that night, Nat was miserably sure she was going to spew—if there was anything left of Ranger's cornbread in her middle, that was. She swallowed something hot and rancid, peering out the window, and found a half-familiar cobbled expanse leading to a bright glass-and-silver revolving door. Two crimson-uniformed bellhops and a doorman stared at the taxi, their heads tilted at exactly the same puzzled angle, and the big slab of security with mirrored sunglasses touched his earpiece, his colorless lips twitching.

The door looked just the same as it had the very first time she'd seen the Elysium, and for a moment she was sure he'd driven her all the way back to Ohio. On the other hand, this building wasn't brick but thick adobe with a red-tiled roof. The doorman glided for the taxi, one white-gloved hand extending.

"Very fast," Nat managed. "Is this . . ."

"Welcome to Elysium Beverly Hills, ma'am." The driver turned his head, and his profile blurred like clay under running water. Only the bright baleful orangish eye of the cigarillo and the fact of a hat stayed the same, though now the latter was a battered straw cowboy number. "I got other fares tonight, so if you don't mind, I'd like to get to them."

"Th-thank you." Nat reached blindly for the door, but it flung itself open as if the car itself couldn't wait to get rid of her. The doorman caught hold, a solid jolt pushing him back on his heels, and springs groaned as the taxi rocked.

"Anytime, ma'am," the driver barked, professional merriment practically spitting through each syllable. "Havva nice night."

Nat spilled out into a smog-tinted evening, her boots meeting old, river-rounded cobbles. This courtyard was also different, she saw with a jolt of relief—the blank walls enclosing it were adobe as well. A cheerful red-and-white striped awning stood guard over the slowly spinning door, which looked just as hungry as it had in Akron. Dusty red tiles crowned sly-peeking nearby roofs; a fountain plashed sweetly, liquid music underlaid by a low, keening moan.

"Welcome to the Elysium, ma'am." The doorman delivered each word robotically, without inflection. "Pleasure to have you with us. Baggage?"

Do divinities just not pay for anything? Is that how this goes? "N-no." She made it two steps away from the taxi on trembling legs before the door slammed, tires squealed, and a yellow smear rocketed away, bursting out of the courtyard's far end and screeching into a hard left turn. "Just my backpack. Thanks."

The water-sound came from a massive white-and-crystal fountain set farther back in the courtyard amid potted orange trees. Water rationing was evidently not in effect, because foaming silver cascaded lovingly down its sides. Standing in its central dish, a female figure draped in sodden black raised her arms, turning slowly as she moaned again. The sound cut through the evening's warmth, and Nat shivered.

"Best to come inside, Miss Drozdova, if I may be so bold." The doorman shifted from foot to foot, and though his tone never wavered, the set of his shoulders expressed deep caution. "Señora Llorona is perhaps not in the mood for conversation tonight."

What the hell? Nat blundered in his wake, her stomach still sudsing like her mother's ancient Maytag. Once they stepped under the awning the doorman relaxed and indicated the revolving door.

Nat braced herself. There was no Dmitri to hide behind, now.

"*Mi niiiiiiñoooos.*" A plaintive cry rose behind her, accompanied by the rilling of water. "*Oh mi niiiiiiiños pooooobres . . . mi niiiiiiños, donde estaaaaaaan . . .*"

Nat flinched. The voice, a beautiful alto, staggered under a weight of devouring grief, anguish fluting in the vowels and the consonants ragged with rage. She halted, half-turning to glance over her shoulder, but the doorman caught her elbow.

"No, miss," he whispered frantically, no longer robotic. "Don't look. Please, *don't* look."

It was hard work to ignore the sobbing. Every bit of empathy Nat possessed demanded she turn back, try to help somehow. But the doorman tugged at her elbow, hissing slightly as if the touch hurt, and she stepped into the revolving door's bright silvery maw instead.

ON THE HUNT

The worst part wasn't having to take the burger with him, though it meant the fries got slightly soggy waiting for Bonney to wrap everything up. Nor was it the deep frigidity outside Deadwood, Baba's storm spreading as the beldame felt her oats.

It was her time of year, after all.

No, the worst was gripping the wheel-yoke with one hand, his fingers no longer tingling pleasantly and the windows all the way up since there was no tempting, teasing smell of vulnerable warmth and sweet jasmine filling the car's interior. Even being able to slip into his thiefways, a familiar umber sky lowering overhead as the tires smoked and glowed low punky red, didn't help.

He carried no fragile cargo now. But where had the damn girl *gone*?

Not my fault, Bonney said, grinning under that stupid fucking shovel-hat of hers as her eyes spat blue sparks. *She needed to go, that's all.*

He should have known the civilizing bitch would take any chance to do him a disservice; she had no use for his type, squeezing them out or clapping them in respectable straitjackets with unseemly haste. He enjoyed taking those she thought were oh-so-straight-and-narrow, tempting them to dip their fingers in one pot after another—oh, very discreetly, of course.

Some of his best uncles were politicians, here as well as in the old country.

It probably tickled Nell pink to set the *zaika* loose, but it was the worst possible twist at this particular point in the game. *Those who eat* weren't the only danger, and little Nat was trained to be a shivering piece of prey. Maria had done the job well; the girl would probably offer her own throat for the flint knife without any hesitation at all.

And there would go all his chances of vengeance, not to mention . . . anything else. He slipped out of the thiefways and back in, hunting, but there was no sign of his little doll no matter how many times he stutter-stepped between his particular pocket traveling-dimension and the rubes' world.

Mortals thought theirs the only reality, the idiots, but every power had its secret ways.

Near Salt Lake City the storm lost him again, even Baba's grasping crimson-nailed fingers slipping free of a thief's collar. He would have liked to show Nat this desert town, its gaudy main temple and its sagebrush-scented wickedness under a thick lacy crust of rectitude. There were affairs to be handled here, if he had time to stop—but he didn't, so he pressed on after a short halt on the outskirts, watching a gray dawn rise exhausted in the east and sniffing deeply.

California, she'd said, and the thought that it might be misdirection was laughable. The girl didn't know how to lie. Her face was as transparent as any rube's.

He had to hand it to darling, hungry Mascha. She'd created the perfect victim. If Dima didn't have his own flinty pride, he might have done the same thing.

There were, he discovered, sitting on his black chariot's warm throbbing hood overlooking the freeway just outside Herriman and smoking while he watched the sun rise through fringes of nasty brush-broom clouds, thefts even *his* gorge rose to contemplate. Few they were indeed, and though he ruled them all, he did not have to give his blessing to any.

He smoked two cigarettes down to the filter, his bootheels braced on the fender and his dark eyes narrowed. His shoulders hunched slightly, and except for his solitude any rube passing by in this part of the country might think him a young man out on mission, with a car instead of a bicycle and a vice their pale, wife-accumulating god winked at in his chosen few. Offering a promise of something better after the Cold Lady took you in her arms was one of the better scams; Dima, however, preferred to make a contract with the here and now.

It was simply more efficient, and far more profitable.

His boot-toes twinkled angrily while he inhaled, blew out clouds of scented smoke, and waited for a little internal twitch that would tell him where to go. All his uncles and nephews, all his other faces—even those repulsed by his particular methods, magnets disliking their twin—were on the alert.

Even if they didn't know quite what they were looking for, a single glimpse would suffice. Long honey hair with more than a hint of curl, big dark trusting eyes, lucent skin, that baggy blue wool coat of hers, that battered black backpack and those heavy graceless boots—the instant one of them saw her or caught a thread of out-of-season jasmine, a warm breeze where none should be, a forgiving comfort . . . he would know.

Finally, Dima slid from his perch and stretched, each joint cracking like a distant shotgun blast. The car roused, the driver's door banged shut with an ill-tempered bark, and he revved the engine, his hands wrapping loosely around the yoke's two butterfly-halves.

"California," he murmured, and smiled. It wasn't a very nice smile, and his *zaika* might well cower if she saw it.

Dima liked the golden state of opportunity. He liked the workers in the fields, dreaming backsore and bruise-fingered. Then there were the greedy cities with their asphalt veins, the rich along the craggy coast, the movie stars and Candy's starlet-harlots in Los Angeles. There was Frisco to the north with its wide-open bars a good pickpocket could fleece at will; further northwards there were the extremists, the Humboldt uncles and nephews who served him well, and the penny-ante players. Everywhere, there were the chickens ripe for plucking and fucking. The entire state was hustle, from the fields to the boardrooms, and though the honest might sometimes outnumber his kind, there was plenty for everyone concerned.

If, that is, you had the balls to take it.

Yes, he liked California plenty, and it had been a while since he'd visited. One of his other faces handled most of the business on this coast. He supposed he should thank his quicksilver *zaika* for the vacation.

There was nowhere she could hide from him. The black car gave a chortle as his mood lifted. His chariot rolled into motion, slipping into the thiefways with a tearing sound, and as dawn strengthened over Utah the secret bootlegger's roads of the entire continent gave out a single stinging, singing pulse.

The Dead God was on the hunt.

ANY BAGGAGE

The Beverly Hills Elysium's lobby accepted her without a sigh, and though the outside was a little different the interior was the same right down to the large central fireplace, the darkened bar behind its smoked glass panels, and the front desk with its carving of reeds and river so detailed she expected it to move. Hushed expectancy hung over every surface, from marble floor to thick red carpet to lovingly polished tables and deep comfortable furniture. Fresh flowers quivered in tasteful vases, and Nat felt very small, not to mention extremely disheveled.

Even the ebon, gleaming-bald man behind the main desk was familiar, and his smile was warm and pleased. "Welcome to the Elysium, mademoiselle. It's wonderful to see you again." A young man and a girl, both in the ubiquitous scarlet uniform, flanked Mr. Priest and smiled encouragingly as well. The girl's hair was cropped short; the boy's was shaven close just like his boss's.

Maybe Priest was a divinity. He didn't carry the blurring, buzzing sense of power Dmitri did, but he certainly looked more *there* than regular people.

Rubes, Dima's voice whispered, and she shook her head.

"Hi." It was an entirely inadequate greeting, Nat realized. *Oh hell, how do I ask how to pay?* "It's, uh, nice to be back."

"We are a refuge for the weary, and proud to be so." His smile didn't alter; he hadn't beamed at Dima like this. "It's Priest, mademoiselle. Your regular room, I presume?"

"I . . ." *Oh, what the hell.* The worst it could cause was a little embarrassment. "I don't have any money."

The girl to Priest's right inhaled sharply, almost as if Nat had cursed.

But Mr. Priest's urbane grin never faltered. "Would you care for some, then? We can make a delivery; simply let us know the amount required. Do you have any baggage, mademoiselle?"

That is not the response I expected. "No more than the next girl, I suppose." She almost clapped her hand over her mouth; this wasn't the time for jokes, no matter how relieved she was. Her mouth had a mind of its own these days, though, and merrily bolted onward like a big black horse with carnivore teeth. "I'm sorry. I'm really new at this."

"Everyone learns, mademoiselle." He leaned forward slightly, managing to give the impression of a confidential whisper without altering his ramrod verticality by more than a degree or two. "Including divinities, powers, and principalities. Sixth floor, as usual? Was the suite to your taste last time?"

"Oh yes. Very." Nat restrained the urge to bob a curtsy. Suddenly, she felt greasy all over, and longed for a hot shower, not to mention a decent bed. "Oh, and if Mr. Konets comes by, can you . . . can you not tell him . . ."

"We are very discreet, mademoiselle." Mr. Priest's handsome face turned grave, all merriment vanishing. His shoulders stiffened slightly. "Your privacy will not be intruded upon here."

Oh, thank God. She winced—breaking the habit of casual blasphemy was going to take a while, especially inside her own head. "Thank you."

"But of course. I must remind mademoiselle that this is a place of rest. All feuds or battles are left outside the doors; while inside these walls all are welcome, and all are held to the same standards. Nonconsensual violence towards another guest or an employee is strictly forbidden and will result in banishment; all formal Ring matches are, of course, exempt. All amenities are included in your stay; whatever is required will be found." The bald man in his sharply creased deep-indigo suit took a deep breath; the speech rolled from his tongue with the smooth cadence of a trained actor's Shakespearean soliloquy. "The bar is open to all; we do ask for some slight moderation in imbibing though we understand it might not be possible in all cases. Meals are served in the restaurant at usual times or in the Ring; if you wish privacy while consuming, simply pick up the phone in your room and we shall be happy to deliver. The boutiques upon the second floor are ready to assist any guest; the pools are open at all hours though we do ask that strict silence be observed in the sauna. The rooftop garden here is open; Mademoiselle's elder sister graciously consented to its upkeep, for which we thank her."

Elder sister? What? Nat's jaw threatened to drop. "Oh. I didn't . . . sister?"

"If you like, we may notify her of your advent?" Priest's hazel eyes were warm and forgiving. His hands rested on the bare countertop, nails buffed to a mellow shine. "She would be very eager to see you."

The sense of the world slipping away underfoot was sadly familiar by now. "Okay," Nat said, through the rushing in her ears. *Sister. I have a sister? Of course Mom wouldn't tell me. But why didn't Mom try eating her?* "I might as well. Thank you."

"It is my pleasure." He said it just as sincerely as he had the first time and made a small movement. "George, please show Mademoiselle Drozdova to her suite. Enjoy your stay, mademoiselle."

The shaved, scarlet-clad boy gave her an encouraging smile, slipped through a swinging gate on the far side of the massive counter, and beckoned encouragingly.

There was nothing else to do, so Nat followed.

SOLITUDE

It was almost exactly the same as in Ohio—the bedroom with a wide white damask bed on acres of thick emerald carpeting, sitting room and bedroom with enormous bay windows looking over a night-jeweled city skyline with a glitter of ocean in the distance instead of a river. The faint good scent of cut grass was the same too, as was the white leather couch and two white leather chairs crouching before a glassed-in gas fireplace in the sitting room. The furniture's wooden bits still looked like birch saplings pressed into different shapes and left to grow over decades, their papery boles glowing. Again, no television, and once the door closed behind George—who thankfully didn't seem to expect a tip—Nat Drozdova was left in blessed silence.

The bathroom was, if possible, even more luxurious—giant sunken marble tub with whirlpool jets, a glassed-in shower with four different chrome heads pointing at marble tile, shelves of high-end toiletries from no brand she'd ever heard of, a vanity with rosy bulbs giving a flattering light as well as a bench with a green velvet pad in case she needed to paint herself for a night out.

As soon as Nat saw the bed, though, all other considerations became secondary. The black horse's gallop still throbbed in her bones, a dim faraway rhythm like a distant train. It had been a long damn night on top of a terrible, terrifying day, and though that uncanny sense of well-being and energy still filled her physical frame the rest of her felt like it was dragging through mud. Her eyes were dry as if she'd cried herself into quiescence like she used to in middle school, her neck ached, and if divinities had souls, hers was weary right down to the floorboards.

Even if sleep wasn't a necessity, sometimes it was the only answer to your problems.

There was one more difference between this suite and the one in Akron. There was no connecting door to another room. The wall where it had been was smooth and blank, and if the Elysium was one weird interdimensional place with a lot of doorways, the change was either the best renovation job ever or the aperture had never existed in the first place.

The urge to drag some of the furniture across that space just to be safe was overwhelming, but most of the birchwood pieces looked disturbingly like they had grown from the floor itself. So she simply slid her coat off, tossing it over the end of the bed, and dropped onto the covers, snuggling into piled, decorative cream and green pillows. They didn't smell like industrial fabric softener or the exhalations of other travelers; instead, a cloud of sun-dried linen scent enfolded her, and the young Drozdova immediately fell into a deep, dreamless state indistinguishable from mortal sleep.

X

For a moment, Nat was certain she was back in the little yellow house, safe and snug in the single bed Leo had built of scrap lumber. She was also certain it was summer, because warm sunlight fell across her face and the quiet was total, which meant Mom and Leo were both out in the garden because she'd overslept. Anticipating her mother's disappointment brought her into full consciousness with a jolt, sitting straight up on a soft white bed scattered with fluffy pillows. Somehow she'd turned it into a nest overnight, and sunk into the exact middle like a weary baby bird.

Her head was clear, though her mouth was full of a thin, watery copper taste and at some point in the night she'd wriggled out of her bra, tossing it vaguely in the direction of her backpack. The white sheers over the window moved restlessly, a soft breeze slipping over every surface. Flames in the gas fireplace flickered; whoever paid the bill apparently didn't mind leaving it on all the time like the one in the lobby.

She was alone.

At home there was always Mom and Leo, due at any moment if not already there. At work there was no solitude, even in the bathroom—retail or office workers were supposed to be ever-available. Even in transit, on the bus or subway, someone was always around. In Dmitri's car there was the constant agonizing fear of the gangster divinity eventually turning on her; even at the Elysium in Ohio there had been the fact of the connecting door.

Nat had never realized just how much of her life was taken up with navigating between other people. It was . . . nice, to be all by herself, if slightly frightening. She didn't have to wait for the front door to close and someone to call *hello, house;* she didn't have to keep her expression neutral or her shoulders protectively hunched. She could probably take all her clothes off and dance around singing at the top of her lungs, if she wanted to.

Would someone in another room complain about the noise? A low, husky laugh surprised her. It took a moment to realize it came from her own throat; she pulled the backpack into her lap and unzipped its top.

The unicorn mug was still there, gilt-glowing as she held it in sunshine far too golden and vibrant to be winter. So far, California was just as bright as advertised; she traced the unicorn's horn gently, a wondering touch.

What did you put in a grail? Wine? Water? Hot chocolate? Anything you damn well pleased?

The wooden box holding the Knife all but leapt open. The

flint blade gleamed slightly, as if oiled, and she touched the handle with a tentative fingertip.

A pleasant warmth flooded from the contact, hitting her shoulder and spreading down through her chest. Both Knife and Cup vibrated, as intensely real and *there* as a divinity. The sense of rightness intensified, and if gazing into the Well had kick-started some weird internal process, the two arcana were magnifying and hurrying it.

"Holy hell," Nat whispered. Whatever she had to find in Los Angeles was probably just as powerful, just as *right*. Maybe all this newfound strength would save her mother.

Or maybe it was meant for some other purpose.

If her mother wanted to . . . to eat her, why send her on a cross-country scavenger hunt? It seemed a little counterproductive, and if there was anything Maria Drozdova despised, it was inefficiency.

"She wanted me to bring everything and the Heart back," Nat said, testing each word. The sunlight strengthened, skirting the edge of painful brilliance; going south for the winter wasn't just for birds. "She can't eat the Heart, but she can . . ."

She will eat you, Drozdova. After you bring her what she wants, so she can bargain with Baba Yaga to allow the theft of a native-born child.

Having uninterrupted time to think was a terrifying luxury. So not only would Nat bring back the Heart, but also the arcana. Trading the Dead God's Heart to Baba Yaga would do . . . what? It didn't matter, if Nat would be consumed afterward. Maybe divinities just needed de Winter's rubber stamp if they wanted to eat their children? It was a gruesome thought, and Nat forced herself past it, to the logical end.

Maria Drozdova would be able to live in this new country without trouble, because her daughter would be . . . eaten.

"Dead," Nat whispered. "Dead and eaten. Right? That's what that means."

Panicked denial turned her stomach over. She wasn't hungry, but she could have done with a cup of coffee before contemplating *this*. Maybe that was why she'd never been alone before; it led to all sorts of things. Like thinking for yourself, or realizing that the bleak knowledge of a mother's hatred had always been pulsing inside Nat's own bones, like a black, malignant mass.

Like the cancer human doctors swore was eating Maria bit by bit.

Don't be ridiculous. Mothers don't eat their children.

But here Nat was, sitting in a divinity hotel, holding glowing arcana and being pursued by shadowy mouthless scavengers. She'd turned a jukebox on with invisible power just by looking at it and asking nicely, not to mention held an entire city street motionless while Dmitri's car slewed between frozen vehicles. She'd gotten rid of Friendly, and danced with Jay before he was nailed to an X of raw lumber and a woman in green spilled from his dry-husk corpse.

There were hungry stepmothers in fairytales, gods who ate their own progeny in old myths. It wasn't that much of a stretch. And now Baba de Winter's behavior, not to mention Dmitri's, made a lot more sense.

You think Maria Drozdova would do this for you, little girl?

Go figure, she'd finally gotten rid of the gangster, only to find out he'd been absolutely right and damn near helpful, too. Not to mention also almost kind, in his own particular fashion. Even his attempt to teach her how to begin using this power.

This *divinity*.

Nat laid the Knife back in its case, closing the wooden box slowly. It didn't take long to repack her bag, both arcana safely stowed in clean laundry. She could wear this outfit for another day, it wouldn't do any harm. The Elysium—and wasn't that name a laugh and a half, folks—probably had laundry service.

Or if she found a laundromat, maybe she could just ask the washer politely and save herself some quarters.

World wants to obey, zaika. *Just ask.*

She could wash her face and get some coffee, at least, before getting back into her boots and figuring out where to find—

But the outside world, never content to simply leave well enough alone, had other ideas. Nat stiffened, her chin rising, a bare moment before a series of crisp knocks resounded against the suite's door, floating through the sitting room to reach her.

Shave and a haircut. Pause. *Two bits.*

At least whoever it was had a sense of humor. Maybe it was Dmitri; her heart gave a panicked, unsteady leap at the thought. Nat slithered off the bed in a rush and padded in sock feet for the entrance, hoping there was a peephole. If it was the gangster, maybe she didn't have to open the door.

Not that she'd be able to hide in here forever, but having the option—any option at all, really—was a pleasant change.

SUNNY FIELDS

I t wasn't what he wanted to be killing.

Dmitri Konets stalked between rows of plywood shacks, a cold breath slithering through mortal dreams. The straight razors—one with a handle of bleached, the other of blackened bone, since he was hunting half amid the rube world and half in the shadows of their fever-dreams—gleamed as he leapt, silent as a hunting panther, and a scavenger shadow's rotting veil-body dropped, neatly cloven in half. They were thickening along her trail, the cold mouthless bastards, and if he winnowed them *just* enough they would lead him to a girl growing into divinity by leaps and bounds.

It was a balance, leaving enough of them alive to follow his tender little *devotchka* but not allowing their numbers to reach truly dangerous proportions. Of course their crowd was inexhaustible, but it took time for them to coalesce.

Unfortunately, the physical and less-tangible misery of migrant workers in slumshacks tucked out of sight on land owned by the rich but farmed by callused brown hands at pennies per day was good fuel for scavengers. The tiny thieveries committed to ensure daily survival tickled him as well; the larger thefts by sunburned overseers and managers were a little less pleasing.

Of course the biggest burglaries, committed on spreadsheets and in boardrooms, were interesting and filling in their own way. But they weren't on the menu tonight.

Sleeping mortals felt him as a chill amid bright nightly fantasies of a better life, and they would never know his lithe, deadly killquiet was keeping *them* safe, too. The scavengers wouldn't hesitate to cluster a born-lucky mortal full of more than the usual measure of bright warm life, battening on any excess of pleasure or happiness. His *zaika's* passage brought good golden luck, true—but she also irresistibly drew this cold wave in her wake, and would until she achieved her full status. He'd tracked this group of freezing carrion from the vineyards, and they were moving steadily west and vaguely south instead of simply drifting.

Which meant they knew, in their witless blundering way, where their most prized prey was to be found.

Dima, skipping across a malodorous alley between rows of slumped shelters built of scavenged materials, bent and cleaved through another shadow. Straightened, extending in an effortless lunge as one veil-draped specimen slightly stronger than its brethren turned to give battle, possibly driven past even its mute grasping patience by his relentlessness. He sliced it into petal-folding pieces before bursting into the camp's central square—these mortals replicated their home villages in all but name, carrying their culture north with their own gods.

One listing, anemic water pump for the hundred and fifty souls crammed into living here; the sanitary conditions hardly deserved the name. Under their care the sunny fields near Fresno produced acres of fruits and vegetables sent to supermarkets in less-congenial climes; here, where they gathered well after dusk to choke down a few calories begrudged by their masters, disease and malnutrition ran rife. To the "employers" it didn't matter, of course—there were always more where these serfs came from, these chickens believing the promise of *El Norte*.

Truth, justice, freedom in America? Certainly—if you could pay for them, and the price wended ever upwards. Keeping the workers exhausted was a good way to make sure they didn't rise with torches and sharpened implements, turning on their tor-mentors.

And wouldn't Dima eat well *then*, too? He almost wanted to provoke a few of them into the act, but he had other work before dawn.

The cold didn't bother him, and weariness was not a danger. Battle was as good as Bonney's burgers, and almost as filling as thefts. Konets leapt; his silvered boot-toes flashed as he landed with a silent crunch on the back of a stretching, rotten shad-owshape, its claws scratching a plywood shack-wall like a cat demanding entrance.

Stray or pet felines wouldn't offer any aid in this chase. Their loyalty was to the one who provided better prey, not to a fellow hunter. Still, they watched—he caught sight of tail-flickers every now and again, lambent eyes hurriedly closing, fur-sliding forms slipping into deep shadow and stepping *between* as felines were wont to do.

They had thiefways of their own.

The battle took a breath on the edge of a broccoli field, one last scavenger drifting away hurriedly as its companion died under his flashing blades. Dmitri straightened, flicking the always-stainless razors as if to clean them of blood.

It was unnecessary—the mouthless clawing eaters held no life-giving fluid—but the fillip pleased him. He whistled, softly, and on a nearby access road an engine sprang into purring life, headlights dim-shuttered in deference to his stealth.

He would follow this lone survivor, watching as it swelled to hive off more of its kind. Yet more would clot-coalesce in due time, and when their numbers reached a certain threshold he would winnow them again, and again, as many times as it took to find his prey.

It was like hunting with dogs in the old country, and for once the thought of his birthplace pleased him. The void in his chest gave a soft, painless lurch, and the driver's door of a low-slung black car closed with a crisp sound. Perhaps a rube sleeping nearby woke at the sound, sweat-drenched, a nightmare moan still caught on chapped lips.

Or perhaps not. The mortals could sleep soundly now, for a few minutes at least, before they were called to work in the fields again.

MARISOL DE FLORES

There was no peephole. Nat hovered near the door, caught between uncertainty and curiosity. A soft, pregnant silence was broken by a faint drumming—fingertips marching in quick succession against painted wood.

A voice filtered through. "Drozdova?" A pleasant soprano, which ruled Dmitri out, unless he was a helluva ventriloquist. "You don't know me yet; it's Marisol. I don't mean you any harm."

Why would you say that first off, then? Nat swallowed dryly. There was a silvery chain on the door; she'd hooked it up last night as well as throwing the dead bolt.

Now she was glad. But if it was another divinity, a chain wouldn't do any good, would it? Priest said "no nonconsensual violence," but plenty of people decided to risk eventual punishment for a short-term gain.

Gods probably weren't any different.

Nat unlocked the door, turned the golden knob, and peered out through a sliver of empty space. The chain stretched full-length, taut and creaking.

A tall, tanned woman with a long fall of straight black hair stepped back, obeying the unconscious dictate of personal space. A pair of red heart-shaped sunglasses was pushed up to keep that glorious hair back, echoing ruddy highlights in the knee-length flow. Her dark eyes sparkled with merriment, and her lips were candy-gloss pink. Her face was oddly familiar, high cheekbones and a lush mouth; thready golden earrings dangle-swung as she moved.

Her white-and-red sundress had a sweetheart bodice and a long full skirt, its straps melding to tender, smoothly muscled shoulders. Her nails were rosy, and her cork wedge sandals incredibly stacked. She grinned, a flawless pearly smile, and the divinity on her was almost as powerful as the sheer warm goodwill she radiated.

"Oh my goodness," she breathed, peering through the tiny slice of open door. "Look how beautiful you are. Hello."

What the hell? Nat's jaw all but dropped. She was, in her mother's words, catching flies with her silly mouth.

"I'm Marisol," the woman continued, after an awkward pause. "Your elder sister, after a fashion—it gets confusing, you know? You're Spring, I'm Summer." Her smile didn't alter, and neither did that deep, incontrovertible sense of benevolence. "I'm so glad you're here. Normally I'd be in Florida, but something told me the City of Angels was better this year. And now look, I was right." She cocked her head, the long waterfall of hair swaying.

Oh, boy. "Uh," Nat managed. *Divinity* didn't quite cover this lady. She was, purely and simply, a goddess. "Hi."

Another tight, awkward silence hummed between them. Marisol's smile didn't fade, but her perfect coal-black eyebrows drew a few millimeters closer to each other.

"Let me guess," she said, quietly. "Maria never told you about me."

That's the understatement of the year. But now the eerie familiarity made sense, because this woman looked a little bit like her mother. Dark instead of blonde, tanned instead of pale, curvy instead of willowy, but still . . . the resemblance was overwhelming. Nat hauled her jaw back up, and found she could speak. "She never told me about anything."

"Well, that would make it easier for her, wouldn't it." Watching this woman grow somber was like a raincloud passing over the sun. Marisol took another half-step back, just as Nat might when eyeing a skittish stray creature in a vacant lot back home. "I'd've talked her out of it, except she'd never listen. Stubborn as her own storms, your mother. When I heard you were coming out west I thought, *thank goodness Maria didn't go through with it.* But . . . that's not quite right, is it."

Oh, hell. Did everyone know her mother's plans except Nat? It was depressingly par for the course. "She's still alive." Nat's hands tingle. "Uh, let me get the door. Okay?"

"Sure, take your time." She even sounded like she meant it.

Like she had all the time in the world.

Nat's fingers were clumsy, but when she got the chain free and swept the door open, the woman showed no sign of impatience or anger. Her high-gloss finish was enough to make even a supermodel feel washed-out and pimply, but that forgiving, high-wattage smile bathed you in such a glow it was almost worth it. She stepped over the threshold, glanced at the suite, and her grin returned. "Oh, wow. I love it, it's so fresh. We should get off on the right foot, don't you think? Hi, I'm Marisol de Flores." She extended one graceful hand, thin gold bangles chiming on her wrist. "I'm Summer. At least, on this continent. I've got a couple other faces, especially up north, but so do you. And I'm so, so happy to meet you."

The moment their fingers touched a flood of heat passed through Nat's body, soles to crown. The fear-copper in her mouth faded, the tension in her shoulders eased, and her sock toes tingled happily. "Wow. Hi. I'm Nat, Nat Drozdova. I guess I'm Spring." *At least, once Mom dies? Or until she eats me? Is that how this goes?*

"You don't have to guess." Marisol's laugh was like warm caramel. "You just *are*, no matter what anyone else says. You'll get used to it."

Will I? Nat swept the door closed. "So you know what I'm looking for, and—"

"You're on a restoration tour, I'd guess. I've got the chariot safe and sound, and let me tell you, it'll be a relief to get it out of the garage. But you're probably going to fetch that damn diamond too. I heard you were traveling with Konets." The woman turned in a complete circle, her hair swaying heavily. How she balanced on those towering wedges was a mystery; her ankles looked too slim to hold the rest of her. "Not like he's going to put it back in his chest, but I'd suspect it's the principle of the thing. Men are so *touchy*."

"You've got that right." It popped out of Nat's mouth, surprising her, and Marisol laughed. It was impossible not to chuckle with her, impossible not to relax. "But he's not that bad. He was even trying to teach me, I guess."

"Huh." Marisol examined her from sock-clad toes to rumpled head, a slow unhurried appraisal. "I'll bet he was."

A flare of different heat rose in Nat's cheeks. "Not like that," she hurried to add, but Marisol chortled again, shaking her head.

"Little sister, you have no idea." Summer's laughter was like warm velvety caramel, coating every word. "Listen, I know you're busy and just here to pick up the car, but I'd love to have breakfast. And since Maria didn't teach you anything, it's my job to help as much as I can, right? You must be so confused."

Lady, you have no idea. Nat's eyes prickled; she forced the sudden tears sternly back into their home as if she was eighteen again and Mom had just informed her a graduation gown and class ring were too expensive, plus they wouldn't be worn more than once anyway. "They say . . . I mean, the horse said . . ." Trying to explain, even to someone who knew about this shit, was almost impossible. "He said Maria wants to . . ."

"Yes." The goddess sobered again, her luxurious pink-glossed mouth drawing down at the corners. A hard hot light now shone in her dark eyes, and her tanned hands curled into fists before she shook them out with quick flickering grace. Her striped skirt fluttered, and the green-and-white suite was suddenly full of dry baking heat, scorching as a magical desert broken only by a single ever-blooming cherry tree with a listing stone well caught in its imperfect shade. "What she planned is disgusting, and I told her so. I'm glad it didn't work."

Let's not celebrate too early. "I . . . I just . . ." Everything she had ever wanted to say balled up in Nat's throat. Her mouth worked for a moment, and when the other woman stepped closer, she froze.

Marisol's arms wrapped around her; the goddess's skirt brushed Nat's jeans. She was warm and soft, and smelled like fresh air, baking bread, and dry hay with an undertone of musk. "Oh, sweetheart," she murmured into Nat's rumpled hair. "Take a deep breath. It's going to be okay."

I wish I could believe that. Nat closed her eyes, swallowing hard. The heat-haze around the other woman was pleasant— who, after all, didn't like summer? And apparently she'd known Maria Drozdova. It didn't do any harm to relax for a single moment, to let her guard down just a tiny bit before snapping it back up.

Because she didn't really know what this divinity wanted, after all.

So she breathed in that pleasant, forgiving warmth, and tried her best not to sob like a baby. She succeeded, too.

Mostly.

SAY HELLO, BABY

It was certainly better than traveling with Dmitri.

For one thing, Marisol didn't smoke or sneer. She didn't eye Nat's backpack like it was a tasty snack just waiting to be devoured, and she didn't make snotty little comments either. Instead, she slipped her arm through Nat's and ushered her through the Elysium's lobby—blowing a candy-gleaming pink kiss to Mr. Priest, who nodded with a wide, pleased smile—and out the revolving door, ushering her "little sister" into a tiny red sports convertible with the top down.

Los Angeles was full of palm trees nodding conspiratorially and traffic parting before the crimson convertible's purring hood like the Red Sea in front of a holy man on a mission. Even the light was different here, but whether the thick gold was natural or just a function of being in a divinity's proximity, Nat couldn't tell.

Not that it mattered, at this point.

Plenty of the palms were wrapped in Christmas lights and plastic Nativity sets crouched in many a yard, whether overwatered green or burned straw-yellow. It was after Thanksgiving, yet people out here were strolling in shorts and tank tops; cars clogged every available bit of pavement and the city couldn't decide what it wanted to be. Like New York, each block was a world of its own—residential, commercial, industrial alternating with dizzying speed as Marisol gunned the engine and the little deuce coupe swept through on a warm hay-scented breeze.

Nat could almost-see how the world leapt to obey Marisol's bidding, traffic bunching up or cringing aside as the red car zoomed through. No talking was possible with the wind combing their hair, but somehow neither Marisol's knee-length mane nor Nat's tumbled waves gained any knots from the hurricane. The slipstream-sound was like riding her childhood bike again, freedom and glory with every pump of the pedals, and when Summer flicked the radio on a driving rock beat throbbed through the speed-roar but didn't resolve into any recognizable lyrics or tune.

It was *wonderful*, and Nat hoped she could travel like this some more.

Summer's house was on stilts over the rocky fringe of a golden-sand beach, and Nat gasped at the Pacific's heaving blue glitter. There was a deep gray smudge-storm on the horizon, but the angular pile of supermodern glass walls and warm hardwood floors basked in a column of sunshine. The garden was full of spiny succulents amid basking rocks, and though the nearest neighbors had decorated for the holidays, Marisol's domicile was blessedly free of any wintry reminder.

Pulling into the garage under the house's pilings plunged them into sudden gloom, and Nat flinched before her eyes adjusted. The little red car stopped with a jolt, the engine's throaty roar cut cleanly as if chopped with a razor knife, and Marisol's laughter was just as sweet and husky as it had been at the Elysium.

"It's nice to drive with you," she said, reaching into the tiny space behind Nat's seat for a fringed leather purse she definitely hadn't been carrying before. "We're going to have so much fun. I hope you visit after you're done with your tour; I have so much to show you. There's this place in San Fran where the oysters are to *die* for. Oh, and we'll have to do Rodeo Drive too. And go swimming—there's a bay tucked away in Malibu I've simply got to show you. We'll have to go up to Carmel when the weather's bad and have hot chocolate at my little shack there. And Tijuana too—you wouldn't believe some of the stuff they've got, there's this one place where the tequila is practically like silk. And Chinatown! We've got to do Chinatown, or what's left of it."

What, all at once? Nat peered at the other half of the garage. A canvas-shrouded shape, much bigger than Marisol's sporty cherry-colored number, sat in the dimness; otherwise, the cavernous space was bare. A row of cabinets stood along the back, dusty with disuse; Summer didn't seem like a garage sort of person.

Leo would have loved all the space, and put up a pegboard for tools. The thought of him was a pinch under her breastbone; Nat reached for the door handle, almost dreamily.

"Oh yeah." Marisol rose from the driver's seat in a fluid wave, her hair a long black undulating flow. She was impossibly graceful; Nat felt like a gawky schoolkid by comparison. "You feel it, don't you? I'm pretty sure Baby will be happy you're back."

"Baby?" Nat managed to get out of the low-slung vehicle without tripping or bonking herself on anything. She could barely look away from the canvas shape; its edges rustled.

"Yep. My little gift to Maria when she arrived on these shores, an upgrade to the cat-sled. But I told her, if you're going to do *that disgusting thing,* give me Baby back. You don't deserve her." Marisol's wedges clip-clopped on smooth concrete as she skirted the convertible's rear, her dress and the purse's fringe swinging merrily. "But since you're here—oh, I'm so happy, Nat. You have no idea." Those whisper-thin, musical golden bracelets twinkled as she gathered up dusty canvas, giving it a twitch, and with one swift movement, she yanked the covering entirely free. It lifted like it had a life of its own, and Nat exhaled sharply.

It was a blue car. Not just any car, though. It was a blue '68 Mustang coupe, or so close it made no difference. Its hood ornament was a silver cat stretched out in full gallop, and its sleek curves shone through a screen of rust and pitted paint. The tires sagged, the rims were bent, and the windshield, not to mention the windows, held a milky cataract glaze. Its bumpers sagged, the chrome cloudy, and all in all, it was a sorry sight.

That's Mom's car. Oh, my God. Nat's jaw dropped for the second time that day, and she found herself moving like a sleepwalker, step by slow step, closer to the poor, rundown wreck. "Mom always talked about this car." She sounded like a little girl, breathy with wonder.

Leo would have loved tinkering with this machine. Was it like Dmitri's black, shine-growling chariot?

"I'll bet she did." Marisol busied herself with folding the canvas; it shrunk in her slim brown hands. "Go ahead. Say hello, see what happens."

Nat couldn't have stopped if she tried. Her hands tingled almost painfully; she stepped reverently close and flattened them both on the driver's side of the hood. "Hi," she said softly, aware of the ridiculousness of talking to a busted-down hunk of metal that probably hadn't moved for years. "I've heard a lot about . . . oh. Oh, *wow*."

Her palms sealed themselves to pitted paint. The blue car shuddered, metal squeaking, and a tremor ran down Nat's neck, jolting through her arms before passing into heavy machinery, paint, glass, and bodywork. There was no sense of draining, merely a deepening of that endless, utter *rightness*.

It was like a special effect. The damage of sedentary age reeled itself back, dents popping out, chrome brightening, glass clearing. Fresh life ran through blue paint, and the tires made soft breathy sounds as they expanded, the rims squeak-groaning as they flexed. Puffs of dust rose inside the cab, cracked upholstery turning plump and seamless, and from under the hood rose a medley of pinging, crunching, sparking, and other shifting metallic noises.

Nat tried to lift her hands; they wouldn't budge. "Am I . . ." *Am I doing that?*

"Of course you are." Marisol performed a few hopping, happy dance steps, the canvas now a neat square clasped to her middle. "You're *Spring*. You're renewal and germination. You used to have a cat-drawn chariot, but this is ever so much better."

"What does it run on?" Maybe the other woman would get tired of her questions, but Nat couldn't help herself. "I wondered what Dmitri's—"

"Oh, his is different. But we're not mortal, we don't have to fill up at every pump. She'll endure as you do. I'm gonna close the door and go make breakfast. Come upstairs when you're done."

Yeah. Nat leaned against the hood, her arms straight and stiff, her palms throbbing. "Thank you." The words were too pale for the big bursting feeling inside her chest. A car. A *beautiful* car. There had to be some sort of cost or drawback to the gift, but at the moment, she didn't care. "This means I can outrun those things, right? *Those who eat.*"

"Once you've finished your tour they won't bother you." But Marisol's expression clouded, and she glanced at the driveway under its drench of gold brilliance. "You've got time for breakfast. I'll help you all I can, little sister, but some things you've got to do yourself."

"I know," Nat murmured. The car, humming under her hands, seemed to agree, and the garage door descended slowly, closing her in deeper darkness.

PLEASANT BREAKFAST

He hadn't been to Pasadena in a while, and the town's outskirts had mushroom-spread. The winds of urban gentrification had also torn through downtown a few times; it was a relief to be out of the fucking sticks. A small brass bell tinkled on a swinging glass door as Dmitri stalked into the diner where one of his uncles had once shot a man, and found the place's bones still remembered him even though the rest of it had changed out of all recognition.

The sun was well up; his hands pulsed with last night's murderous work and his boots were grimy. The muck would flake free in the next hour or so, and his suit would heal itself in fits and starts unless he wanted to be fresh again in less than a heartbeat, stepping out of damage and dirt with a slight effort.

At the moment, he didn't. Sometimes it was pleasant to roll in the filth and let it dry naturally. The scavengers were stupid, but there was a certain charm to even that manner of combat. It was like rube video games, very little risk but pleasant reward in performing as well as possible.

An already-fatigued rube waitress, scanty blonde ponytail gathered low at her nape, eyed his dishevelment, compared it to the rest of him, and visibly decided he wasn't worth pissing off. "Coffee?" she drawled, and saved herself a serious bit of ill-luck by hurrying to set a bundle of silverware wrapped in a napkin and a gummed paper band in front of him as he settled at the breakfast bar.

"Yes, please." He was polite enough, considering. The bell on the door jangled again, and he knew who it was even before a finger of chill touched his dirty back. "Two."

The rube, her bloodshot gaze rising over his shoulder, backed up a few steps, turned sharply, and marched for the coffeepot with determination.

The stool to his right squeaked slightly, accepting a sticklike frame. Baba's black silk shirtwaist dress would look old-fashioned to the rubes, yet would imply a certain amount of money. It wasn't her hard-edged business suit, but neither was it her party attire. Her gray hair, pulled severely back in a bun the size of an overly generous cinnamon roll, held only a single iron stick thrust through its nest, but that pin was sharp and its head bore a single deep-red glitter. She folded her thin, swell-knuckled hands on the bleach-wiped counter and studied the long rectangular window to the kitchen, where a heavy copper-skinned cook with a ferocious black mustache was absorbed in a sheet of newsprint looking suspiciously like a racing form. Tattoos crawled up the cook's beefy forearms, mostly in blurred prison blue.

He was a nephew, of course. Dima almost smiled.

The rube waitress came back, her thick-soled white shoes squeaking. Two mugs of coffee were placed with more care than they warranted, and she reached below the counter, probably for plastic-coated menus. "Getcha something to eat?"

"Pancakes. Bacon. Hash browns, crispy. Four eggs over easy." It had been a long night. Dima gave his most charming smile; the rube didn't melt, but she did straighten, nod, and scrawl on her anemic order pad with a tired blue Bic.

"You, ma'am?" At least the girl was respectful; Baba might sew a rude bitch's mouth shut just for the pleasure of the act.

"Toast. White, dry—*no* butter. Triple order of bacon, very

crispy." Baba reached for a dish of shelf-stable creamer tubs, her fingernails gleaming chocolate-cherry like the gem on her hairpin. "That will be all, Sydney. Thank you."

It was no great trick—the rube had a name tag—but it made the mortal woman flinch. She finished jotting on her pad and hurried for the kitchen window, where the cook sighed, putting his paper aside.

They had the place to themselves this early, in the valley between predawn truckers stopping for a bite and those with more leisurely schedules just beginning their day. Baba folded her hands around her coffee; Dima dumped four packets of sugar into his—real bleached caneblood, none of that ersatz shit.

It wasn't wartime, after all.

Steam hissed; kitchen implements clanking and clanging like prison doors. The cook began to hum, an old ranchero song about wandering without a woman. Sydney retreated to the other end of the counter, finding makework with ketchup bottles, napkin dispensers, and syrup pots needing refilling. The breakfast rush would start trickling in soon, like snowmelt cascading off mountainsides when winter's grip loosened just a little, just enough.

Baba's dark eyes half-closed; she stared into her mug like it was her shining, scrying desk top in the Morrer-Pessel building. "You've been a busy boy."

Dima snorted, but softly. The rubes didn't need to hear this parley. "No less than you, old woman."

"Hmph." She didn't disagree. The beldame's long, pale, naked toes, each nail painted just as carefully as her fingertips, rested against the brassy-colored rail running along the counter's bottom. The rubes wouldn't even notice she was barefoot. "Maria's trapped in a hospice bed. Intubated. It must be maddening for her."

It was his turn to make a noise of non-disagreement. He didn't add *it serves her right*. What was the point? Baba knew

Maria's sins—if such a word could apply to one of their kind—better than anyone.

She's my mother, Dmitri. Can you just not? Oh, his *devotchka* had a tender heart. How long would that last?

Outside the café, Pasadena woke in lazy stages under a bright winter dawn. No snow, no ice, but Baba's presence was a chill against the nape, a current of cold water clasping a startled swimmer's legs. None of the migrant workers he'd brushed against last night would remember more than a vivid nightmare or two; some of them might even enjoy a sudden spate of cooler weather.

Oblivious, all of them. Which was as it should be.

"You gonna visit her soon?" he finally asked, as she obviously wanted him to. The beldame had some end in mind, or she wouldn't be bothering with a rube breakfast.

All this trouble for one wayward little girl. He might have expected the old woman to simply let things take their course, one way or the other. Maybe she was bored, or maybe a nice pliable *zaika* was more to her taste.

It was an open question.

"It occurred to me," the harridan of winter said softly, lifting her mug, "that you might want the pleasure."

So that's it. Dima considered his own coffee—hot, sweet, dark as sin. There was no tang of traitor's blood or other offering in it; the waitress's misery was faint spice at best. The nephew in the kitchen might have something to offer, especially if he desired some luck at the races.

He didn't shift in his seat, but his silence was telling. She would know he felt some interest. "What's the price?"

"Consider it more of a courtesy." Baba's lips, the exact shade of the last mostly deoxygenated blood wrung from a shuddering mortal heart, pursed slightly as she blew across her own drink. "Since it was my inattention, after all, which allowed her to subtract that certain item."

Of course the beldame wouldn't admit she owed Dmitri anything, even if it was an unalterable truth. "You want something in return. Like a promise not to hurt the little girl."

"Do I?" Baba's low, husky laugh was almost pleasant, except for the thin sliver of ice at its heart. "Maria stole it, Maria pays. Everything nice and neat, balanced just so."

Even Winter had her own strange sense of justice. It was part and parcel of her function; otherwise she might go around slapping the black hand upon her fellow divinities with abandon. She was made to keep a particular equilibrium, just as his *devotchka* was.

Just as Dmitri himself. "Maria hid her own arcana, too. Deep, in taproots. Sent little girl to collect them."

"How interesting. She certainly didn't think *you'd* be willing to provide transport. Marisol's in town, by the way." Baba took a sip, her eyebrows raising. "Not wintering in Florida this year."

Now there was news. That flame could burn more than one scavenging moth, but he didn't think it likely this country's incarnation of summer would bestir herself to more than a few gifts before settling back into off-season torpor. Flora would be better, but the divinity of harvest and fruition had other business.

She *always* had other business.

"I thought you wanted me to look after little *zaika*."

"Oh, Dima." Baba did not laugh again, but sharp chilly amusement feathered the edge of his name. "At a certain point, children have to walk on their own. Besides, you'll see her again before this is finished."

"That a promise, or a threat?"

"Merely a certainty." Baba's pointed chin turned a few fractions; she gazed at the rube waitress. "Like the cancer in little Sydney's pancreas. It won't be long now."

Especially not as they counted time. "How much of this did you have planned, old woman?"

"No need for a plan when the pattern is so clear." Baba's shrug was a masterpiece of ambiguity. "Maria's not the first to try this."

"Some succeeded." He could name them effortlessly enough. After all, the secret knowledge of every theft was his.

"A few," Baba allowed, taking a decorous sip of her thick, creamer-splashed brew. "How many won't if Maria is an example, though? The arc bends towards justice, *moy vnuck*. Just too slowly for mortals to see."

"You're philosophical today."

"It must be my age."

The cook slammed a palm over the order bell, and Sydney hurried to bring her two customers their loaded plates on a big round plastic tray she handled with a wince. "Here you go. Pancakes, bacon, hash browns, eggs. Dry white toast and triple bacon. Can I bring you anything else? Orange juice?"

Baba looked at the rube, her dark eyes glinting, and the silence stretched uncomfortably as the cook clattered through cleanup and whatever preparation was needed for the anticipated morning rush of hungry mortal mouths. An invisible, powerful current swept through the diner, married to a frigid breeze. Sydney, her mouth falling open slightly, trembled like a rabbit caught in the hunter's snare.

His *devotchka* would never look this washed-out, this dispirited, this hopeless. Even with Maria alive Nat burned with incipient divinity, fresh and stainless. Was that why he was unwilling to hie himself all the way back across the continent to attend to what was, after all, only a loose end?

I'm sorry. You must want it back really badly. His little *zaika* apologized too much; Dmitri tried once more to imagine growing up with Maria in that tiny yellow house, thinking yourself a rube and probably battered daily with a foreign divinity's harsh, furious hunger.

I don't need your fuckin' pity, he had snarled, and it was still true. He had promised to vent his wrath upon the one who stole what belonged to him even if Baba held the bauble again, and that promise demanded keeping.

So did a few others.

"No," the beldame said finally. "Thank you, Sydney. You're a good girl."

The waitress blinked and straightened. A faint flush crept into her wan cheeks. Dima could almost taste the now-shrinking tumor hiding in her body's secret hollows.

Baba took, yes. But she could also give, when she had a mind to.

"Th-thank you." The rube waitress fled through the swinging door to a hall lying alongside the kitchen, probably completely unaware of why she was so unsettled. Being a rube, of course, she'd find some mental hook to hang the morning's strangeness on, and forget any breath of the uncanny as soon as possible. She probably didn't even know she was ill, yet.

And never would know she had been, or that a miracle had freed her.

Baba gave him a sidelong glance before unwrapping her silverware. "Not a word, little boy. Let's have a pleasant breakfast for once."

He shrugged, reaching for his own implements. The nephew in the kitchen knew his trade, at least—the bacon was crispy and the eggs perfectly over easy, the hash browns fried to a lovely golden crust. It was almost enough to make up for Nell's burger turning lukewarm, and the soggy fries.

He even used more than the bare minimum of manners. The little brass bell on the door jangled merrily as rubes filtered in for feeding, Sydney returning to her work with renewed vigor and only one troubled glance at the pair of strange customers.

By the time he finished with the last scrap of bacon and sliver of egg, Baba was contemplating her own empty plate. She finished her diluted coffee in three long swallows, her scrawny throat working, and tapped twice on the countertop, a crisp fifty-dollar bill springing into existence underneath her claw-nail the second time.

The beldame was generous today, but Dima didn't remark on the event. He cradled his own coffee, waving aside Sydney's inquiry—*more, sir?* The cook was too busy to look at his racing form again.

"Think about it," Baba said, slithering off her stool. "She won't last long."

The brass bell jingled sharply as she left. Dmitri made a face at the sugar-slurry remaining in his cup, the very dregs of boiled American coffee. It wasn't like the old country's heady, heavy, perfect black sludge.

But it was his now. He had paid for it, after all.

Promises had sharp edges, even for divinities. They were, after all, a form of honesty—and even a thief had to know what truth was in order to effectively lie.

Baba left the money there, tucked under her empty plate. It would be easy, almost reflexive, to slip it into his own pocket. On another day he might have.

His suit was no longer torn and dusty. His boot-toes glittered bright silver, and his sharp friends were safe in their dark homes. So was the gun, nestled under his left armpit. Everything in his proper place, but something was missing—something other than the steady pulse in his chest, the heart he was, after all, better off without.

It was no great trick to slip sideways, like one of Spring's own allied felines. The thiefways lay under every inch of the physical; all it took was the will to step through. No bell marked his departure, no mortal took any notice.

Sydney, clearing dirty plates, silverware, and two coffee mugs, gave the door one more uneasy glance before sweeping up the fifty-dollar bill. It was a huge tip, almost obscene, but every food service worker knew strange things happened where people gathered to satisfy their bellies and pay for the pleasure.

You took what you were given, with only a token shake of a weary head.

Waitresses have their own protective divinity too, though perhaps she was not watching that morning.

But not even Baba Yaga could be sure of that.

NO SURRENDER

Yesterday she was riding a black horse across a desert and running away from hungry shadows. Today, Nat had sesame waffles and fresh-squeezed orange juice with a woman who vaguely resembled her mother, but without Maria Drozdova's terrifying, ozone-smelling temper or brisk chill efficiency. The supermodern kitchen wasn't cold or soulless, especially since they could watch the Pacific rolling in and out while they sipped espresso from a shiny, very expensive silver machine, which ground the coffee beans, measured them, dispensed the dark fluid and its honey-colored crema, and finished the whole process with a pleasant beep.

It was nicer than the Elysium, even.

Afterward, the dishes merrily clattered into a sleek silver dishwasher on their own, cradled by invisible hands, and Nat's amazement was met with Marisol's deep, velvety laugh. *Dishes are boring,* the divinity said. *Let's take Baby for a spin.*

Getting behind the wheel of the blue Mustang was nervewracking—what if there was an accident, what if she'd forgotten how to drive? She could just about coax the Léon-Bollée into working, but to her vast relief, Baby was a lot easier. For one thing, she was an automatic, and for another, the deep thrum of her engine was like a favorite, mostly remembered childhood song.

Marisol settled in the passenger seat, her tanned arm lying

along the open window, and she glanced at Nat as if asking permission before flicking the radio's knob. The speakers crackled, there was a brief burst of static, and Bruce Springsteen began singing about dancing in the dark as Nat brought the car to a halt at the stop sign at the end of the cul-de-sac.

"Which way?"

The divinity grinned and pointed left. Warm wind poured through open windows, the wonderful sound of freedom just like her childhood bicycle's windrush in Nat's ears, and somehow the roads had jumbled themselves together because the next thing Nat knew they were on Highway 101 and heading north at a steady pace.

It was good. In fact, it was flat-out *great*, and the fact that the car had been a rusting hulk just a few hours ago was beside the point.

It was almost possible to believe this was how her life had always been, one beautiful miracle after another, a steady succession of wonders. But somewhere behind her were the blind, wriggling veil-draped shadows and their icy hunger, not to mention a dark-haired man with a razor-sharp smile who was bound to be very, very angry indeed.

Even further behind there was New York held immobile in snow and ice and her mother lying on a bed in the Laurelgrove, waiting for Nat to obediently bring a blood-tinged diamond and Spring's arcana home.

And then what?

Baby took the curves easily, humming with joy; her engine-sound throbbed up Nat's arms and filled her with an uncharacteristic sensation. Light, and almost . . . happy? Was that it? Oldies throbbed through the speakers, and each one called up good memories—dancing with Leo while the Beatles sang, Mom humming along with the ancient Bakelite radio while soup bubbled on the stove, Nat's earbuds in and a suitable song playing while she rode a bus in summer or braved the subway, riding her bike in the park as someone's boombox granted everyone a few bars of rock 'n' roll, the best music in the world.

A good rock beat made you feel more steady, more solid, more *there*. Even normal people could feel like a divinity when the drums throbbed, the bass popped, and a catchy tune forced fingers to snap and feet to tap.

Marisol pointed, and Nat saw the turnoff a moment later. Tires crunched on washboard-rutted gravel, but the ride was eerily smooth. It was good, Nat decided, to have a car of her own.

If this other divinity wasn't going to suddenly take it away, that was. Like Maria going through Nat's bedroom while her daughter was at school—*you do not need these, you are grown up too big, stop your whining.*

The gravel road climbed, switchbacking hard, up a tawny hill crowded with wind-tortured trees. At the crest, it widened into an attempt at a parking lot or just a turnaround, and at the other end of a dusty, pebble-strewn space was a plain white adobe church with red roof tiles, its squat tower holding a rusty bell. The cross above the bell was blackened from lightning or some other fire, and the heavy wooden doors above a flight of worn stone steps were ajar.

Baby came to a neat stop in a cloud of dust the color of corn-meal; her engine died with a final growl that said she'd be more than happy to start again whenever necessary. The ensuing quiet was full of the ocean's mutter married to the wind, a low dry-brushing drone.

"There are powerful places everywhere," Marisol said softly. "You'll feel them when you need them. Baby's got a good nose too, she'll sniff out all sorts of helpful things. You've probably already noticed you don't really need sleep now, or a few other mortal things—though sometimes it's nice to pretend, isn't it? Let's go inside."

"It's a church." Nat wasn't sure if it was an objection or

just stating the obvious. "Mom—*Maria* sent me to Catholic school."

"Of course she did." Marisol's lip curled for a moment; the pink gloss never seemed to need reapplication. "They're good at guilt, and suppression. I suppose she'd've chosen something Baptist down south, or a charter school up north. Anything to keep you from blooming before the right time."

If you knew all this, why did you let her do it? "The right time?" Nat made herself let go of the wheel; there was no ignition switch, and no key. It wasn't necessary.

But it was a little weird.

"Not to put too fine a point on it, a baby's just a mouthful." Marisol's nose wrinkled, and for once she wasn't smiling and sunny. Her nose was a little sharper, her mouth thinner; the heat inside the car turned dry and oven-hot for a moment, a parched wind stirring Nat's hair. "She needed you at precisely the right stage of development. Just on the verge of coming into your power, but not strong enough to . . . well, to fight her off."

That makes sense. Nat shivered despite the golden warmth and reached hurriedly for the door handle.

The mission church was empty except for a few dusty wooden pews ranked in the approximation of solemn rows. The altar was deserted, but a hole high up let in a column of thick soupy sunlight. It was too bright for an otherwise windowless structure, and the air was hushed, expectant, full of ghostly incense and half-heard chanting. Ocean wind brushed across the broken tower, making the bell creak on its mounting; eventually it would fall, crashing through masonry and wood to thud onto the dais.

The fine hairs all over Nat rose. She let out a soft wondering sigh, pausing right next to an ancient, bone-dry stone font set on cracked pavers.

"See?" Marisol was hushed, too. Though the older divinity's glow dimmed the reality of her still shone through, the sun behind a thin lens of white cloud. Nat's hands, paler, still gave off a faint gleam. "Belief lingers. It's pleasant, and necessary for some of us. But not you, and not me."

I got that. "Is there a Jesus, then?"

"Oh, there's about fifty of them." Marisol shook her head, pacing down the nave. Her hair moved like a living thing, rippling to the tender tanned hollows behind her knees. "Every time there's a schism, a new one hives off. I don't know how they stand it." Her wedges made hushed sounds; she continually moved as if dancing. What would it be like, to be that graceful?

Hiving off? Sounds gross. Dima had said that too, about Baba. Was it like Jay's husk birthing a slim woman in green?

Nat followed in Marisol's wake, hitching her backpack higher and quashing the nervous urge to cross herself. Her peacoat, flannel button-up, and thermal undershirt were neatly folded on Baby's backseat; it was warm enough for just jeans and a pink cotton T-shirt. Nobody would break into a divinity's car, especially to steal a few clothes, but she was still uneasy.

"I was like you once," Summer continued, taking a hard right and gesturing at the front row of pews. Dust puffed away on a sudden warm breeze; she sank down, arranging her candy-striped skirt with quick habitual movements. "I remember my mother. She came with invaders, but that wasn't her fault. She taught me what I was, how to control it. It was . . . like breathing, or learning how to swim. I can't imagine how confused you must be."

Nat settled on the pew next to her, cradling the backpack. "Can I ask how . . . what happened? Did she . . ."

"She faded. It was very gradual, like a mortal aging. Then Winter came for her—not your Baba, *she* came much later, but the Lady of the South, Coatlicue Invierna. She was the most beautiful thing I'd ever seen, next to Mamacita." Marisol's right hand rubbed at the thin gold bangles on her opposite wrist, a soft thoughtful touch. Her mouth wobbled briefly, dark eyes shining-full. "I cried a lot that year. The maize rotted in the fields; Cente-otl was annoyed but there wasn't anything to be done, you know? Grief takes her own time. Just like the rest of us."

Nat touched the other woman's warm, bare shoulder with tentative fingertips. All the polish had worn off her nails, a faint pinkish shine taking its place. "I'm so sorry."

"Oh, you're a kind child, indeed." Marisol sniffed, heavily, and wiped at her soft tanned cheek, her own peach-colored nail varnish gleaming solemnly. "I'm telling this so you understand, little Nat. Maria could have chosen something different. She didn't."

"Yeah." Nat stared at where the altar had been, her hand dropping back into her lap. There was a heavy scorch of long-ago disaster there, the same as the half-blasted cross. She couldn't imagine Mom willingly getting older, allowing wrinkles to crease her beautiful cheeks.

No, Maria fought. She fought everything—weeds, dirt, spending any money at all. You could even respect the flinty strength it took, the depth of dedication necessary to go to war with the inevitable. There was no surrender in Maria Drozdova.

Ever.

How much was there in her daughter? It felt like Nat had been surrendering all her goddamn life.

"I love my mother." Her own voice startled her in the ancient hush; she whispered as if it were a shameful secret. "I could let her do it." Would it hurt? A brief stinging and no more pain, ever? Or would it be agonizing—chewed up and drained like a wad of tough steak?

Marisol was silent for a long moment. "That's up to you," she said, finally. "It always has been, even if it doesn't feel like it. But it takes age to understand as much. Even young divinities have to learn."

Maybe that was the price for having a mortal shape. Dmitri

would probably snort and say something cruel, or just wave a dismissive hand, probably decorated with a trapped cigarette spewing perfumed smoke.

How far behind was he? Of course a god of gangsters would have ways of tracking someone down.

If all else failed, he could probably just follow the scavengers. A shadow drifted over the golden sunlight. Marisol sighed, wiping at her cheeks again. "You should probably get going. Do you know where . . ."

Nat did, as a matter of fact. "North." She even had a suspicion who she'd meet, and if it turned out to be right . . . what then?

Trusting your own instincts was a real bitch. You couldn't blame anyone else if it all went horribly wrong.

"I'd love to have you here longer. But it wouldn't help." The older woman's sigh was like leaf-heavy branches rustling before a short summer storm, a thick green scent of petrichor rising through dust. "Take 101, not the interstate. It's a lot nicer."

"I can take you back to your house," Nat offered, awkwardly. Was Marisol really giving her the car? It beggared belief.

It's pleasant, and necessary for some of us. She tried to imagine growing up knowing about all this, tried to imagine her mother teaching young Nat how to do the dishes with invisible hands or make traffic clear in front of the Léon-Bollée.

Her mental inventiveness, usually so vivid, couldn't manage *that* trick.

"Oh, I'll just whistle and my own ride will show up. That's never a problem." Marisol turned slightly, and her smile wasn't quite as bright. It was just as warm, though, and the tinge of sadness only made it deeper. The smell of rain thickened; the sound of the sea had changed, too. "Come back and visit once you're done, if you like. I'd love to show you around. There are good things about this kind of life too, you know."

Maybe there were, but so far even the luxurious bits were

terrifying. "I'd like that," Nat said, and found out she meant it. "If I survive."

"I think you're going to be just fine." Marisol stretched, a picture of languid grace. "You're my little sister, after all."

Nat rose, slowly. "You sure I can't give you a ride?"

"I'm going to stay here for a bit. Think about things." Summer shifted her attention to the scorched altar-dais, her profile sweet but achingly sharp, her expression with an edge of piercing nostalgia almost approaching bitterness. "It's a thoughtful kind of place. Oh, by the way, I put some things in Baby's trunk. I know you probably like to travel light, but a girl needs *some* luggage. Consider it catching up on a few birthdays."

It might have been nicer if you showed up before now. But there was no need to be nasty; Nat hunched her shoulders. "Thank you. I don't know . . . I mean, just, thank you."

"You're going to do just fine," the divinity repeated, and for a moment Nat almost believed her.

She left the chapel before Marisol could change her mind about any gifts, blinking against the sunlight. It was much cooler without Summer's steady radiant heat, but Baby's engine roused as Nat approached. The chuckling purr even sounded happy to see her.

At least someone was.

Nat closed the driver's door, settling on the bench seat that had just the right amount of give. Her fingers curled around the sky-blue steering wheel, the horn's raised circle in the middle bearing a carving of a complex, almost-Celtic knot, and she took a deep breath. The radio was off—maybe Baby knew she wanted a little quiet.

"Looks like we're going north," she said, and the engine gave a happy giggle, for all the world like she was saying *okay, let's go, give the word.*

The gearshift moved easily. Baby's transmission dropped into drive and the car banked like a plane in the wide, weed-starred gravel expanse. The mission church sat in the rearview, full of a secretive inner glow. Behind it, dark clouds boiled far away over the ocean's salt plain, diamond lightning stabbing almost playfully.

Nat pressed gently on the accelerator, and small rocks scattered as Baby leapt to obey.

THE
KEY

KEEP DRIVING

The 101 is old as American highways go, and knows the value of a little meandering. The Pacific stretched blue and innocent on Nat Drozdova's left for a while, breathing cool salt through the driver's side windows as the storm receded; Baby took each curve easily, gently, like a boat on calm water even though the speedometer was pegged at max and Nat suspected that wasn't even half the story.

The first few times she met other cars on the road were nerve-wracking. The blue Mustang simply blinked past them, a slight fluttering sensation like butterfly wings filling Nat's stomach. It was like being in Dmitri's car, only without the devouring fear or constant sickmaking tension. It was also like being home when both Mom and Leo were out, but without the waiting for the front door to open, letting even beloved authority invade a temporary refuge.

Most of all, it was like freedom, and the only thing more intense than the intoxicating pleasure was the bald edge of fear underneath.

Nobody ever talked about how lonely absolute liberty was.

At Gaviota the highway took a sharp right-hand curve, turning inland. The smell of saline and kelp gave way to sage and creosote, sand and manzanita; clouds drifted over mellow sunshine with almost clocktick regularity as Baby flashed through small towns, past ancient signs, ditches sometimes on one side and sometimes on the other. Two lanes in either direction, a narrow meridian turning green in places where winter rains dipped into the most golden of states, and Nat found herself humming along with the radio as the road turned into a gray blur under smoothly spinning tires.

I could do this forever, she thought, and Baby seemed to agree.

The sun began to fall from its noontime height, and when she glanced in the rearview a chill slipped down Nat's back.

It was the same feeling that pushed her past the boarded-up house at the end of the block back home, its weedy front yard full of dead rustling yellow weeds even in spring and the rotting plywood over its windows slipping drunkenly but never quite managing to fall free. Mom had always threatened to march her in there at midnight, and more than once young Nat had been forced into eating something disgustingly adult and healthy, or foregoing some childhood pleasure, because it wasn't worth the risk.

Now she wondered what was *really* in that malevolent, ramshackle building with its gabled roof, but she had more immediate problems.

A tiny point of crimson hung in the rearview mirror's crystalline depths, billowing shadow dilating around its baleful gaze. The bright dot was far away, but a wire-brush of anxiety scraped Nat's nerves.

She jammed the accelerator to the floor. Baby took a deep breath, shaking herself like a dog whose owner had just picked up a beloved ball. *Finally,* her engine seemed to bark, and she lunged forward. Traffic thickened as the highway jolted towards the ocean again, signs for Pismo Beach flashing past, and the crimson dot receded.

Maybe I should just keep driving. To hell with Mom, to hell with Dmitri and his stupid Heart, to hell with everything except the road and this beautiful car, shining in a mellow winter afternoon as she shot north on a road that remembered being a dirt track under pilgrims' rope sandals and the clip-clop of donkey hooves. The scavengers were chasing her, maybe the gangster god was too, but all she had to do was elude them for long enough, right?

Each mortal car or semi, van or truck she flicked past was a victory. Dima was right, the world wanted to obey. It longed to arrange itself to her pleasure, it flat-out *ached* just as she'd always yearned to help her beautiful, distant, dissatisfied mother.

Oh, hell.

Nat was already pointed north, towards yet another piece of the puzzle. She could decide to stop at any moment, really.

But maybe not just yet.

Baby chuckled with glee, blinking past a lumbering red semi hauling refrigerated freight. One moment behind, the next ahead, hopskipping like a kid on the playground, the Drozdova's chariot drew away from her pursuers, receding like a winter-hibernating creature's dream of sunshine and plenty.

THE LARGER INSULT

His thiefways were full of burnt umber no matter the hour, a deep lungscorch of smoke echoing his fury. The sun was a hazy red disc hanging low in a dry, vaulted sky; bright spatters, near and far, echoed from the mortal world, each sending up a coil of incense vapor. Arid, stubbled fields stretched in every direction, dust blown in lazy spirals whisked to nothingness by a hot wind. Occasionally, a scarecrow or dangling gallowsdoll on a jagged, half-broken pole shifted, a limb popping up to indicate a nearby act of thievery, prayer, murder, or some other appetizing event.

If the thiefways ran through a city, buildings of every description would crowd close, jagged broken windows ready to be slipped through, doors hanging ajar, every lock burst and every piece of pavement bearing spidery cracks. Stepping sideways into this unland was easy as breathing for Dima Konets, and sometimes he let a cherished mortal worshipper catch a brief glimpse of all the blasted glory, where venomous glitters—different than the glowing, worshipful acts of stealing—were valuable things crying out to be taken. Reaching through the rotting veil and subtracting those bright items were child's play—the best thief left no traces, because he was, strictly speaking, never there at all.

Roads here were dusty too, dirty eggshell-colored stripes holding them to their tasks. The black car, solid and real instead of fuming-indistinct, idled easily while waiting for him to decide. His fingers tingled, his hands wrapped around the thrumming vibration of the steering yoke.

While a mortal could catch a single shuttered blink of this place with his blessing, they could not stay. Nor could a young divinity not of his kind travel this way. It was a lonely kingdom, indeed.

Those who eat clotted in another realm stacked tissue-thin next to this one, yearning in an unphysical direction after a tender morsel rapidly gaining too much strength to be easily consumed. They were now his only way of following her; the new Drozdova, in her wise innocence, had taken nothing from him.

Not even a silver cigarette lighter.

One road stretched north, vibrating between the tired, filthy whitish lines impersonating a highway's painted borders. Another veered eastward, and at the end of it was a hospice room full of torturing mortal machines, an old divinity denied any form of graceful release. By now darling Maschenka was probably wishing for the black hand to descend, for an end to the suffering. She was hopefully writhing on a mortal bed, helpless and furious, her bloodshot, fading eyes like a woolly mammoth's as it sank starving into hot bubbling tar.

An unfulfilled promise nagged at him. *I will repay the one who took it from me. I will fill my mouth with her blood.*

When the girl found all her mother's arcana, would she bring a fist-sized, bloody diamond back to Baba de Winter? He might never see the goddamn thing again, merely sensing it behind the mirrored wall in the beldame's office, its throbbing a faint narcotized ache.

Even holding the pulsing gem one more time might tempt him to do something . . . rash.

What would it be like, to see an aggressive young thief take over his realm? To witness the uncles and nephews paying court to another, maybe to see some *molodoy pank* smiling a razor-sharp smile at little dark-eyed Drozdova? To feel his essence drawn away, slowly but surely, until it was him waiting for the black hand, Dima the ruthless waiting for the scavengers to descend?

Baba might even make it painless for him. Or she might not.

There were other dangers, too. The little girl was lost in a garden of wickedness, wandering among sharpspine trees and hungry rocks. Though slim, there was always a chance *those who eat* would find her despite all the help Summer or others disposed to do Spring a service could be moved to give. And even if Konets did not close his teeth in her tender jasmine-salt flesh, he could still perform a trick or two, taking back what was his and having the power to decide.

He could *win*. A hollow victory, but still his.

Did little Drozdova fully understand what her mother intended? If she was stupid enough to bare her throat to the flint knife . . .

He did not think his *devotchka* was so cowardly, or so unintelligent. But could he, of all divinities, take that chance?

A thief's dilemma. Either way, he was fucked. But one kind of fucking was more enjoyable than the other, maybe. Sometimes the only freedom a man had was choosing which way to take it.

His fingertips drummed, velvety-soft and sensitive, nails clipped short and blunt, his hands able to sense the slightest vibration as a safe's dial was spun and tumblers clicked into place. Quick enough to subtract a single dollar from a closed wallet in a deep pocket, skilled enough to flick a straight razor through a throat without a single drop of blood remaining on the bright, hungry blade.

He could have stolen the heart from that cabinet, but he'd disdained. A bargain was a bargain, and an agreement which benefited him was one he could elect to hold himself to. *If* he chose, and that choice was his alone.

Mascha had the sheer *effrontery* to do what he had not, and to plan a nauseating theft nearly two mortal decades in the making, too. Not only had she taken the Dead God's Heart, but she was infringing on his rights, damn her eyes and all the rest of her.

It simply could not be borne.

He could not decide which was the bigger insult—Maria's robbery, or her daughter's refusal to take even a small gift.

"*Idiot,*" he hissed in the language of the old country, and all the thiefways cringed. "*Make up your fucking mind.*"

The trouble was, he already had. Resentment burned jaundice-bitter on his tongue, like an unnecessary, imperfect lie. The black car's engine revved, dust-smoke spurted; diamond headlights cut yellowbrown gloom.

The road not taken shrank to nothing behind him, and Dmitri Konets did not look back.

TIME TO THINK

S he veered onto 880 while passing San Jose; San Francisco passed too in a wraithlike blur across the water from Oakland, lost in billows of salty fog tinged with a nose-scouring whiff of dead fish. Nat was certain there was an Elysium in that fair city as well, but it was far too early to stop. Besides, traffic was awful, and it took all of Nat's concentration to flicker through stop-and-go, jumping from one clear spot to another. It was like learning to ride a bike all over again, or to drive the balky old Léon-Bollée; having to think about each tiny movement was exhausting.

After a while your body figured it out, and all you had to do was know where you wanted to go. But in the meantime, her eyes were grainy and her neck ached.

Apparently there were limits to even a divinity's sense of deep, inalienable well-being. Or maybe the past few days were catching up with her. 880 turned into 580; Baby veered across the John Knox, a thin strip of concrete over cold, unseen ocean. Just as she thought it would probably be a good idea to find the Elysium in Frisco after all, land returned, the crowd of cars drew away, Baby found 101 again and climbed a series of bluffs. The day was darkening under veils of white vapor.

I'll come back, she promised the City by the Bay; she hadn't even seen the Golden Gate. It would be something to go home and tell Leo she'd driven across that span as well as the Brooklyn Bridge.

That was a good memory, a warm sunny day and horns blaring as the old black car trundled along on a bed of its own exhaust, Leo grinning proudly in the passenger seat and teenage Nat biting her lip. *Ignore them,* devotchka, Leo kept saying. *You're doing great.*

The happiness was tinged with brassy-tasting fear, though, like nearly all her memories. Frisco's fog turned to drizzle as Baby reached a comfortable hum, not needing to flicker through clotted traffic anymore. The sensation of staying still while the world whirled away underneath a sleek metal ship was overpowering, and she wondered what Dmitri was up to at that moment.

Probably something terrible. And cursing while he did it, or smoking.

Getting home after that particular jaunt across the bridge had been awful, even though they'd stopped for ice cream on the way back. Mom had been furious, white-faced, her golden hair lifting in an angry cobra-hood halo. *I told you never to touch my things,* she'd hissed at her daughter, and that set off another fight with Leo while Nat hid in her closet upstairs, hugging her knees. All the good feeling had drained out of the achievement like water from a broken cup, and that night a violent late-spring storm stripped the leaves from most of the trees in the neighborhood, not to mention Princo Park.

If the little yellow house was indeed crumbling, what was happening to Nat's room? Her ancient laptop held together with silver duct tape, her discount-store clothes, the bed Leo had made, her tiny cheap desk for doing schoolwork with the green-shaded lamp he'd found somewhere? Her ancient teddy bear, clutched each night even though she was an adult and hidden safely each morning because *you've outgrown your toys, Natchenka, give me that and stop your sniveling . . .*

The thing about driving alone was how it gave you so much time to brood. The entire lens of her life had shifted, and things that used to be just-how-it-is were now distorted monsters, looming over her with long clutching claws and slavering jaws.

Or maybe the nightmare-creatures had always been there, and she'd just been oblivious. Now she saw them clearly for the first time, in all their misshapen, hateful glory.

Where was Leo? Was her mother still in a hospice bed? Nat could call the Laurelgrove; the number for the front desk was burned into her fingers. Her prepaid cell was gone, but a divinity could get a brand-new smartphone, couldn't she?

The crick in her neck and dusty irritation in her eyes eased as she left Oakland far behind. The windshield wipers started, waiting until just the right moment to sweep the glass clean of fog-dots and trickling. Nat found herself brushing at her cheeks. There was salt water inside the car too, apparently.

Green glimmered through the fog, stutter-flashing like an old-fashioned movie projector with a slipped cog or two. The road dipped, rose, threaded through city-clusters and small towns. Though it was winter, the breeze through Nat's half-open window was warm, and smelled of fresh-cut grass.

Was Marisol helping? Or was something else happening?

It didn't matter. Baby knew the way to go.

X

Her back began to complain near the California border, after the wet green blur of Humboldt and the slight turn inland past Crescent City. At Smith River the road lunged back towards the coast again, and a moving band of silvery rain beaded on Baby's hood, tracing veinlike fingers down her crystalline windows, now fully rolled up. It was chilly enough to need the heater; Nat turned a dial and was rewarded with deep hay-scented warmth. Still, getting out to stretch seemed like a good idea, and the malevolent crimson dot had vanished from the rearview mirror.

She had a little breathing room. The highway never veered too far from the shore now, but sometimes the ocean's glitter hid behind wind-twisted trees, their backs turned and their limbs companionably interlinked, heads bent together like old women conferring about coupons.

WELCOME TO OREGON, a green-painted sign called hurriedly before vanishing, and she stroked the steering wheel absently, as if petting a stray dog who didn't mind a little affection. "Let's find a gas station," she murmured, and was rewarded with Baby's deep mechanical chuckle of agreement. There was no fuel gauge, and Nat had the idea there wouldn't be a hatch for a tank, either.

If she achieved full divinity status, she'd probably figure out what the cars ran on. It might even be something that wouldn't give her nightmares.

Baby veered to the right and slowed. The rain intensified; there was none of California's gold here, just gray and taupe. Winter was back with a vengeance, though far milder than the snow of her hometown. There was a bright-green BP station at the end of a long gradual rise—Nat tapped the brakes and Baby jolted back into regular-mortal speed, her engine's hum rising to a purely normal pitch.

Parked with her nose towards a white metal box proclaiming FRESH ICE & NIGHTCRAWLERS, Baby settled into somnolence, metal pop-ticking as it cooled. Now Nat was faced with walking into a store on her own and maybe getting some snacks.

How on earth was she going to talk to normal people again after all this?

Digging in her backpack for her wallet, her fingertips brushed the Cup. Electricity zinged up her arm and she gasped, snatching her hand back. *What the hell?*

Carefully, cautiously, she peered into the backpack's depths. The unicorn mug glowed golden, casting a thin dappled light against the car's roof; Nat squinted disbelievingly, a laugh caught in her throat.

Nestled in the mug, a roll of crisp green lurked. She had to dig a bit, but eventually came up with a handful of what appeared to be perfectly ordinary twenty-dollar bills. Even their serial numbers looked entirely legitimate.

Holy shit. Better than an ATM. Wouldn't Dima like to get his hands on *this*—or would it work for him? Was this why Mom had always been so worried about money?

Nat folded the bills in her palm. She made a fist, stared at the back of her hand for a few moments, and when her fingers fell open again, the twenties had turned to fifties, ol' Unconditional Surrender Grant looking dyspeptic as usual.

World wants to obey, zaika. *Just ask it nice.*

"Holy *shit*," she breathed aloud. There was nobody around to mock her; hell, there was nobody around to *see*. A tan-and-brown Chevy Silverado sat at the pumps, its owner probably inside; the world was a blur of silvery rain, dripping green, gray stone, bright electric light from the convenience store windows, and the shock of a small miracle trembling paperlike in her hands.

It took a few moments of breathing deep, her forehead resting against Baby's sky-blue steering wheel, before Nat could gather the courage to zip up her bag and reach for the door handle.

A portly middle-aged man with a blue baseball cap exited the store, cast an incurious glance in her direction, and headed for the truck with long swinging steps.

Nat waited until he was gone in a cloud of rumbling exhaust before getting out, stretching and taking a deep lungful of fresh, chilly air. Tiny beads of water caressed her hair—she hadn't bothered to braid it, and the humidity would bring out all the stubborn curl her mother disliked so much.

Had Maria Drozdova liked anything at all about her daughter?

Nat swung the door closed, a good solid heavy sound. Would the car still be here when she came back out? It was a risk she had to take—but Marisol didn't seem like the kind to retract a gift.

It didn't matter. If Baby vanished, she'd find another way to travel. There was no going back.

There hadn't ever been, and maybe figuring out as much was what *growing up* really meant.

THE MAKERS

Buying lemonade and cheese curls from a monosyllabic minimum-wage employee in a green polyester vest was oddly anticlimactic, and southern Oregon passed in a gray blur afterward as the sun sank towards the Pacific's cauldron, reddening as it descended. The forest reached down to swallow the highway, and each vista—pounding surf, wind-gnarled trees, great stacked masses of rock—was more beautiful than the last as a short winter afternoon drained away. Baby's headlights pierced gathering gloom as she hummed along at more-than-mortal speed, the road curved back and forth like a lazy snake, and when Nat cracked her window the roaring breeze was full of cold moss, driftwood salt, and dripping.

The butterfly-flutter of flickering through traffic returned, though there weren't many pairs of bright white diamonds or ruby-red taillights to be found even as towns thickened on either side of the highway, streetlamps guttering into life. Golden windows glowed, mortals going about their winter evenings; it was lonely until the trees returned and the pavement became the floor of a tunnel between black-wet trunks. The curves would have frightened Nat at this speed if Baby hadn't taken them so surely; the tugging intensified, a twitching in Nat's middle.

"It's getting closer," she murmured, reaching for the radio dial.

Baby didn't disagree. Her speakers began to throb softly with

Stevie Wonder singing about superstition, and Nat was startled into a laugh. The sun dropped below the horizon in a glory of crimson, orange, and indigo, a show she might have enjoyed watching but had to settle for glimpses of.

Full dark fell, broken only by song changes. Whatever station the blue Mustang was tuned to didn't have ad breaks; there was no DJ gabbling. Still, in the hush between song-fade and opening bars a murmur often rose, like a busy coffee shop on a weekday morning.

Maybe she should have felt dejected, or creeped-out. Instead, a soft sure glow ignited in Nat's belly, driving the chill damp away.

An orange spark lit in the wet, tree-tangled distance. Baby left Highway 101 on a nameless ribbon of pavement, turning unerringly inland towards that small flickering light. The gleam flitted out of sight behind a series of hills, returned as the road curved, and vanished again.

That's where I'm going, she realized, and Baby purred her agreement.

It felt like Nat had been driving forever, humming along with golden oldies and a few newer songs. Whoever was choosing them had exactly her taste in music; she hadn't heard a bad song yet, and no repeats either.

It made her wonder what Dmitri listened to in his black car. Or if Baby played something else for Mom—Vedel or Tchaikovsky, maybe, or folk songs from the old country Maria sometimes sang in the garden on soft summer nights, while she rocked on the porch swing and stared across her rigidly pruned, well-weeded garden.

The funny internal sensation of entering another divinity's space thumped in Nat's stomach. A single lane of unmarked pavement crumbled at its edges, slithering between giant moss-hung trees. Even at night there were so many different shades of green here, discerned only when headlights picked out a saturated edge, a trunk sheathed in wet blackish bark, a moss-covered boulder. Hushed and dripping, a cathedral of forest swallowed the Drozdova and her chariot.

)(

The paving fringed away; gravel took its place, relatively smooth at first, then washboard-bumpy and weed-scarred. Eventually wagon-ruts hopping occasionally over thick-knotted roots rose under Baby, who took them with a faint rocking motion, a rowboat on a ruffled lake. Nat held fast to the steering wheel, glancing nervously from side to side. The headlights didn't do much for lateral vision, and she had the uneasy sense that the trees were moving behind Baby's taillights.

Closing in.

The orange glitter slipped between trunks, played hide-and-seek as Baby dipped into a valley, then approached in hopskip jumps once she climbed the other side. The wagon ruts disappeared, the trees pulled back all at once, and a level meadow appeared, tiny pollen-pieces of light lifting from waving knee-high grass—not fireflies, just glimmers riding invisible updrafts.

A campfire glittered some distance away, the will o' wisp an actual flame and not just swamp gas after all. Baby approached obliquely, then came to a halt, headlights courteously averted from the orange-and-yellow smear. She didn't quite shut off, though, her idle low and soft, somehow tentative. The tugging was all through Nat now, not just in her belly but drawing on each vein.

Maybe the car wasn't the one who knew the way after all.

"It's all right," Nat said softly. "We've come a long way. Rest a bit."

The engine halted with a sigh. Silence fell, not even a ticking of cooling metal breaking the profound hush. The tiny foxfire lights rising from the meadow winked out at some indeterminate point far above; clouds fringed into lacework and a three-quarters moon peered over the heads of dripping firs.

Even though she'd pulled on her waffle-weave thermal and flannel button-up back in Oregon, Nat shivered as she rose from the driver's seat, the sound of Baby's door unlatching loud in the stillness. She shrugged back into her peacoat, though the shivers fled almost immediately, that warm, forgiving strength spreading out to her fingers and toes.

Closing the car door quietly wasn't possible; still, she tried. She set off across the meadow, glad of her boots.

The campfire crackled, mouthing well-seasoned food. Silver conchas glittered against a dark hat, and the flames were reflected in a lean, proud-nosed man's dark eyes. He sat on the smooth dry trunk of a felled tree; beside him was a dark shape on a hunching granite boulder worn almost to satin smoothness by the passage of time. Long hair like Marisol's glinted with bluish highlights instead of red; the second man stared at the fire instead of Nat, feathers framing his almost triangular face. A slight unamused curve tilted his thin lips, and his nose was even more knifelike than Coyote's.

The fringe on Coyote's jacket stirred restlessly. Nat approached the fire, her hands dangling loose and empty, her backpack left on the passenger side of Baby's front bench seat.

Something told her that was the safest place for it.

Nat halted just at the edge of fireglow. Flames popped, the sound melding into a rattling buzz.

She'd never heard a diamondback, but she suspected it was a lot like that blurring, dangerous sound. An atavistic shiver worked down her back. Could divinities die of snakebite, or was it just really uncomfortable?

I don't think I want to find out.

Coyote leaned back, his long legs stretched towards the fire. He looked just the same as he had in Ohio, right down to his soft-soled boots, except now only a single beaded necklace, yellow and green, peeked from under his shirt collar. "Took your sweet time, buffalo girl."

"Hello again." Nat tried to figure out the applicable etiquette, and failed miserably. The tiny rising light-pinpricks from the meadow avoided her, swooping lazily as they ascended. The fire's heat was blessedly normal, uncomplicated. Even the smell of smoke, tinged with a cedary aftertaste, was entirely good and wholesome.

But so, so strange.

"This is my cousin Raven." Coyote's brief, graceful movement indicated the man next to him. "Sometimes we're just different faces. Not here, though."

I've heard about different faces. One problem at a time, though, and she had all she could handle right in front of her. Nat tried a tentative smile. "How do you do?"

"How the fuck do I do *what*?" the black-haired man said, softly but with great vehemence. A pale smear was a white dress shirt; he wore a glossy black suit jacket over it, and blue-black trousers with fringe like Coyote's coat. His dark irises glowed red at their borders for a moment, live coals warning *don't touch.* "White girls, man. Fuckin' sit down so we can get this over with."

"He lost a bet," Coyote added, helpfully, pointing his toes like a young ballerina stretching. "Said you'd never make it past San Diego."

"Thanks for the vote of confidence." Nat found a handy log to her left, its bark stripped away. It looked safe enough, and she settled gingerly upon its pale bar. That put her own boots uncomfortably close to the fire, but at least the flames had stopped buzzing. The radiant heat was pleasant, just on the edge of too much yet balanced against the chill on her back.

Coyote threw his head back and yip-laughed. Moonlight gilded his throat, flashed off the silver conchas on his hat.

Raven shook his head, hunching thin shoulders, but a smile twitched on his thin lips. "You're right," he said, as soon as the laughter's echoes lost themselves among hushed, dripping trees at the meadow's dry fringes. "She's a funny fuckin' white girl."

"I told you." Visibly pleased, Coyote settled himself a little more securely on his own seat. "Nice car, Drozdova. What you want for her?"

At least Nat had an answer for *that*. "She's not for sale." The log had a divot just right for sitting on, and she wondered how many other people had rubbed their behinds on it.

Or if it had appeared just for her.

Raven snorted, his hands dangling loosely. He crouched atop the boulder easily, knees splayed to either side as if his hip joints were other than human—they probably were, and despite the firelight, his feet were lost in thick shadow. "Thought you white people were all about buying and selling."

"A fair assumption," she allowed. You had to agree with the truth. "But Baby's not for sale, sir."

"*Sir*, she says. Like I'm a fuckin' preacher." The shadowed man shook his hair back as the fire popped, sending up a burst of crimson-orange sparks. "Just tell her, get it over with. I've got business in moonlight tonight."

"Night'll last as long as it lasts, cousin." Coyote studied Nat through smoke and rising sparks. "It wouldn't killya to be polite. This here's a brand-new bonafide. Shame about her feet though. Should have hooves."

"Pff. *That* one's not a deer woman." Raven shifted, and a dry brushing sound like feathers across a taut drumhead flattened the campfire's smoke, pushing it to Nat's right. "Probably doesn't even know what that knife she's carrying is for."

It was like listening to Mom and Leo on nights when they weren't quite arguing, but it was only a matter of time. Nat hunched, crossing her arms over her midriff, and stared at the fire. The wood was corkscrewed; ancient knotted roots and shapes suspiciously close to horrified openmouth faces lingered on tortured loops and curves. The flames shifted color—driftwood, probably, though they were a fair bit inland.

Orange at a distance, different up close. Would anyone normal see this burning, follow it through the wet, quiet forest?

"She'll find out soon enough," Coyote said, and the silence returned.

Finally, Raven sighed, moving again. He drew his knees up a little further, heels shifting on the granite boulder, and nodded sharply. The posture might have been uncomfortable, but his face didn't change. "Well, Drozdova?" The challenge in his tone was familiar, mocking as Dmitri's. "Gonna offer your throat to your hungry white mama?"

It was almost a relief to have someone just spit it out, without pussyfooting around. "I . . ." Nat couldn't make herself argue, or defend Maria. There was no defense for some things, no matter how much you loved someone. But she didn't aim her reply at Raven. "You knew. Back in Ohio, you *knew*."

"Of course. I'm not a dumbshit." The laughter had fled Coyote's easy tenor; a growl lingered under the words. "White mamas always eating their babies. They eat everything, the assholes."

"I ate the sun once." Raven's outline blurred, swelled, and shrank again as he shifted. The light turned blue on his jacket, and his hair rustled softly as it moved. "Don't recommend it."

"That's a story for another time," Coyote sniffed. "You gonna smoke, or just sit there and talk about has-beens?"

"I could talk about how your wife lost your testicles, *cousin*." Raven's laugh was a harsh croaking caw, and he turned his head, eyeing Nat sidelong. "Bet the girl would like to hear that one."

I drove cross-country for this? Still, the pulling in Nat's bones had softened. Right here on this log, looking at this strange shapeshifting fire burning through yellow and blue at its tips, was where she was supposed to be. The same sure, soft internal knowledge also told her Maria Drozdova was still alive, all the way on the other side of the continent.

Maybe not for much longer, like everyone kept saying. But Nat hadn't failed completely, not yet. Maybe there was a way out that didn't involve being . . . eaten.

How exactly did something like that happen, anyway? Did it involve knife and fork, or her mother's jaw distending like a snake's, or . . .

Did she even want to know?

"Thought you had other things to do tonight." Coyote's gaze rested on her as well, bright and pitiless.

"I do." The other man sighed, a deep, aggrieved sound. "So we just give her the thing, end of story."

"No story ever ends." Coyote leaned down, and a stick appeared in his deft coppery paw. He poked at the fire, loosing a tide of multicolored sparks. "What if I want to keep it?"

"It ain't yours, cousin." But the hatless man kept a beady eye on Nat, probably waiting for her to object, to say something useless. "You wanna be like them?"

"Seems like the only way to get ahead. We were here first, and what did it get us?"

"We came from elsewhere, too." Raven's tone softened, though not by much. "The People brought us—more fools they, but we can't control what others carry."

"Listen to you, being all philosophical." Coyote sighed, finally looking away from Nat, out into the night. He tossed the stick into the fire; it curled up like paper, emitting a faint whispering protest as he dug in the pocket of his fringed jacket. He produced a small blue package, and Nat almost smiled.

Cigarettes. Maybe he changed them every time, like Dmitri. What, she wondered, would the god of gangsters make of these guys?

If he was here, nothing would get done. The thought sounded a bit like her mother's voice, but it lacked some essential venom. *He is, after all, a man.*

Coyote tapped up a single slim cylinder, twist-closed at both ends. Then he tossed the pack to Raven, who caught it with a flutter, his unseen feet scraping stone, a harsh whisper. "You want one?" the man in the black suit asked, somewhat grudgingly.

"Is it polite?" Nat cupped her elbows in her palms, hugging harder. She'd never been camping, but sitting in front of a fire like this would be enjoyable—if she was alone. No divinities, no mothers, no normal people, just the night and the soft sound of dry wood turning into heat and light. "I don't want to offend."

"Miss Manners." Raven's croak-caw laugh lifted again, bouncing against the trees and echoing. "Oh, my. Girl, you are fucked for sure."

"He said that too." Nat tipped her chin in Coyote's direction. Her own calm was almost frightening, but then again, screaming and running wouldn't get her anywhere. She was stuck in this lunacy, and the only thing more frightening than the dreamlike terror throbbing in time to her pulse was how *inevitable* it all seemed. "Pretty sure you're both right."

"Least you admit it. Might be hope yet." Raven tossed the pack back to Coyote, lifting his selected coffin-nail to just under his nose, sniffing deeply twice. "I don't think you want to smoke just now, though. Give you bad dreams."

"And you're too young, anyway," Coyote weighed in. He stuck the cigarette—it looked like one of Leo's hand-rolled—between his lips, and tucked the pack out of sight. A short inhale, the tip suddenly glowing orange as the fire, and he held his breath for a moment before smoke slipped from his nose in two jets. "Not like us."

"Showoff," Raven said, but not very loudly, and he lit his own with a flicking fingertip. The feathers framing his face fluttered gently; a ripple went across the meadow's grass, making the lifting sparks dance and bob.

Nat didn't point out she'd seen the without-a-lighter trick before. Maybe she was wrong and Dmitri would get along with these guys. All the same, those shadowy things were following her, and her mother was dying. She wished they'd hurry the fuck up.

The two men smoked, exchanging conspiratorial glances. They were visibly waiting for her to say something, daring her to protest, to be a pushy bitch. Or maybe they just operated on a different timescale than . . .

Than mortals.

There. She was finally thinking like Dima, his mouth pursing before he spat *the rubes*, like it was something shameful to be born human. Like anyone had any control over what they were plonked on earth with.

Did that make her mother innocent, too?

Finally, Raven made a short, annoyed sound. "You gonna just sit there all night, then?"

"I don't want to be rude," Nat reiterated. "I'm a visitor. Even though I didn't ask to be born here."

Coyote's mouth gaped wide; he made a short chuffing sound and a perfect smoke ring drifted lazily free. Raven's head turned; he regarded Nat sideways again, contorting his lips. A jet of smoke from the corner of his mouth shaped itself into a broad-fletched arrow, flickering across a drench of firelight to whoosh through the ring, both shapes dissolving in hot spark-laced updraft.

"I wouldn't worry." All the mockery left Raven's easy baritone. One crimson-ringed eye fixed her with a steady glare; the shadow of his head briefly blurred like clay under running water. "When the white mothers have choked swallowing what they gave birth to, when the white fathers have beaten and raped until they can murder and rape no more, we will still be here. We are the makers, and we are eternal. Them? They're scavengers."

Coyote nodded, his cheeks caving in as he sucked on the

cigarette. "Still, even scavengers have a place." The words rode a scree of smoke, almost indistinguishable from the fire's breath.

"I don't want to be like them." It bolted free of Nat's mouth, and she hunched even more. It wasn't quite the truth, and she was almost compelled to spit the rest of it out. "I don't want to be like *her*."

Oh, Mom, I'm sorry. But I don't. I can't. Following the realization came the inevitable next step. *And I won't.*

The nuns said it was a mortal sin to disobey, to rebel against God's plan. Maria Drozdova would no doubt agree, with only a small proviso: *She* was the goddess of the little yellow house, and her word was law. Any defiance Nat attempted ended in abject failure, sobbing in the stifling darkness of her closet while Mom raged and Leo did his best to ameliorate.

But Nat was no longer a child. Everything was a sin, which meant nothing was—if the game was rigged from the start, why bother following any rules at all?

"I'd say that's your problem." Coyote sighed. It smelled half like unburned pipe tobacco and half like skunky weed, and the tiny lights rising from the meadow drifted ever higher.

Guilt settled even deeper on Nat's shoulders, another inevitability. What had she expected? "What if I want to live?"

"Now there's a question," Raven said, softly. He shifted again, with a faint clacking sound, and took a long drag off his own smoke. "What if you do?"

"Then my mother dies." The sentence stung Nat's tongue, hurt her lips. Of course she could lie, even to herself, and say she wanted them *both* to live. But that didn't seem to be a possibility.

No, Nat realized. It really wasn't an option, and somehow she'd known as much all along, the knowledge buried like most unexamined childhood truths.

But still, it was her mother. And she loved Maria, didn't she?

I love her. But I'm afraid of her, too. And I don't want to be eaten.

"I've died before," Coyote said. He trailed his fingers through a raft of exhaled smoke. The vapor clung to his skin, granted temporary solidity. "Ain't that bad."

"Not pleasant, either." Raven's shape blurred again, and Nat was suddenly glad it was nighttime and the fire's playful shadows hid whatever he was doing. "If we're being honest. Might as well."

"Yes." His cousin nodded. Orange light flashed against silver conchas. "Might as well. Guess we've wasted enough time."

"*Finally.*" There was a snapping sound, like a heavy beak clacking shut.

Nat, tense and expectant, almost flinched. "Did you talk to my mother? When she left . . . whatever she left here?"

"Maria Drozdova's too high-and-mighty to talk to the likes of us." Raven's eye gleamed, the red waxing, a perfect circle with an abyss at its heart. "Just stuck her garbage here and left. Typical." He pointed, a quick jabbing motion, and his nail was long and thick, coming to a sharp, sharp point.

Nat looked over her shoulder. A mass of the tiny meadowlights coalesced into a stream, ribboning across high, dew-heavy grass. Past Baby's sleek blue gleam, a huge tree-shadow loomed—a night-black cedar, its trunk easily as big around as the house Nat had grown up in. Bobbing little foxfires ringed the tree; the pull in Nat's veins, bones, and the rest of her sharpened. "Oh," she said, and sounded like a total dipshit.

She felt like one, too.

When she turned back to the fire, Raven was gone. His boulder-perch glowed in pale moonlight, deep grooves scored in its surface.

Claw marks.

"Give you a piece of advice, if you'll take it." Coyote stretched, fluidly graceful, the glowing tip of his cigarette perilously close to his lips.

"Okay," Nat managed.

"One way or another, you're gonna die. You wanna do it on your own terms, go south, and see Georgia."

Georgia. Okay. "Thank you." Her throat was dry, the words a croak as harsh as any corvid's throatcut call.

The divinity bark-yipped another laugh, and his bottom lip moved with elastic authority. The burning stub vanished into his mouth and his strong white teeth clapped together. The campfire popped, Nat started violently, and there was a soft sound of collapsing air.

Now she was alone. The flames whooshed, collapsing. The campfire flattened to smoldering coals, all illumination gone except for the moon's bleached face and that bobbing river of tiny will o' wisp lights, heading for the tree.

It took all her courage to rise, and to turn her back to the dying blaze. Walking amid the tiny bobbing lights wasn't so bad—they didn't touch her, though they clustered in a tight ring as if urging her onward.

The tree loomed larger and larger, fringed cedar branches stirring slightly in a breeze she couldn't feel. Baby's headlights flicked on, casting Nat's shadow against gleaming, drenched bark. A single star was caught in living wood, glittering like sharp silver boot-toes or silver conchas on a black top hat. Resin oozed around it, the tree slowly weeping at the intrusion of a foreign body.

Nat's fingertips touched cold metal. The thing fell into her palm, much heavier than it should be. Now it was dull iron instead of bright silver, and she turned it over in her hands.

It was a key. It melted from a heavy antique number with a thick haft to a perfectly prosaic modern house-unlocker and back, shimmering like the Grail as it decided what it wanted to be. Finally, it settled somewhere between, a broad flat bow and the wards like prickle-sharp cat teeth on a long, gracefully fluted stem.

"Thank you," she whispered, hoping it was the right thing to do. Sap made a soft oozing noise, sucked back into the cedar's trunk. The pull throughout Nat's body subsided, settling into deep warmth and a heady sense of thundering force, power spilling up her arm, smacking her shoulder, cascading down her back in harsh ripples. Her breath came hard and fast, her heart skip-pounded, and her nipples were high hard peaks under her T-shirt. She blinked, almost blinded by Baby's headlight glare in sudden darkness.

The tiny lights had winked out, and there was no sign of the campfire anymore. *Of course,* she thought, dazed. *Wouldn't want to start a forest fire.*

A harsh, croaking laugh echoed across the meadow, married to a soft brushing rustle.

Nat whirled and bolted for her car.

KIDNAPPING AND THEFT

Abig green sign, a green-painted building—of course, where else would Spring halt after so much of California's dust-taupe and dry olive, oleander and madrona, hills sage-scarred and golden? Even the hushed cathedral halls of the redwoods, dripping with solid inches of cold precipitation, might not please a creature of tender new velvet and gentle rains.

The rube behind the BP's counter was a hefty middle-aged woman with a graying blonde braid, a polyester vest pronouncing her an hourly serf and her plastic name tag bleating POLLY; her tired customer-service grimace was faintly ameliorated by a breath of jasmine under the reek of spoiled milk, cheap beer, and stick pepperoni.

His *devotchka* hadn't blessed this woman, but there was no sharp ozone of Spring's lightning displeasure here either. Dmitri went aisle to aisle, sniffing, and when the glass doors whooshed wide the chime of *someone's here* held a sharp edge. The stink of *politsiya politruk* wandered through like it had a right to stick its fat pink glistening nose in, but this far west it wasn't Friendly— who was probably still slugging it out with Barry in Ohio, at least one of them enjoying the dance.

Muscle twitched and rolled under a tan uniform, and the blank mirror-face of the helmet reflected only lazily drifting smoke instead of the convenience store's bright fluorescent glare.

It was Chip, Friendly's extremely southwestern cousin, with his gleaming leather gloves and his high shiny jackboots.

Chip liked to dress well, and that gleaming helmet was constantly polished by freeway wind. It must have irked him to be even slightly out of his jurisdiction—but making the rules, or enforcing them with neck-snapping violence, meant little things like the letter of the Law could be briefly set aside.

If necessary. If the payoff was good enough.

Bright packaging disguising cheap sugar and looming expiration dates ruffle-rustled uneasily, and tinny canned Muzak from dust-choked speakers grated on Dima's ears. He hadn't even touched so much as a candy bar yet. "Little bit out of your territory," he said, quietly, and Chip's helmet swiveled, a twitching, insectile movement. The rube behind the counter made a small sound, staring at what to her silly mortal gaze was a motorcycle cop who'd forgotten to take his headgear off.

"Konetsss," Chip hissed. "Been looking for you."

Oh, I'm sure you have. Dima retreated a step, behind an endcap stacked with beer boxes. Drinking warm piss on the road was a tradition in these parts. "Liar. You sniffing after little Drozdova." Everyone always thought *he* was the cheat in the great game; it was partly amusing and mostly maddening. It was his job, his function, his meaning, and his pleasure to take what could be subtracted from others; you could ascribe it to mortal greed or even simple hunger.

But no, everyone *blamed* him, and the guardians of private property and corporate interest got all the pets and praise for "keeping the peace" and "protecting." As if they ever protected anything but themselves, as if peace was anything other than their grinding profit out of the blood and meat of the unfortunate.

"The chargesss are kidnapping and theft." There was a slight click; Chip had drawn his pretty little sidearm. "Sssurrender yoursssself, Konetsss."

So that was today's game. Of course Friendly and all his other faces would love to get their hands on the Heart, and if they could somehow slip their shiny silver cuffs on Drozdova, who knew what they could accomplish? Their ascendancy might well become total; Dima's *devotchka* was just enough of a mannerly little girl to follow orders from men who meant her no good.

Maria had made sure of that. If Dima had chosen the other road, he'd be back in New York by now, and maybe the Drozdova would slow down for red and blue lights in her rearview.

Well, then. Even though a thief preferred not to meet the *politsiya*'s overwhelming force directly, there were times when you had to remind the snuffling, snorting, pawing *politruks* that they were simply another variety of thief.

And, as such, they were his little brothers, not the other way 'round.

Dima's right hand rose, full of matte-black gun. His left tingled, the bleached-bone razor giving a sharp migraine glitter. It was annoying, but he was going to have to make sure the mortal behind the counter wasn't hit.

Today, at this moment, it pleased him to let a heavy-hipped rube who had served the Drozdova keep her miserable mortal life while he taught a mirror-faced pissant his proper place in the pantheons.

"I am going to tear your little head off and shit down your throat, *Chip*." The words held a howl of steppe-winter, the edge of a prisoner's best shiv, and the soft finality of a boss declaring war. "Then I'm going to set your little bicycle on fire."

The Law-licker made a sound like an angry diamondback married to a plunging siren, and Dima dove down an aisle full of overpriced travel-sized "health" items—harsh shampoo, analgesics and decongestants and Dramamine, Band-Aids and Pepto-Bismol, tampons and four-packs of harsh splinter-filled asswipe. Spinning, uncoiling in a leap as bullets plowed into linoleum or pop-pinged off metal shelving, drawing the fire after him as Polly the rube shrieked and crouched behind the counter—*wise girl*, he thought, and his laugh shattered the glass doors of the cold cases, a foaming tide of soda and cheap beer bursting free to flash-freeze as his pale razor flicked. The wall of carbonated ice cracked as Chip plowed into it, shiny jackboots scuttling; Dima laughed again and landed with a jolt another aisle over, bright bags of candy hanging on arm-racks and boxes of solidified sugar standing on shelf-edges like good soldiers.

A step aside into the thiefways, popping out with a short plosive sound behind the bumbling bug as Chip's arms and legs crackled with temporary growth, segmented and shining; the soda-ice, full of sharpglass spears, crumbled under the cop's assault and scored his muscular hide. Dima shot him twice—*pop, pop*—and flickered back into his private realm, appearing again in the aisle full of crisps, chips, and savories.

Bags exploded as Chip—his fury turning frozen cola, beer, and cheap wine into spatter-slush—plowed around the corner and howled, each of his two upper arms holding blazing revolvers needing no reloading. His legs had separated, the multiplied jackboots' shine sadly stained, and a hairline crack wandered down his mirrored face. He siren-howled again, the wall of sound almost clipping Dima as it roared down the aisle. Shards of processed starch in several different flavors turned into shrapnel, scraps of foil-backed packaging flying like confetti—Dima giggled and skipped sideways again, reappearing behind the stupid *politsiya* fucker and smacking another bullet against his helmet-cranium. The bleach-handled razor cut silent-quick, carving up the bug's tan-clad back in a deep line. Red ichor full of golden traceries sprayed free, but Dima was already in the thiefways again as Chip's segmented spine twisted and the pig-bug tried to pistol-whip him.

They had little trouble with unarmed civilians. But Dima Konets, not to mention the more gifted of his uncles or nephews, was another matter entirely.

Polly the rube was still screaming when Dima popped out of the thiefways—not behind Chip again, for the little bastard was ready for that and jabbing with a pair of legs, the jackboots becoming leather-clad spikes whistling with deadly intent. No, the divinity of those who took what they could and gave nothing back resolved in midair *above* the petty Law-sucker so foolish as to step outside his jurisdiction by even a hair, and Konets's boot-toes gave a venomous glitter as he dropped like a falling star.

The idiots with their shiny badges, their gleaming metal brace-lets, their helmets and batons and pseudo-military armor—they had things like *borders* and *jurisdiction* and *proper procedure*.

Dima and his followers merely had the will to take, to sur-vive, to endure. Turning on the tormentors with desperate force at the right moment was a skill, like judging whose pocket to pick and which house to toss, how to tickle a safe the right way and when to put a muzzle against the back of a head and whisper *your money, your life* or *my uncle says hello*.

A crunch, a spray of stinking fluid, and if Friendly or his brother-faces ever managed to catch him, they would pay this and a thousand other insults back with interest.

He almost wished them luck. Taking what another had well predated their kind. They did this for pay, Dima's kind for sur-vival, and the difference was total.

Chip screamed, his carapace crackle-cracking. He wallowed amid shattered shelving, among dunes of chips and crisps, a tide of sticky fluid edging around the corner from the violated cold cases. Some of the fluorescent tubes overhead buzz-blinked; others out-right broke, glass glittering as it fell, grinding itself finer and finer.

Dima hopped on Chip's back again, a gleeful stamping dance. His dark hair flopped free, his white teeth gleamed in a murder-ous V-shaped grin, and if Polly the rube had been peeking, her mortal heart might well have stopped at the sight. He ground down with both feet, and a sharp *crack* was a deadly deep diago-nal crack blooming on Chip's blank mirrored face.

He could have completely crushed the motherfucker, but his next iteration coalescing from mortal belief might be less stupid and hence, more troublesome. Better to simply incapacitate, and administer a lesson in the wages of stepping outside your bailiwick.

Polly, crouched with her hands over her graying head, made a thin whispery noise she probably thought was a shriek as Dima's boots landed on the front counter. His hand flicked out, sinking into the cabinet overhead that held cartons of cigarettes; he grinned down at her as he stamped twice, leaving vast stars of breakage in the heavy glass covering notices like WE ID IF YOU LOOK UNDER 40 and ALL RETURNED CHECKS WILL BE CHARGED A FEE.

Some of his disciples worked in the banks. Now *there* was a racket.

He fished a pack of Pall Malls from the shredded cabinet, humming as Chip thrashed and wailed. Dima's melody became words. "Better run, Polly." Little red pinpricks danced in his pupils, bearing a distinct resemblance to hellfire. "You a lucky, lucky girl. I suggest lottery ticket. Buy one soon."

That was all he'd give, even for a rube who had perhaps pleased a solemn-eyed Drozdova. Cellophane crinkled; he bit into the pack, enjoying the melting plastic coating his tongue.

Just like American cheese. Dima hopped down from the counter and sauntered out the door, chewing and grinning. Chip's motorcycle quivered as his gaze fell upon it, and a few moments later he was in his own comfortable black chariot, pavement throbbing under gleaming tires as orange flames crawled over a shattered hulk of metal and glass left in his wake. Whatever was in the cycle's tank screamed as it ignited, sickly green threading through the orange and red flames, and all told it was a lovely evening.

Even if it was raining.

SPRING'S COUNTRY

It wasn't so difficult after all, not with the Key. All she had to do was wonder *how fast can I go*, and Baby burst with a yowl of glee from the dark, dripping tree-tunnel over the wagon-rutted road into bright moonlight. The internal *thump* of entering a divinity's space spread, tingling in Nat's arms and legs, and she recognized this place as if she'd known it all along.

The moon didn't move as Baby purred over gentle curves, dropping into shallow valleys. A dirt road with slim ribbons of gravel at its edges held no washboard rattle or pop-pinging stones; the ride was as smooth as the hills looked. The stars were dry fires in a velvety sky innocent of any city stain, and the good sweet smell of a warm evening after winter had loosened but before summer's sweating grasp was everywhere. The cropped, tender grass was all silvered green under the full moon's beneficent gaze, and the key Nat had taken from the cedar's trunk was safely stowed in her backpack, vibrating slightly in the Cup's warm embrace.

Perhaps she'd dreamed of these rolling hills, this road, the soft satiny grass. The sense of rightness was overwhelming, wringing joyful tears from smarting eyes, buzzing in her bones, filling her head with sure knowledge she couldn't remember learning *or* forgetting.

If this was the way divinities traveled, she only wondered why

Dima hadn't before. But his route was probably a lot less pleasant, and besides, Nat had been . . . mortal? Or mostly mortal, and maybe couldn't stand the strain of the trip?

Did she dare to call herself *human* now? It could give you a headache to think too deeply about.

Now she had Spring's arcana—Knife, Cup, and Key. It *felt* right, all three vibrating with warm, forgiving force. Not just correct, but complete.

The next step of the riddle said *a salt-black tree*, but the cedar didn't seem to count. Coyote said *go south, and see Georgia*.

So far she'd followed the riddle faithfully. It was Maria Drozdova's game, and Nat knew what happened whenever her mother thought she might be losing. There was no outright cheating, of course.

But Mom made you wish you could lose, and curse any bit of luck. Any victory against the goddess of the yellow house was paid for later, one way or another.

Consequently, Nat hated board and card games with a passion. Pinochle, gin, even the one time she'd tried Monopoly were all terrible ordeals on South Aurora; Leo only played chess in the park.

A dam had broken inside Nat's head, and while she drove through Spring's verdant country with Baby's windows all down to catch a soft breeze, edged with just enough crispness to refresh, the memories crowded her like predators clustering a running deer.

Stop lying, Natchenka . . . don't give me that look . . . you must have cheated, little girls shouldn't cheat . . . I will march you into that house at midnight . . . your attitude, Natchenka, go to your room . . . clean this up, filth is disgusting . . . have you gone to Baba yet, have you gone . . . cats don't talk in this country . . . you and your imagination, little Natscha, go dust the parlor.

Sometimes the low sweet sound of the slipstream impersonated her mother's voice, scraping Nat's ears and producing an un-happy growl-edge to Baby's engine. Nat gripped the steering wheel, her hands aching.

How far away was New York from this strange place, this dimension built for fast travel? Did her mother, lying on a bed in one of the Laurelgrove's most expensive rooms—because a window was an absolute necessity, Maria needed natural light—somehow feel Nat traveling in this secret place, under that pale perfect mooncoin with no meteor scarring?

Spring's Country, indeed. It was as good a name as any. Baba de Winter probably had snow-covered hills and a round chariot with chicken legs, striding along and casting a terrible scratch-edged shadow. Marisol? Her country might be akin to the coast highway, bright and warm, the top on her convertible down and her glorious long black mane an untangled banner.

"*Natcheeeeenkaaaaaa,*" the slipstream moaned, and Nat wanted to rub her grainy eyes. But her hands wouldn't unclamp from the wheel.

Her first unicorn mug, "accidentally" broken while she was at school. Those nights when she half-woke and Mom was standing over her bed, head cocked, blue eyes lambent in the dark—child-Nat had been both uneasy and comforted, because at least the goddess of the yellow house was paying attention to her miserable, misbegotten daughter. The aggrieved sighs when Nat grew out of another pair of shoes, the glare when a hungry child had the temerity to ask for seconds, the parent conferences Maria bothered to attend in order to dazzle a nun or one of the infrequent male teachers. *Oh, Natchenka has such an imagination, you grade her so nicely, we know she's not that bright . . .*

Each time Nat thought she had a handle on the entire mad, impossible affair another memory would coldcock her, driving the breath out of her lungs and making her eyes fill with hot saltwater.

This was probably what therapy felt like. Nat wouldn't know, it was too expensive. *You think money just grows, Natchenka? You think I am made of it?*

Maria never laid a hand on her, though. Sometimes she prodded Nat a little ungently, especially when her daughter bumbled while weeding, but that wasn't like real *abuse*, was it? Just a steady drip, drip, drip of caustic irritation and impatience, just making it clear Nat was a burden and a mistake, just . . .

Just tenderizing the meat?

Nat flinched, swallowing hard. Her throat burned with bile, her hands shook, and though the deep sense of utter physical well-being flooded her, there was nothing in it to make the memories hurt less.

She had to wait until the proper moment, Marisol said. If Nat hadn't made plans to move out, scrimping and saving—and that was another thing, taking three-quarters of her daughter's paychecks to help with the "house bills"? What was *that*, when a divinity could literally make cash, or did you need your arcana to do it?

"Get out of my space, Natscha!"

Nat jumped, honeydark hair bouncing as she peered wildly in every direction, still gripping the steering wheel. Her heart leapt into her throat, pounding wildly. Baby's engine roared.

Crackling black spiderwebs poured down the soft green hills; a rumble of thunder rose in the distance. Bright diamond lightning forked, and the windroar of swift passage was full of ozone and perfume, the peculiar smell of Maria Drozdova's anger.

"Get out!" The cry scraped down Baby's side; the car slewed, her tires biting powdery dirt, sending up a spume of gravel, finding the road again with a fluid feline lunge.

What the hell? Nat's fingers cramped. The lightning struck closer, thunder washing over hills like those awful black cracks. If the scavenger-shadows were around—

"I . . . said . . . get . . . OUT!" A banshee scream tore across the road, digging a gaping crevasse. Nat practically stood on the

brake; the mental image of her mother on the hospice bed—stiff and skinny, her bloodshot blue eyes wide and rolling as her back arched and a terrifying wail rose around the plastic tube forced into her throat—was sudden and Technicolor-vivid.

The hills blinked out, the moon snuffed like a candle. Rubber screamed, brakes squealed, and Baby rocked to a stop, sending up a long roostertail of night-gray dust. The hay-scented breeze vanished, replaced by sagebrush, exhaust, and a distinct dry-rasping undertang.

It was still night, but high scudding clouds held the orang-ish reflection of citylight. Pavement seamed with veins of hot-tar repair ran in either direction, and it was a mercy there was no traffic because Baby was cockeye across the wholly normal, wholly *mortal* road, a thin gravel shoulder diving into a deep ditch a fraction of a foot away from the blue car's shining chrome bumper. The only sounds were Nat's jagged breathing and the car's dissatisfied grumble.

And thunder over far-off hills, like some giant creature turn-ing over in its stony bed.

If Nat died in a car accident, would Maria Drozdova become young again?

OhGod, Nat wanted to whisper, but that was stupid. Instead, her mouth opened, and what came out was a single, drawn-out syllable. "*Fuuuuuck.*"

Baby's rumble said she agreed. A flash over shadows that might have been hills waited eight long seconds to send more thunder tiptoeing through the hush. Baby's headlights dimmed once, twice, as if cat-blinking.

Nat fumbled for the gear lever, her neck creaking as she rested an arm on the bench seat's back, peering out the rear window. Thankfully, Baby reversed with no problem, and Nat got the car at least in the right lane, though if anyone came along at high speed they were probably both goners. Slowly, in fits and starts, the trembling all through her diminished. A faint pull began—

fortunately, the way she and Baby were already pointed. There was no more lightning, but she didn't know where in the hell she was.

If her mother wanted Nat to hurry up and bring the Heart, she was certainly making it difficult. But then again, frustration could make you work against your own best interests. It happened all the time.

Including, apparently, to divinities.

Maybe Maria could tell what Nat was thinking. It was a parent's trick, helped along by the fact that most toddlers are really bad liars. Being with someone twenty-four-seven since birth probably had something to do with it, too. Or maybe Mom somehow just *felt* someone in Spring's Country, since it was hers too.

"But for how much longer?" Nat heard herself murmur, and her right hand flew up, cupping over her mouth and sealing tight as if she could trap the words, jam them back down her throat, negate them somehow.

Baby idled comfortably, content. Her headlights showed the ruler-straight road tapering to its vanishing point like an art class illustration of perspective. The scent of sage rode a knife-sharp chill—Nat had read that desert nights were cold, and the air here was much, much drier than the dripping Northwest forest. How far had she traveled? Could she get to anywhere in the world from Spring's Country, or just anywhere in America?

A pale approaching sparkle in the rearview forced Nat to shift the car into drive and press on the accelerator, despite the fact that she had no goddamn idea where she was. Still, at least this road was traveled, and indisputably human. Even if she was lost, there would be a sign sooner or later.

Nat was also, still, completely alone, except for that distant headlight-glimmer in the rearview mirror's watery depths.

The solitude was frightening to a New York girl who had never slept away from home until a few days ago. Just how many she couldn't tell—did time warp in that in-between space of moonlight and soft hills, or just distance?

And yet . . . Nat Drozdova found out she kind of liked the loneliness, and couldn't wait to eventually find out more about her private traveling dimension. Especially once her heart stopped pounding, her hands stopped shaking, and Baby's head-lights discovered a freeway on-ramp sign, whispering its location into the desert night.

𝕏

She was in New Mexico. Just north of Albuquerque, in fact.

And another soft tugging, different than the arcana-urge, was building in her bones.

NOT DEFEATED YET

Winter's hand lay heavy upon an iron-gray, perpetually unsleeping city. Meteorologists nattered on about precipitation, inversion, and trends; newscasters bubbled with glee while retail workers groaned inwardly. The houseless shivered, attempting to burrow into any shelter they could find, and any mortal might be forgiven for thinking there had never been any such thing as summer, only the endless cold.

Freezing rain coated skyscrapers, roads, houses, stores, and any other surface unlucky enough to feel the weather's ire, twinkling viciously as a divinity's sharp silver boot-toes. The keyholes of parked cars or outside doors were coated, windows filigreed, roofs groaning under a fresh weight. Every drop was merely feather-heavy, true—but there was strength in numbers, especially when added to a blanket of snow compacting under the assault.

The peculiar hiss of droplets solidifying as they hit glass slithered against the window of a hospice room. Safe on the other side, an elderly man dozed on a pink-cushioned bench—it had taken tortuous mortal hours to reach the Laurelgrove again, and Leo would not attempt a return to the shattered, slumped ruins of a yellow Brooklyn house.

As long as the electricity lasted, though, the machines inside mortal buildings kept to their work. Lightbulbs blazed, heaters struggled to breathe through vents and rooms, and hospital machines continued transcribing the electrical ephemera of heartbeat and lungfill with greenish traceries while singing in soft rhythmic beeps.

On a much-bleached cotton blanket, a thin hand twitched. Papery liver-spotted skin moved uneasily, drawn tight over bones become almost wholly mortal. Yet a flame still burned in Maria Drozdova's wasted body. Her belly, oddly distended, echoed the motion, and had she been fully conscious the agony—something inimical pulsing, enclosed in flesh becoming perishable—might have triggered another round of frantic medical activity, vital signs described and palliatives administered.

Her eyelids fluttered, rose halfway. Blue sparks filled her pupils, answered by two tiny reflected dots on the ceiling's acoustic tiles, though strictly speaking, the elder Drozdova was not . . . *there*.

All her flinty will and iron determination focused inward, clutching at a subtle, invisible space that had been her sole domain since her forgotten coalescing, so long ago upon another continent. Silent alarms blared, and all her waning resources collected like raindrops running down a window.

But it was so cold, and her strength had faded alarmingly. She hadn't expected the process to be so quick, or so agonizing. The child should have returned by now; not only was the maggot dawdling, she was also invading the *Strana Vesny*, and she had stolen her mother's beautiful blue chariot.

Get out, Maria Drozdova howled, the cry struggling through layers of weakness, shadows with papercut edges crowding her fevered almost-dreams. The lovely green hills, the bright vernal moon, the crisp stainless road and glitter of cool water between grassy banks, was warping and shifting to obey a new incarnation.

Get out, you little bitch. This is my *realm. Get out, get out, get OUT . . .*

The last straining effort paralleled that which had brought the worm forth on a tide of golden-laced ichor a little over two mortal decades ago, a wringing expulsion. Maria's spine arched, the machines at her bedside belatedly noticing distress and hurrying to remedy inattention. Her pulse skyrocketed, and a gurgle spilled around the plastic proboscis plunged into her throat.

Leo, chin almost touching his sunken chest, did not wake. He was an old man, after all, and exhausted from the effort to reach his beloved's side through a wintry city wasteland.

Maria's feet writhed under the bedding; her hands lifted, fluttering arthritic birds. A choked whimper, the blue glow in her pupils intensifying before she sagged, lapsing into semiconsciousness.

But the invader had been repelled upon the very last shore. Unintended consequences ruined many a carefully laid plan, yes—but though the elder Drozdova was weakened into mortality she was not quite extinguished.

She was not defeated yet.

Everything now depended on the tearing, pulsing, agonizing horror lodged in her vitals—and on her careful training and shaping of a child.

Once her daughter reached the salt-black tree, all could yet be made well again. Though many had struggled against Maria's pretty, pale hands, in the end they all offered their throats to the flint knife. How could they not, when her loveliness surpassed all mortal imagining?

Old Spring's pupils dimmed and her eyelids resealed, the machines' quieting clamor failing to attract any mortal attention on a busy afternoon since the event passed swiftly, equanimity returned. She lay and dozed, her teeth—discolored, but still strong—worrying at the tube forced past her lips.

TRUTH, CONSEQUENCES

Rose-fingered dawn spread into gray sky an hour later. The horizon burst into full crimson-and-pink fury, clouds lingering over mesas and olive or cypress forest-smears. The desert was strangely green, not at all what she'd expected, but winter was the season of rains. Every surface held a fine patina of dust, but the light was beautiful—it drenched every facet and curve, robbing shadows of their terror. The air warmed quickly, too; Nat rolled the windows down and turned the heater off as soon as the sun had cleared the horizon's rim.

Baby hummed southward on I-25. Any human habitation meant water, which meant clots of green far dustier than California's. Reddish rock frowned on anything resembling a slope; Nat's first sight of a roadrunner was a distinct letdown.

The little brown bird didn't so much as beep-beep.

Now that she knew how fast Baby could go, she held the chariot to a comfortable—though entirely inhuman—speed. Las Nutrias, Contreras, La Joya, San Acacia—the towns clustered the eastern edge of the freeway, sometimes just a flicker before they were gone. Traffic was sporadic once they were free of Albuquerque's predawn sprawl, and the signs for wildlife refuges, national parks, and flash-flood warnings didn't shout. They drawled, having all the time in the world.

Elephant Butte, another sign giggled, and Nat laughed along like a kid. Baby peeled off at the interchange, surefoot as a stretch-galloping feline, and before Nat knew it the blue car was slowing, waxed thread slipping through the eye of a needle. *Cemetery Road*, the signs whispered; the town was named *Truth or Consequences*.

It figured. Nat's breathing slowed, a curious comfort folding over her. Out here, like in the Dakotas, there was enough space for everything to be on a nice neat grid, very few surprises or weird angles. Turn after turn rolled under the tires; Baby circled the town as if hunting.

Good thing the car knows where to go. Just after the thought came another laugh, bubbling up from a deep hidden wellspring. Whether the car knew, a divinity could sense, or Nat's prosaic, mortal unconscious was coming through loud and clear was academic.

It all ended up in the same place.

On Baby's left was a sluggish glitter—a largish creek or smallish river. A tiny skip in the car's steady humming echoing all through Nat's body, the warning loud and clarion-clear; she all but stood on the brake, whipping the steering wheel. Gravel crunched, a spray of roostertail dust rose, and she almost clipped a listing sign for a whitewater rafting company with the passenger-side mirror.

A wide unpaved turnout snuggled against the river's curve, its fringes crowded with dry bushes and thorny scrub. Baby rocked to a stop facing the water; there was a chuckling collection of stones submerged in the flow. Come summer Nat could probably hop across on foot without getting wet past the shin, but now . . .

The Drozdova chewed her lower lip gently, staring. Despite the dust, Baby shone pristine. Even her windshield was untroubled by bug-spatter. Nat rubbed her hands together as if cold, contemplating this new puzzle.

The tugging was clear—she had to go across the water. It was equally clear that looking for a bridge wasn't the solution.

She was a divinity, after all. Was she supposed to get out and walk on the surface tension, or . . .

There was nobody around, the town busy waking up and going about its mortal business. Broken beer bottles glittered fiercely, trash turned into diamonds while paper and other detritus busily melded into taupe and dusty green. It was a pretty shore nonetheless. Past a screen of thirsty, hunched olive-green bushes on the other side was another rutted dirt road, and what looked like a farm field.

And past that? Desert, rising red rock, and more dust.

The sense of direction in her bones buzzed impatiently, like manicured fingernails drumming on a gleaming-empty, mirror-surfaced desk.

Oh, what the hell. She had very little to lose at this point, frankly. *Is there a god of tow trucks?*

Nat slipped her boot-toe off the brake, inhaled sharply, and stamped on the gas.

Baby's hind end sent up a roaring fan of small stones and dust; the car leapt forward, yowling like a cat in heat. There was a slight shifting sensation, a bunching and an elastic release. Twin sheets of brown water curled high on either side, sparkling with white foam at their edges, and the jolt of landing was accompanied by a wrenching right turn. Metal squealed, flexible as a feline spine, and Baby snort-chuckled.

Should have given me a difficult *task,* that noise said, and Nat—sweat greasing her lower back, collecting in the hollows of her elbows and behind her knees—giggled as well, a high wild glassy sound. Power, bright as white wine, sang all through her.

Was this what *divinity* meant?

A network of dirt roads—some larger, some smaller—veined the desert. The hills swallowed a blue car with a laughing woman inside, and traces of tender green from droplets scattered in her wake drove their roots deep.

Ж

One tiny, almost-hidden road climbed with switchbacks, goat-graceful and assured. A dry rasping buzz on either side penetrated engine-hum and the crunch of tires; Nat barely had to keep her fingertips on the wheel. Finally, Baby crested the hill-top at an angle and turned again, finding an almost-driveway passing through a break in ubiquitous Western three-strand barbwire fence stretching between weathered gray posts. The sunlight turned sharper, noon instead of dawn, and though the shadows were finely edged they were not hungry.

Not here.

Baby halted, her nose pointed at a small round adobe crouched on an apron of flat land starred with rock piles somewhere between erosion-carved and artistically stacked. A similarly round garden wall curved protectively close. Behind the wall, cactuses tangled together in vibrant profusion, wicked spikes protecting strangely fragile green skin. A large fire-blackened saguaro-esque monster lifted four arms around a central pillar. Far away from any of its cousins, it glowered on the right side of the garden, and each of its spines held a faint electric shimmer.

No mailbox. No sign of life other than the cacti and a few hardy, spiny bushes outside the garden's enclosure. The adobe's front entrance was an impossibly black arch holding no door in its lips; its red roof tiles were dust-free and burnished under a flood of glaring sunshine.

Baby's engine settled into silence. Nat reached for the door handle and paused. That buzzing from the rock piles was probably snakes.

I am not very brave, she realized dismally, and shuddered.

Still, she'd come this far. Was the big forklike thing the

salt-black tree? It didn't *seem* like it, but there was no instruction manual for this divinity bullshit.

Just as her fingers curled over the handle, a flicker of motion in the doorway's deep gloom made her breath catch.

It was an old woman, tall and sticklike, with a frowsty mess of iron-gray hair. She was incontrovertibly a divinity, and she looked very familiar indeed.

The sound of Baby's door opening was loud in the humming stillness. Nat was painfully aware she was braless in a not-very-fresh T-shirt, and was thankful she was wearing jeans. Not that they'd do anything against a snakebite, but . . .

"Well?" The woman's voice was a harsh, impatient cigarette-rasp, high and hard as if warning off a traveling salesman. "I've got light to catch, child. Come in, if you're going to."

Nat closed the door and set off for the house, patting Baby's hood once as she passed. *Guard my backpack, will you?*

She didn't want to leave the car's safety, but there was no help for it.

TRUTH AND GEORGIA

G eorgia." The woman's slim, iron-strong hand was warm and leathery. Her knifelike nose was familiar, and her irises were so dark her pupils seemed almost brown in comparison. Wrinkles fanned from the corners of those eerie eyes and bracketed her mouth; her neck was a column of tendons. Her hair moved uneasily, gray curls sandpapering each other. "And you're Maria's child. Took you long enough."

"Hello," Nat managed faintly. "You look like . . ." This close, the woman resembled Baba de Winter even more strongly, only tanned instead of pale. Instead of Baba's thread-fraying silk gown or pinstripe business chic, Georgia wore a loose dun button-up shirt and a pair of heavy canvas pants, both bleached to sand-color by long exposure to dry sunglare. A huge, black-veined turquoise set in tarnished silver peeked between the shirt's top vee, the first two bone buttons undone.

"You think I only have one form, granddaughter? Or that you do, for that matter?" The old woman shook her head, turning into the house; clearly, she meant for Nat to follow. "It's uncomfortable to be around them, though. Magnetic repulsion."

The darkness was a high cool foyer with a red-tiled floor, stone stairs with risers worn into shallow U-shapes by long traffic on the left, an arch full of murmuring to the right. Every edge was worn and rounded; the woman's shadow was a sword in the much brighter archway at the hallway's far end. Nat hurried to keep up, hoping she wouldn't scatter sand inside—there was no mat to wipe your feet on. "That makes sense."

"*Sense,* she says." A buzzing, croaking laugh, almost like Raven's but indisputably female, bounced off the smooth walls. Nothing hung to break their thoughtful, pale purity, no paintings or photographs, not even a nail.

The brightness at the hall's end was a semicircular, airy kitchen, an antique black cast-iron cooking-stove-plus-oven crouching along the wall with its mended tin chimney rising to pierce the ceiling. An oblong window over the deep utility sink— holding a pump-handle that had once been painted red—was full of more potted cacti drinking in golden light. A butcher-block table, its top polished satin-smooth even in the scars from constant use, had two old metal barstools tucked underneath. Every surface was clean and bare; the sink had a tiled apron to its right and a metal dish drainer holding one glass, one plate along with a fork, a spoon, and a very sharp knife in a tiny wire cage next to two bowls, one much larger than the other. The dishes were earthenware, an indeterminate shade between brick and terracotta.

You could breathe in a house like this, despite the almost painful cleanliness. It was the home of a woman who lived alone and knew goddamn good and well why she did, as well as liking it that way.

The kitchen window gazed onto a bare stone courtyard. Outside in the bright new afternoon a glowing-white empty canvas sat upon an easel; the only clutter was a triangular wooden table to its right holding a jumble of brushes, paint tubes, scrapers, and other artistic tools.

"Tea?" Georgia coughed, a dry rattling sound of amusement. "Or something stronger? Surprised you made it across the river, but then again, I shouldn't be."

"I'm fine with anything—" Nat began, but the old woman whirled from the sink, her lip lifting and sharp white teeth gleaming as her hair writhed. A shadow passed through the window's indirect glow.

"Don't fucking lie here, little girl," Georgia hissed. "That's the only warning you'll get."

Oh, fuck. Nat's throat was so dry it clicked as she swallowed twice, painfully. "Vodka," she said. "Neat, and very cold."

A charged silence descended. The old woman sniffed, then turned back to the sink. "Mealymouth," she muttered. "If there's anything I despise, it's those discreet little falsities. Have the fucking courage to say what you mean."

Hard to shake a lifetime's training, ma'am. Nat forced the words down.

They didn't want to go. The sisters at school had always been big on manners and nice little white lies, and of course there were things you knew better than to say at home. Retail and office work was the same; the entire mortal world wanted a woman to play nice, go along, be polite.

Out here in the desert, you could say exactly what you wanted. Who was around to hear it, after all?

Of course, Mom got away with behaving badly. Probably because she visibly didn't give a fuck, she was so far above what Dima would call *the rubes.*

It must be nice, Nat thought, and an uncharacteristic vibration started in her chest. It wasn't quite uncomfortable, but definitely unsettling. It halted, then returned, a fitful buzz.

"Sit down." Apparently mollified, Georgia turned away from the sink. Both her strong, thin hands were now full of lambent yellowish glasses. She indicated the table with an irritable little motion, and Nat hurried to obey. "What are you here for?"

She almost answered *I don't know,* but realized just in time that was a lie. Nat accepted one of the glasses, now heavy-full of liquid; condensation was cold on its slick sides. "To ask you where the salt-black tree is. And to see what else I can find out."

"Ah." Georgia nodded, pulled out one of the stools with a

dragging screech, and settled on it with a quick, birdlike movement, her bony hips twitching. "You want your mama to die, girl?"

How the fuck could she answer that? Nat took a deep breath, pulling the other stool from its home. Thankfully, it didn't scream at her, and she found the words she wanted were available after all. "I want to survive."

"Not quite an answer."

"I love her." Nat hitched a hip carefully onto the seat, observing a prudent distance from the old woman. "But . . ." Her throat threatened to close, and that buzzing in her chest mounted. "I think . . ." All she could produce was a strangled whisper. "I think I hate her too."

Saying it was terrifying, so she bolted half the vodka in the condensation-greased glass.

It was indeed cold, just this side of freezing, and it went down easy. It exploded in her chest, next to that strange mounting vibration, and her eyes watered as if she was about to cry.

But not nearly enough. It wasn't tears, and it wasn't the alcohol. It was something in between.

All this time, she'd been so frightened of Dmitri. He was scary, sure, but nothing compared to this.

"So you *can* tell the truth." Georgia snorted, took a hit off her own glass. Whatever was in it was sticky, and glowed rubescent. "They try to beat it out of you, don't they. After a while you stop fighting back."

Was that what happened to you? Nat didn't think asking would get her anything good. "Or you move out to the desert."

"If you have to. One way . . ." Georgia shook her iron-colored head, her hair settling into slight twitches instead of that nauseating, hypnotic dry writhing. Her eyes were very bright. "Or another."

There didn't seem to be much to say, so Nat stared into the remaining vodka. The cut-paper shadows probably wouldn't dare to step into this woman's yard, but this definitely wasn't a place to hide.

Georgia didn't seem to like guests very much.

"Each one of us has to learn," the old woman finally said, softly. She studied her own drink like it held the secrets of the universe, and who knew? Maybe it did. "You think it's pleasant, being what we are? Power's got to be paid for. Some of us think we control things, but we're *in service*, and don't you forget it. Even the Eternal, even that Cold Bitch herself. If you can't do the job, get out of the way and let someone else."

"Like my mother." Nat wondered what the greenish, barefoot Cold Lady would say to this woman; she also wondered if Georgia would scare even Dmitri Konets into behaving.

"If you want." Georgia made a slight, shrugging motion; clearly, she didn't care either way. The old woman cast a very dark shadow on rounded tiles; Nat's own held tiny golden sparkles at the edges. "Some day you might find yourself dragged to another shore by mortals. What would *you* choose?"

"I don't know." Nat suppressed a flinch—even truth could feel guilty, sometimes. If she had some of Mom's stubbornness, it was a good thing, right? Obstinacy had brought her this far; it had dealt with Dmitri and even forced a galloping-black motorcycle-horse to bring her back to Ranger's. Not to mention everything else. "I hope it would be the right thing."

"Oh, everyone's got some idea of the right thing. Usually it's close to what they won't admit to wanting." Georgia rolled her dark, dark eyes, a strangely teenage expression. When she shifted, the stool creaked as if she was much heavier than her slimness looked. "That thief-boy, now, at least he's honest about what he is."

Yeah, and I'll bet he's fucking furious right now. Nat couldn't scrape together an ounce of fear at the thought, not while she was sitting here. "Yes. At least."

"You could learn a lot from that." The old woman set her glass on the table with a slight, definite click. "Finish your drink, I've got painting to do."

Nat lifted her vodka as politeness demanded, and stopped. Lowered it. "Where do I go next?"

Did a flicker of a smile touch the old woman's bloodless lips? Perhaps. "Depends on what you want."

So she was going to make Nat say it. Fine. "The salt-black tree." *I might as well.* "I want the Dead God's Heart."

If she was being honest, she wanted a lot more. Nat *liked* the deep warm sense of well-being, she liked Baby and driving with the windows down. She even liked Spring's Country, though she couldn't go back until her mother . . .

Until her mother was dead. Which might happen sooner or later, but either way Nat had promised to find the jewel for Baba.

And once she held it, what would the gangster god do? What *could* he do to her? It probably couldn't be worse than being eaten by your own mother, could it?

"Louisiana." Georgia's black gaze fastened on Nat's face, as if the younger woman was a toddler, easily readable. "New Orleans. Look for the woman with the power. She doesn't like liars either, mind you."

I'll try not to be one, then. But for fuck's sake, couldn't any of these divine assholes be polite to *her*, for once? Even Marisol hadn't said *please* even once. "Thank you."

Georgia's thin, sharp shoulders twitched as she laughed again, a dry brazen scraping sound. "You're going to die."

The buzzing in Nat's chest mounted another notch. "Thank you," she repeated, almost primly. "For the vote of confidence." They all found her so fucking funny—nobody dared laugh at her mother, though.

If Nat managed to survive, could she make them shut up? Or maybe she could just get in Baby and . . . go, avoiding all their impossible little quests, their cryptic pronouncements, their goddamn cackling.

It sounded nice. It sounded, in fact, downright amazing.

"But that's all right, little Drozdova." The skin on Georgia's skinny neck twitched, as if something underneath was shifting. That mass of writing gray curls moved again, restlessly. One lifted, a questing viper-head. "We all do, sooner or later. At the end, even the Cold Bitch will lay down her burden."

It didn't seem possible. "Even you?" She was getting just as weird as the rest of them. Did they just sit around all day having philosophical discussions?

"Especially me, and on that day I'll probably even be glad about it." Georgia's mouth pulled down at the corners, bitterly. She picked up her glass again and finished off its cargo in three long, sucking swallows, smacking her lips at the end. "Here's the last thing I'm going to tell you: There's dying, and then there's dying. That's it."

That sounds about as useful as flies on meat, thanks. One of Leo's sayings, and thinking about him made the buzzing in Nat's chest worse. She hadn't eaten since Marisol's, and now she was downing vodka and about to drive again. Did divinities get DUIs?

Did she need to sober up? Staying here would be a very bad idea, though.

Nat exhaled sharply, clearing her lungs. She lifted the glass, and the remaining vodka, just on the edge of ice-slush despite its alcohol content, filled her mouth before sliding down her esophagus in a muscular wave. A supernova detonated deep inside her, and the buzz-rattle deep in her ribcage was so loud she was almost afraid the other woman would hear it.

When she lowered the glass, sucking in a breath full of desert sage, dry spice, and rasp-scaled heat, tears filled her eyes. Her vision blurred, and for a moment another shape moved behind Georgia. The enormity of that shadow all but choked her.

Because it was familiar, and because she knew what to call the thing coiled inside her own body, its tail held high and buzzing. It had a wedge-shaped head and shining flat eyes; the blurring button-rattle was its final warning.

Striking quick as lighting and driving its fangs deep was what followed.

Georgia's bony hand flashed out; she subtracted the empty glass from Nat's nerveless hand. Two long, unpainted fingernails scratched lightly along her granddaughter's left wrist; the contact burned, though razor pinpricks didn't break the skin. "You didn't think I'd let you leave without a gift, did you?" Baba Yaga's other form—or maybe Yaga was Georgia's, who knew—gave an arid chuckle. "Now get out of my house, and go do what you're going to."

Nat slithered off the stool, her boots hitting tiled floor with twin fang-thumps. She backed away, her right hand clapping over her mouth because the urge to hiss-scream boiled in her middle with the vodka, and once she began she might never stop.

She staggered down the hall, reeled out into bright desert sunshine, and heard a thick slamming sound behind her though there wasn't a door in the entire dwelling. The cactuses, startled by her reappearance, froze like dancers petrified by a sudden cessation of music, and the black saguaro-monster spat two blue-white sparks from wicked hand-long needles, the brief crackles vanishing in midair.

Nat ran for Baby. The chariot's engine was already thrumming, eager to be flying again, dying to be gone.

And still the buzzing filled the young Drozdova's bones; now she knew its name. The twin marks on her wrist throbbed as she spun the steering wheel; Baby's engine roared.

A few moments later, nothing remained before Georgia's little round house but churned dust settling with little slithering sounds, and another scarf of dry cackling laughter rose to the innocent, powder-blue sky before ending with a shimmering sibilant sound.

HERE WE ARE

There was a lot to love in Texas, at least as far as Dima was concerned. Every man liked to think himself a cowboy, and in the wide-open they could all pretend to be one. A greasy petrochemical scent on the back of the wind spoke of bubbling oil wells, and where there was crude there was money. Where there was money, there was someone looking to take it all—and there were others looking to subtract it from the grasper.

Plus, the barbeque was tasty, and guns were everywhere. It was a carnival, especially with Christmas lights still blinking even though the commercially blessed nativity had passed. Plenty of rubes were frantically returning gifts they couldn't afford, not to mention back at suffering their miserable pittance-paid jobs, and no few of them were looking around and thinking *why shouldn't I just grab?*

With New Year's right around the corner, alcohol was lowering every inhibition in preparation, too.

One of his other faces lived in Dallas, but Dima didn't wander too close to that good ol' boy. He was after different prey, and the tingling in his hands made his black car scream along the outskirts of Amarillo, circling like a shark before diving. Lubbock's smog held the faintest tinge of jasmine; he bisected the town going due south, turned east, and so it was that his hunt finally ceased between Grassland and Post on a lonely stretch of 380, pulled far over on the shoulder while the sun sank in a crimson-orange inferno, the metallic drench of irrigation riding a tepid winter-rancid breeze and dust tickling his nose.

Rubes zoomed past in pickup trucks and SUVs, sedans and hatchbacks. Some bore faint traces of delicious wickedness or bright tasty fear—one even the nasty-yellow cloud of murder deeply contemplated or freshly achieved—but Dima ignored their blandishments and temptations, leaning on the black car's trunk and smoking cigarette after cigarette, squinting into the western distance.

Heatshimmer melded with sunset, and in the last dying glow of the day a blue car shaped very much like a '68 Mustang slowed, headlights sharp with feline interest.

At least his *zaika* didn't just zoom past, disdaining his invitation. She pulled onto the shoulder as well, the dusty plume behind her car catching sunset in a net of gold, and the engine's deep throb was almost as pleasant as his own vehicle's.

Dima didn't move. He stood and smoked, leaning nice and easy.

Waiting.

Between the glare of the sun's nightly Liebestod and the blue chariot's headlights, the driver was an indistinct shadow. The engine's idle didn't halt when the door opened and she emerged—of course, the chariot would be unhappy with its mistress at a roadside parley with one of *his* kind.

Everyone had a fuckin' opinion.

She'd either lost or laid aside the big woolen peacoat. Nat Drozdova had peeled down to a waffle-weave thermal, long sleeves clinging to her arms and jeans to her legs, her boots bearing traces of desert dust. The buckwheat-honey hair was a wild mop now, curls stubbornly resisting taming by either water or braid, and its highlights gleamed golden. Her wide dark eyes held all the warmth of good fruitful earth in damp spring, but also the gleam of an ancient stone blade polished to a razorglass edge.

Jasmine, warm plow-furrows, chill rain, and cut grass tinged the exhaust-laden breeze, overpowering the breath of cars and subtle steady stink of mortality. *Those who eat* would still come for her, yes—she wasn't sealed into a divinity's true force just yet.

But they would have to mass heavily to bring her down, and no few of them would be unmade in the attempt to take this prey. The *zaika* was *kotenoka* now, and though kitten claws were small, they were also needle-sharp.

The Drozdova halted, the chariot's headlights limning her with ice. "I didn't do it on purpose." Anxious explanation hurried the words; behind it, though, a hint of cold snowmelt over sharp stones warned against mistaking manners for weakness. "One minute I was in the bathroom, the next I was in Los Angeles."

"*Da*, Bonney's house be like that." He took another perfumed drag, measuring her from boot-toe to tangled hair. Walking into Baba's office, the morsel made a predator salivate. Now Maschka's daughter provoked an entirely different—but not unrelated— reaction. "How's Marisol?"

"She's nice." Nat's hands hung, empty and graceful, but her long graceful fingers, tipped with tender rosiness, were tense. She watched him carefully; adult felines remembered insults given during kittenhood, and they did not often forgive. "Georgia says hello."

So, his *devotchka* had visited another grandmother. A busy little girl, indeed. Dima laughed, smoke slipping through his nostrils in two curling jets. "Not likely." The desert painter had her own idea of courtesy, and it wasn't passing along gossip.

"Well, she said at least you're honest about what you are." The information was accompanied by a single nervous side step, but other than that, Nat held her ground.

"*That* sound more like her." Dmitri stayed very still. Every hunter knows when a sudden move, even a twitch, will make a shy creature flee. "So. Here we are."

"Here we are." A pained attempt at a smile pressed a sweet little dimple into her right cheek. "The next step is New Orleans. There's a woman there who hates lies; Baby will find her for me."

"I know her, *devotchka*." Of all the powers to send her to, Georgia was choosing . . . that one. But Dima Konets knew better than to question a woman who had made up her mind. "Baby?"

Her chariot growled, very softly. Dmitri grinned, taking a last drag and tossing the butt into the deserted road. Either the Drozdova was holding traffic back or this stretch was naturally a wasteland at sunset; either way, it was . . . pleasant.

"I have the arcana," Nat continued. "The only thing left is the Heart. I haven't forgotten."

Neither had he. "Gonna take it to Baba, then? Or to your hungry mamma?" He took care not to make the words mocking; even a thief could ask an honest question once in a while. The third, the biggest query of all, left his mouth in a singsong. "What on earth will my good little *devotchka* do?"

"I thought I'd offer you a ride." One slim shoulder lifted, dropped; her hands spread a little. "You drove me across half the continent. It seems only fair."

She was, after all, so very young. Two mortal decades were nothing. He'd probably slept—or whatever sanity-saving simulacrum of mortal rest passed for slumber among divinities— longer than she'd been alive. "You think anything about this gonna be fair?"

"It would be nice if it could be, don't you think?" The *zaika* who entered Baba's office a few days ago would have asked it anxiously, braced for sudden displeasure. This woman simply regarded him across a few tense feet of Texas gravel, earnest and quiet.

"I think you gonna end up hurt." Another truth. Why not?

He had the rest of his endless existence to lie, in whatever direction he chose.

A few bits of honesty wouldn't matter in the face of that avalanche.

"Not that it matters." Painful openness, a shadow of agony in her dark gaze. "Both you and my mother want to kill me."

So she had accepted at least one unpalatable truth. How long had the knowledge been sitting behind those big, solemn eyes? He could have pointed out *I promised to repay the one who stole it,* but for some reason, the simple observation lodged in his throat. So Dmitri Konets shifted his gaze over his *devotchka's* shoulder, staring at the sinking sun, already half-swallowed by a planetary rim.

He'd never thought about how much he hated this chunk of rock whirling through space. There was no such thing as *home,* only larger and larger prisons.

Would she ever realize as much? Somewhere else in the universe was another planet with springtime, and maybe even mortals to create strange divinities of their own. It was mathematically possible, philosophically probable, but an utterly useless, not to mention unprofitable, line of thought.

"So you can either ride with me, or follow." The young Drozdova retreated another single, restless step, taking the tinge of warm perfume with her. "Your choice."

"What if I want to drive you?" He hurried to add a codicil, for once. "Like gentleman."

Nat folded her arms, her chin lifting. "Gentlemen take *no* for an answer."

"They all idiots."

"Maybe." Clearly done, she retreated another step, not bothering to look down to place her foot. Only the barest sliver of the sun remained, but bright-dyed scarves still burned above its crown, a drowning man's last desperate wave. "I'll see you there, then."

"You think I just leave my car here?" Dima's baretooth grin was full of final bloody sundeath, but she still looked steadily at him. "And smoke in yours? Lots of smoking."

"I think your car knows how to park itself." Nat shrugged again, half-turned, and walked away. When she reached the blue chariot she drew her fingers lightly over its enameled hood, a caress fit to make any man blind-jealous.

It was easy. A snap of his fingers like breaking a rich man's bone or a traitor's neck, a screech of smoking rubber, a crumple-clatter of angry metal, and the black car vanished into the thiefways until he wanted it again, only the imprint of its tires pressed heavily on roadside gravel. He lit another cigarette as he ambled for the passenger door of Spring's blue conveyance, ready to hop contemptuously aside if she gave one of Maria's tinkling-ice laughs and gunned the engine.

Baby growled once more, but the door was unlocked. He settled on a leather bench seat, eyeing the dash, and Nat's familiar backpack was in the back, prim as a beloved pet. Mortal nylon, fake leather, and plastic zipper had taken on a deep gloss; it was no longer a schoolgirl's desperate little bag but a traveler's trusty companion, quite capable of biting any stray hand brushing too close. That zipper would turn to flint shards, and the thing might keep chewing until its owner decided a petty thief had learned a lesson—or lost enough of their flesh.

Not that he'd stoop to pawing through her belongings at the moment. Dima made himself comfortable, rolling the window down and exhaling a cloud of perfumed smoke while the Drozdova buckled her antique seat belt, worked the old-fashioned gear lever so the orange bar pointed to D, and checked over her shoulder for nonexistent mortal traffic, her honey hair moving over her shoulders with soft lovely whispers.

"I'm not traveling the, uh, the divinity way." Was she nervous? Brittle new self-confidence was almost as alluring as former soft anxiety. The juxtaposition was even fetching, in its own way. "But Baby goes fast enough even for you, I think."

He could have sniffed, made a cutting little observation, or even observed a stony silence. But Dima found he didn't have the taste for any of those options. "Well then," he said, stretching out his legs—plenty of room, you couldn't improve on old-fashioned American heavy metal. "Show me, Drozdova."

The dimple came back, peeking at him, and Baby lunged into motion.

FRAGILE TRUCE

Avelvet-soft southern night swallowed a blue car, full of long stretches of almost-companionable silence interspersed with commonplace observations—*Abilene is nice town, I drove through Oakland, glad we aren't going through Dallas, my mom watched reruns of that show, there was crazy rube in that town once, you want some snacks, no I'm fine I got smokes*—mixed with the heavy incense of the gangster's cigarettes. Nat even tried one as they skirted Waco, and Dima's laugh as her nose wrinkled at the pleasant numbing burn was, for once, not mocking.

Maybe he was just being polite in another divinity's car, or he was tired of driving. He taught her how to flick her fingertips at tollbooths, passing through ghostlike while a mortal yawned or rubbed at their eyes, and watched while Baby blinked through traffic, eventually nodding his slick dark head and taking a long drag. *Not bad, Drozdova. Like you been driving for years.*

It was unexpectedly satisfying to hear, even if he was lying.

He leaned forward every once in a while to peer at the sky; between cities there were long stretches of deep black lit only by diamond fires peeking through thin-torn veils of scudding cloud. Nat saw the Milky Way for the first time on a long stretch near the Texas-Louisiana border, a skyriver of milk hemmed by trees and reflected in still water.

Dima pointed at distant lightning in the direction of the

Gulf, told her the Alamo was a lot smaller than you'd think, said the music scene in Austin was worth catching, and spoke about Spanish moss when the trees thickened and blotted out the sky. The humidity rose, and even though it was past Christmas—or so he told her, she'd lost days somewhere—there were strings of lights in unexpected places and the night was warm.

After Baton Rouge's bright, painful throbbing in wet darkness he turned silent for a long while, smoking and gazing out his window. The sound of the slipstream was different here, and the fecund marsh-smell it carried made Nat's scalp tingle. Her hair was developing a life of its own; she hadn't bothered to comb in what felt like forever.

Maybe pretty someday, her mother had always said, forcing Nat to sit still for pixie cuts until the end of middle school. *But curly hair means curly mind, Natchenka.*

It had been one of her few disobediences, growing her mane during high school as the idea of saving up and moving out took root. Was that when Maria had started to get tired, fatigued, ill?

Gray dawn found them deep in the Maurepas, and the greens here were different than in the Northwest—juicier, teeming, warmer. Veils of hoary moss hung still and sullen, mirrorlike water bloomed with algae, and tree roots straddled empty arches where their fallen ancestors had rotted to provide nutrients. Scrub clustered the freeway's skirts, a thin thread of solid ground spooling through a waterlogged, treacherous shifting probably holding a few divinities of its own. Or at least so Nat thought, aware of the steady hum of bursting life pouring through the car windows along with the reek of rot and decay. Like Dima said, you couldn't have one without the other.

Long drives probably made anyone philosophical.

The freeway curved sharply south, an ocean of heavy saltfish fog catching Baby in long streaming fingers before swallowing her whole, and signs began announcing New Orleans's approach. Finally, Dima stirred. "Elysium in the city." He'd rolled his window mostly up and still spoke softly, serious and reflective instead of mocking and nasty. "Stay there today. Come sunset, we go to party."

"Do we . . ." *Do we really have time for that?*

"The lady you want, she don't come out by day." This new aspect of the gangster god was actually pleasant, unless it was another trap. "Besides, you dress up again. Nice for Dima."

"I'm not visiting another Coco." Nat rolled her head from one side to another, stretching her neck. "I think Marisol packed me something."

"She give her gifts, yes, but only when you right in front of her. The instant you gone, *poof*, she forget." He cracked his long flexible fingers, knuckle by knuckle, muffled gunshots. "Must've liked you, though. Little sister and all."

A few days ago Nat might have felt compelled to defend Summer verbally. But now . . . well, maybe he was right. Marisol had, after all, known about Mom's plan well ahead of time.

Everyone had. Probably even Leo. Families only had secrets if you willfully ignored the obvious after reaching adulthood.

Funny, how she'd never really thought of herself as *adult* before.

"Thing I can't figure out," Dima continued, still in that meditative tone, "is why your mama didn't give you car. She had one, not from Marisol, *da*?"

"An old one." Nat could have laughed at the idea of the arthritic, hearse-like Léon-Bollée attempting this kind of journey. "Very old." Leo was always fixing it, tinkering for hours while Maria was in hospice and Nat was at work . . .

"Still." The gangster glanced at her, returned his gaze to the window. Dense, wet vapor drenched every surface, hung in the air, and turned gold for a brief moment. Somewhere behind the curtain the sun had lifted itself above the horizon, piercing all the groundclouds. "Not like her to let someone else drive you. Especially Dima."

I could have made it run. Sudden knowledge struck, quick as Georgia's leathery-tanned hands. The old woman's nails hadn't broken Nat's skin, but she still felt them, prickling-warm. *Maybe it would even repair itself, the way Baby did, or how the house kept itself together with me there.*

Maybe Leo . . . Nat sucked in a breath, her fingers tightening on the wheel. It wasn't even an effort to avoid mortal vehicles anymore, their indistinct shadows wrapped in thick cotton.

You really could get used to anything. Anything at all.

All this way, and she hadn't had time to really contemplate her eventual return to ice-locked New York. She was supposed to take the arcana, not to mention the Heart, straight to the Laurelgrove and her mother. But if she went home instead, if Baby turned down South Aurora and the little yellow house was a caved-in ruin . . .

Why could she imagine her own gruesome demise in vivid color, but not anything approaching freedom? Even "moving out" had been a hazy, indistinct idea, for all her careful lunch-time research about sublets and roommate-wanted ads, snatching quick bites of mortal food along with rent numbers, adding together first, last, and deposit over and over, calculating.

Even the *idea* of liberty had been enough, really. But reality was approaching at high speed now, and she couldn't blink past it like a wallowing mortal semi. "Dmitri?"

"Hm?"

"Did you ever not know what to do?" She tried to imagine him arriving from the old country, probably steerage in a *Titanic*-sized ship, an urchin or skinny teenager with a nasty, prideful sneer and quick temper. Or had he simply appeared when mortals stepped off the gangplank onto dry land, bringing a cargo of belief with them?

He dug the chameleon cigarette pack, green this time with yellow calligraphy, out of his suit pocket and tapped up a smoke. Their fragile road-trip détente probably wouldn't last past the

Elysium's revolving glass door. When she got her hands on the Heart—*his* heart—all bets were off.

"You think too much." But the truce still held, because he lit the cigarette with a fingertip flicker and exhaled, heavily. "Time to survive, *zaika moya*, not wonder about old wolves."

He was right, but she still wondered. Fog thinned, mortal traffic thickened, smoke curled around his dark head, and he jabbed two fingers at the windshield. The mist cringed away; an exit sign loomed.

He was showing her, of course, the way to the Elysium.

A REASONABLE PRECAUTION

Nat only caught a few glimpses, but the French Quarter was just as rococo as all the movies and books hinted, even under a flat gray morning sky with the humidity hovering near "unbreathable." Two of the streets Dima pointed her down were pedestrian-only, but none of the mortals ambling along even glanced at Baby, whose engine hushed to a library whisper before a sudden right turn through a low arch spat them into a courtyard with a familiar revolving glitter at its far end.

The Elysium New Orleans was sheathed with yellowish brick and bright gleaming glass, wrought-iron balconies starring its face. The courtyard held two fountains shaped like well-pruned magnolia trees as well as the usual trio of doorman, valet, and security guard. The enclosing walls were jaundiced brick like the paving, the revolving door was just as bright and hungry-looking, and once through, the lobby was entirely the same. Marisol had indeed left a gift in Baby's trunk—three antique leather suitcases of varying sizes were dutifully hauled on an antique brass-railed cart by a crimson-uniformed bellboy sum-moned by the doorman.

The valet driver cleared his throat respectfully before inform-ing Baby that the parking garage was in the sub-basement; the blue car's engine roused and she moved away at a sedate pace, apparently hip to the program.

Nat wanted to watch where her chariot was going, but there was no use in protesting at this point.

Inside, Mr. Priest's greeting, right down to the speech about not causing any trouble unless it was in the Ring, was almost word-for-word. His uniformed acolytes were different, though—a smiling woman with an ink-black pixie cut and a young man with a shaved head and a prominent Adam's apple—and this time the rooms were on the third floor, "near the exercise facilities, and with a view," Priest added, smiling modestly.

"Separate," Nat clarified. "No adjoining door." She waited for an objection.

Mr. Priest did not wait for Dmitri's agreement. "Yes, mademoiselle. Martin will handle your luggage."

Maybe there was some residual truce left from their all-night drive, because the gangster just shrugged. "Marie still on St-Ann?"

"Her *levée*'s held near Pontchartrain, nightly. A new lake house, since the recent weather events . . . well." Mr. Priest glanced at Nat. "Does monsieur require a *carte d'invitation*?"

"Two. And a carriage. Traditional, you know." Dmitri's smile was as wide and white as ever, but this time it didn't send a chill down Nat's back.

Maybe she was getting used to all this divinity stuff.

The short ride in the whisper-quiet elevator was an eternity, especially since the gangster locked gazes with her in the mirrored door, tiny red dots swimming in his black, black pupils. Martin the carrot-haired bellboy lugged the brass-railed cart out on the third floor and set off down a long crimson-carpeted hall, his red pillbox hat bobbing. A cut-glass bowl full of fragile white flowers she couldn't identify stood on a spindly ebony table before an antique mirror at the far end.

Dmitri cleared his throat, meaningfully.

"Don't threaten me." Nat was just glad to be out of the car; even though Baby was beautiful, long drives wore on the back and neck, not to mention her legs. The sense of bodily well-being was still eerily strong, but her weariness wasn't physical.

Besides, the deep, unsettling, blurring buzz surrounding Georgia's house was still in her bones. It slept uneasily, and even though Nat had no desire to find out if she could summon the crackling scent of ozone Maria Drozdova could, the feeling might not ask her permission.

You didn't think I'd let you leave without a gift, did you?

"Your room, *mamzelle*." Martin gestured at a white-painted door, its polished brass plate bearing a quasi-familiar symbol. "Monsieur, a moment, and I'll show you to yours."

"Be ready at sunset." Dmitri tilted his head, one corner of his lips twitching upward. It wasn't his usual murderous grin, but it was still uncomfortable. "Wear something nice, eh? But no big dinner." The half-smile fled. "Might not be wise."

Great. "As long as it doesn't end like Jay's party, I think I'll manage." Nat followed Martin into a familiar suite—green carpet, white birch, the gas insert fireplace burning softly, a star in the gray daytime. The young man in the red uniform settled the leather suitcases on a long padded bench at the foot of the bed, and hurriedly retreated without waiting for a tip as if he didn't quite trust her temper—or he suspected Dmitri might be up to no good in the hall.

Either way, Nat had to admit, it was a reasonable precaution.

)(

Two of the suitcases were stuffed with clothes, fitting Nat as if they were tailored. Jeans, T-shirts, sundresses in deep jewel-tones, two drape-y evening numbers—one black, one white—two pairs of canvas shoes, cork-soled wedges just like Marisol's, a big floppy straw sun hat, casual slacks and blouses, two pairs of green flip-flops, a set of raw silk pyjamas, two pairs of kitten heels to match the evening gowns. It was amazing how so much could fit in confined spaces, and she wasn't sure she'd be able to repack it all.

The third case held a travel bag full of high-end skincare as well as shampoo, conditioner, an old-fashioned boar-bristle hairbrush, plus two wide-tooth sandalwood combs. There was also a long linen cover-up for the poolside, a brief black bikini Nat couldn't see herself wearing, brightly patterned sarongs for beach lounging, a freezable eyemask, and other odds and ends along with two plain wooden boxes. The smaller held jewelry—studs that looked like actual diamonds, gold hoops too restrained to be anything but real, a slim velvet case holding a string of baroque pearls, and a teardrop of bright green surrounded by colorless gems, the silver setting ornate but resting high against Nat's breastbone light as a feather. Thin silver bangles matching Marisol's gold ones chimed on Nat's left wrist, and she stared at bright cloth scattered across the plump, pristine hotel bed, the sun hat smoothing out its crumples as it expanded, shoes tangled in material and the evening dresses very aware of their exalted status, laid carefully across velvet pillows.

The bigger wooden box, smelling faintly of cedar, was almost empty except for velvet padding around nonexistent shapes. After a moment, she realized what it was meant to hold—a Knife with a flint blade, a Cup with a unicorn handle, and a heavy iron Key.

Nat closed her eyes.

It was beautiful, luxurious, perfect—but she wanted to be driving. No, that wasn't quite right.

Nat Drozdova wanted to be *home*. The little yellow house on South Aurora was almost always full of suffocating tension, but without that weight she was depressurized, a fish gasping on a stony shore. She wanted her small bedroom, her closet that had never held as much as the suitcases now open and spilling their bounty across satin, damask, and fat, self-satisfied pillows. She wanted the kitchen with the ancient white Frigidaire and the old

Bakelite radio; she wanted the parlor's stillness and the house-plants in every room, even the postage-stamp foyer. She wanted to go out the back door, down the porch steps, and take the hard right turn to the tiny garage, where the Léon-Bollée crouched and Leo's woodworking tools were hung neatly on pegs, sawdust and gasoline-grease smells mixing together to spell *safety*. She wanted the flagstone path in the front yard, the white picket fence, and the hum of the most insomniac city on earth audible the instant one stepped outside any refuge.

Most of all, she wanted to stand in the middle of the master bedroom, breathing in Maria's perfume. Sometimes when she was in a good mood Mom held Nat close, stroking her hair and humming.

My little dumpling, you will do something nice for Mama now, hm?

She still loved her mother. Even now, even knowing . . . what she knew. The painful, unwilling child's affection was a dry weight in her throat, jostled by the rattling of Georgia's "gift" lurking somewhere far deeper.

If you didn't accept a present, what the hell did you do with it? Who did it belong to?

"I want to live," she heard herself whisper, in the deep hush of an Elysium suite.

Did that make her just as selfish as Maria? The sisters at school talked about sacrifice and service, and so did Georgia in her spare, serene desert. But if there were fifty different Christs nailed to fifty different crosses, what was all the agony for?

What was the *point*?

The big window in the suite's bedroom was a French door; a small balcony with curlicued wrought-iron railings looked over a curiously empty, fogbound street. As soon as Nat stepped outside the humidity wrapped around her velvety-thick, almost impossible to breathe through—the Elysium's air-conditioning was tip-top, at least.

The mist smelled of salt, silt, fish, frying oil, and red mud; streetlights like old gaslamps sputtered, uncertain in the fitful daylight. Some had multicolored Christmas lights wrapped around them.

How many days had Nat lost? Dmitri hadn't said the exact date, just *past Christmas*. The subtle inner sense Nat was beginning to rely on more than unconsciously told her Mom was still alive, but . . .

Here she was in the Big Easy, and she wasn't dipping beignets in chicory coffee, listening to jazz, or ambling among crowds of tourists. She was stuck in a plush, gilded prison cell, waiting for dark to fall and another agonizing, horrifying test.

A sound pierced the fog—long mellow notes, observing a stately pace. Nat cocked her head, listening intently.

Music. Shadows moved at street level; she recognized what the musicians were playing and winced just as the soupy white vapor began to thin.

It was a funeral march, familiar from childhood cartoons on the bulky old rabbit-eared television in the parlor. *Pray for the dead . . . and the dead will pray for thee . . .* The shadows moved in stately lines, but they were small, and definitely not human.

Nat's heart pounded. Her hands curled around the iron banister, refusing to let go. The funny crawling sensation on her scalp was each hair attempting to stand straight up, and it prickled down her back, down her arms, spilled riverine down her legs, and made her breathing short and silent.

I cannot fucking believe this. But there it was, right in front of her.

Cats. Tabbies, tuxedos, Siamese, Persians, calicos, shorthairs, longhairs, even hairless sphynxes, every shade and every size, Maine coons to ragdolls to teacup kittens marching several abreast down cracked pavement parting in scabrous patches to show old bricks and the occasional cobble.

People rarely tore up a road and replaced it; they just laid another coat of paving down and called it good. Children, even divinities, were a fresh layer over the older path, Nat thought, and watched the cortege move, slink-stepping with regal patience.

A small gloss-polished open hearse was preceded by thirteen black cats, not in harness but simply walking in unison, their tails high as ostrich feathers. An invisible force drew the carriage along, its wheels making a slight grinding sound, and it was that tiny noise that convinced Nat she wasn't having some sort of psychotic divinity-breakdown.

She was sane, dammit. The madness was in the world itself.

The glossy black coffin bore a tiny gilt crown, winking slyly as the fog thinned still more. It passed her balcony, none of the cats deigning to look up, and in its wake came even more felines, padfoot-quiet, their shoulders moving with the supple swimming grace of predators.

By the time the procession began to straggle, sunshine was peeling off even more fog, and it was tepid-warm for the end of December. New York was probably still snowed under, though without a fresh application of white all the ice would be dingy now.

The final, flicking tail of the cat-crowd disappeared into lifting mist. The funeral march vanished with a long last mournful note, and Nat realized, with a painful internal thump, what she'd just seen. It was an old short story, one always sending a chill through her.

"*Le roi est mort,*" she murmured.

Then I, one of the dinner guests—or Puss, sleeping by the fire—would shout, *am king of the cats!* He'd vanish up the chimney with a bang, never to be seen again. It didn't have to be an omen if it was just literature, right? After Jay's party, she shouldn't have been surprised.

But she was. All the unreality of the last few days crowded her, poking and prodding.

She managed to peel her fingers from the balustrade, took

a few staggering steps inside followed by the returning hum of mortal traffic, and closed the glass door. Nat stood for a few moments, scrubbing at her face, her palms solid as Georgia's, the rest of her brimming with deep, ineffable warmth.

Why a cat funeral straight from folklore should be the straw breaking the camel's back, she had no idea. But it was a long while before she could drop her hands and return to the bed and its cargo of bright gifts. She closed the arcana-box, nestling it back in its home, and set about replacing everything else.

Marisol expected Nat to survive, no matter what else happened. It was, at least and at last, a real vote of confidence. That was how she was going to take it, anyway. Still, she spent the afternoon refolding and repacking, closing each suitcase with a slight, definite thump.

It would be nice to dress up, to play the part, to pretend. But if Nat Drozdova was going to be roped into a country-crossing scavenger hunt, shoved from one square to the next on a rigged chessboard and terrified out of her mind by mouthless cheesecloth-veiled shadows, gangster gods, rattlers, coyotes, and old folklore, she was going to do it on her own terms.

And in her own damn clothes.

COTILLION GIFT

It was almost dusk, and Dima's suit was freshly brushed. His boot-toes glittered, and he had even cleaned his gun, humming with anticipation. Settled at the Elysium's bar nursing his third tall, skinny glass of almost slush-frozen vodka, he didn't move when the smoky-opaque swinging door to the lobby opened and a warm draft tinged with sweet jasmine announced the arrival of Spring.

It was pleasant to anticipate, to draw out the moment when he would turn, slowly, and see what Marisol had given his *devotchka*.

He didn't get a chance. Nat settled gracefully on the stool next to him as the mechanically silent bartender glided forward to provide service. "Coffee, please," the Drozdova said. "I think I might need it."

The 'tender gave soft assent before wheeling away, and Dmitri shook his head. "I said, *wear nice dress*."

"Didn't feel like it." Under a soft cloud of wildly curling buckwheat-honey hair alive with gold, Nat's dark gaze was direct as prey's would never be. A black T-shirt, a worn red-and-gray flannel button-down, jeans, and the same boots she'd worn since New York—neat and clean, certainly, and full of reflected glow from the fire of a young divinity, but hardly party attire. Her backpack, heavy with humming numinous force, hung on one slim shoulder.

Oh, Spring didn't need one of Coco's dresses or Marisol's

gifts; the lily did not require gilding. But it would have been nice to see her like that again. Or to think that maybe, in some small way, she wanted to please someone other than her voracious mother.

The tinge of brass in his mouth wasn't quite anger, so Dima shrugged and took another hit of vodka, letting the cold fill him before the alcoholic fire spread. "Don't need it, anyway."

For some reason that made his *zaika* smile, soft lips curving and the dimple peeking coyly at him again. "Thank you."

Her coffee arrived; they sat almost shoulder to shoulder. The bar was deserted, but the lobby hummed—news of her arrival had spread, and there was a line of carriages before the Elysium's door. Even divinities, powers, and principalities hungered to chew a juicy bit of gossip.

"Here." Dima dug in his suit's breast pocket, his fingertips finding what they wanted and drawing it out of a nothingness deep as hunger itself. "For you."

Tortoiseshell sunglasses, the frame just big enough to make her look like a movie star, the arms sturdy and the earpieces not too tight. Nestled in the pocket since their first convenience-store stop on this voyage, they were burnished by proximity to a divinity, and not a single scratch marred the dark lenses. He set them on the bar, gently.

Of course, she'd turn them down. A careful little girl, taking nothing from Dima Konets. He wouldn't even be surprised, would he? Not shocked, and not insulted, either. Just the way the world worked, with her place in the vast pantheon so different than his.

Nat studied the sunglasses, then examined his face. Dima's gaze wandered away; he finished his vodka with long angry swallows. Next she'd ask *where did these come from*, or simply say *no thanks, I'm good*.

"They're pretty." His *zaika* picked them up, probably looking for the tag. She flicked them open, tried them on, those big dark eyes vanishing. Her dimple remained, deepening slightly; she pushed the glasses up until they nested in her hair. Maybe she'd learned that little trick from Marisol, but then again, rube girls wore them that way too, like a headband. "Thank you again, Dima."

It don't make us friends. He swallowed the words, set his empty glass down. "Finish your coffee. We go to party."

"I've never liked parties," she muttered. "And the last one was awful."

What could he say? "Cheer up. This one likely worse."

"Thanks for the warning." She pushed her mug away with a fingertip, unwilling after all. "Who's driving, you or me?"

"Neither." He slithered off his seat, landed with a jolt, and was glad he'd polished his boots. Strolling in with her on his arm would be a finger in the eye of Friendly's local face, and even Marie might enjoy the show. "We go for little ride with pretty horses, instead. Don't worry, Dima will be right next to you."

"You make it sound like a threat." Yet she followed him, obediently, from the bar.

A tide of whispers filled the lobby; bright avid eyes on burning-vital divinities, powers, and principalities swiveled to follow their progress, some of them perhaps envying Konets his companion's warm grace. There was throaty-voiced Dollaparda near the fireplace, with her plunging neckline and her teased-blonde mane, sequins glittering as her dress hugged every curve and her misty smile full of goodwill; next to her, Quean Bey Moriah was a vision in bright goldenrod, her hair a soft brown cloud and her dainty foot tapping, eager for a dance. Lafitte, with his tricorn hat bearing its bloodred feather and his high boots ready to cling to a heaving deck or kick a hungry alligator, gave a single bright flash of a smile, acknowledging his cousin—there were thieves upon the water, too, and they knew who to propitiate in this part of the world.

Yeller crouched on one of the couches, his shaggy gold hair

rasping as he scratched behind a flopping ear with delicate claws. Yemayja Gulfe lounged indolently on a red velvet love seat; her skirt blue as calm ocean turned into white froth at the bottom, and above it a statuesque brown torso repeated on the prow of many a ship held up a head carved from mahogany, a sapphire nestled in her cleavage winking its semaphore of desire. Even Picasse Matisse halted his constant gossipy whispering with linen-suited Playwright Capote, both of them staring hungrily at a muse who didn't even glance their way, safely tucked to Dima's other side. All of them, and more, watched Spring's advent.

One or two made their peculiar little salutes to honor an Endless, one of the great forces of nature itself come into her power and patently about to visit Marie, who would probably enjoy the sudden influx of guests about as much as she enjoyed anything else.

Dima showed his teeth, warning them all to mind their fucking manners, and maybe a few even took the hint. A Black man with an ash-smeared face simply bared his own strong white fangs in return, winking out on a draft of cigar smoke with a *pop* of collapsing air Nat didn't notice; she was busy eyeing the Elysium's revolving door as if she could unravel its ancient magic.

He would not put it past his *devotchka*, oh no. Dmitri's smile widened, full of predatory good cheer, and he shepherded the Drozdova out into the soft, clinging southern evening.

⋇

The rubes still used open carriages in this part of the world, their drivers harvesting tourist dollars, canvas shitcatchers slung under mortal-equine rumps as if it would keep the streets cleaner. The rube traps were not shining cream or deep glossy black half-pumpkins with springy wheels, though; nor were they drawn by flame-eyed skeletal quadrupeds with bony swanwings and clawed, whisper-quiet padfeet.

Such pleasures were reserved for divinities.

It was pleasant to lounge upon purple velvet, watching the mortal world slide by like hot grease while a whip-carrying coachman—jaunty-tilted hat, long face-wrapping scarf, bottle-green velvet suit, olive-dyed kid gloves, shining boots with silver-clad heels—held the reins. A fresh breeze dispelled cloying humidity but never ventured into an actual chill, and arriving in style held a thrill all its own.

The rubes had only pale imitations of this ceremonial transport, and he would have thought a girl raised mortal would enjoy the upgrade.

But Nat Drozdova sat tense and arms-crossed the entire way, though the moving air lovingly patted her hair and her escort had given her a cotillion gift.

It didn't matter. He was in an *excellent* mood. Very soon, he was sure, he would see a bloody diamond throbbing with its own hurtful inner strength again.

It wasn't every day a man traveled towards his heart in a carriage-and-four, so Dima intended to enjoy it.

HELLUVA TRICK

There was no snow; every tree was green and dusk was wet purple gathering in luxurious masses of foliage. If this was the depth of winter, she could see why retirees fled south; there was no killing frost or black ice. At home this would be a late-spring night, almost fifty Fahrenheit and glad for every single degree. Everyone on the street was dressed as if they feared catching a cold, however—at least, all the normal people, the *mortals*, were.

Or, all the normal humans she saw flickers of during that nauseating ride. Which wasn't very many at all.

The big white half-pumpkin carriage moved with sickmaking fluidity, borne on its own peculiar slipstream. It wasn't so much the speed as the elastic jouncing back and forth that threatened to unseat her stomach. The winged horses with their skeleton sides and clawed feet would probably like to show a rider a shortcut or two, and she shuddered at the thought. Dmitri lounged next to her, grinning like he was having a grand old time, and the city whirled around the conveyance like ink streaking on a greased, spinning dish.

She couldn't even enjoy the scenery, and she wished she was in her own comfortable blue chariot instead.

Gliding, rocking, swaying like a demented cradle, their carriage finally joined a long line of others moving at a steady pace down a long drive between ranks of arching trees, their boughs meeting overhead in complex knotwork to make a tunnel. During daylight, bursting from the shadow to see the circular drive before a house of red brick with white columns marching across its face was probably an Experience, but it was dark, the movement made her gorge rise hot and acid, and she was just trying to keep whatever coffee she'd managed to swallow happy in its home.

Dima had even warned her not to eat dinner. Looked like he'd done her a real solid.

The mansion wasn't as massive as Jay's house, and there was no migraine attack of colored lights. Still, every window was glowing with electric gold, and music floated through their open eyes. Jazz, in fact, and the sheer gorgeous vitality of each note shouted it was a live band. Not just live and in fine form, but having a great time, too. The beat throbbed, the bass walked, the guitar sang, and the horns cried out happily, rollicking along like an express train.

The centerpiece of the drive was a massive cypress, its arms hung with veils of gray moss reminding her of *those who eat*. She shivered, and Dmitri's elbow nudged her upper arm.

It was probably entirely accidental, but it still helped. He couldn't let them get to her.

At least, not just yet.

Each carriage paused for the briefest possible interval in front of the house; their turn came after a mercifully short wait nonetheless spent in constant swaying motion. Getting her feet back on solid ground was a gift, and she didn't even care that Dmitri helped her out of the damn thing *or* that he kept her hand, tucking it in his elbow and warning her with a swift, pointed glance that any objection would be fruitless.

Her legs felt suspiciously like a sailor's after half a year away from dry land, and she had longing thoughts of pulling the new sunglasses down to shield her from the glare when they plunged through the winged doorway into a vast, bright front hall. Rooms stretched in every direction, each with a hanging chandelier—a massive iron confection with dripping beeswax candles, one made of rainbow glass rectangles in a cascade, and over this massive central entrance hall, a giant writhing mass of hanging, incandescent crystals.

Imagining the fixtures descending at high speed was frightening, but anyone unlucky enough to be caught underneath wouldn't suffer long.

There were no stairs separating different levels of divinity here; everyone milled in rub-shoulder congeniality, somehow carrying goblets, tumblers, flutes, or glasses. Dmitri snapped, a crisp shot-sound, and handed her a champagne flute full of pale bubbly; another snap produced two inches of amber fluid in a squat smoked-glass container he sipped at, glowering at all and sundry.

One hand trapped in his elbow, the other weighted down with booze, Nat caught sight of a vast ballroom seething with bright motion. Most of the dancing guests held the same vital *there*-ness of divinities; those with weaker glow clustered in laughing knots at the periphery watching the show. Every possible sartorial statement was on display: suits of every description, three-piece, linen, and threadbare; dresses simple, homespun, or elaborate; a golden-tanned girl in a bikini, sucking on a lollipop, gave Nat a cheeky wink as her bare painted toes scattered sugarsand; a round man who looked like Mr. Moneybags from the Monopoly game grinned in her direction as he raised a foaming iron-bound tankard; a skinny fellow with a glossy top hat and smooth ebon skin under a layer of chalky ash-paint turning his face into a skull's grinned around a puffing cigar; a tomboyish towhead girl in worn denim bib overalls with a corncob pipe hanging from one corner of her mouth—she looked vaguely familiar, had she been at Jay's?—watched Nat somberly; a Black man in a flashy multicolored suit and furry cowboy hat waltzed with a brown woman in a similarly bright dress whose thick black eyebrows met in the middle . . .

"Rules," Dmitri said as he lowered his smoky glass, a quick flicker of pale tongue touching his top lip. "Respect the house, don't start shit you can't finish, and respect *her.*"

Sounds reasonable enough. Nat was just glad to be out of the goddamn buggy. "Her?"

"Me." A pleasant contralto sliced the hubbub in half; the music retreated as a bubble of hush descended upon Nat, Dmitri, and a tall mahogany-skinned woman in a suit jacket and pencil skirt of indigo so dark it was almost black, who glided out of the crowd with a panther's stalking fluidity. Her dreadlocks were as long as Marisol's mane, black as the damp darkness of midnight in silt, and tiny gem-beads on a multiplicity of hair-fine threads wrapped around her neck, descending onto her snowy silk blouse. Her glossy Cuban heels matched her suit, and she weighed Nat with a swift glance before turning her attention to Dmitri. "I've business with the Drozdova. Leave."

"Got business with her too." Dmitri looked supremely unconcerned, but the deep rattle-burr in Nat's bones quieted, and she got the idea this woman was very, very powerful indeed.

And probably had a Georgia-sized temper to boot.

"It's all right," Nat said, and was faintly surprised neither of them ignored her. In fact, both the woman and Dmitri looked at her, clearly expecting more. "My mother probably arranged it this way, Dima."

"*Dima.*" The woman's faint ironclad smile didn't change. The lights trapped in her necklace-beads sparkled, some flashing randomly, others stuttering as if trying to impart a message. "Got a weakness for a certain season, Konets?"

"I am equal-opportunity, *gospozha.* And always available." The gangster's chin turned in the woman's direction, and Dmitri's slow, murderous, very amused grin was back.

Oh, boy. A divinity pissing-match. Nat took the opportunity to slip her hand free of his elbow. "Let me just talk to her, please. And then you can—"

"Three days." The woman didn't fold her arms, but something in the set of her shoulders said she wanted to. Her fingernails were indigo too, the varnish starred with infinitesimal bright points, a galaxy on each digit. "Where she's going, you can't follow."

Just like Ranger's. But three days? Time apparently moved funny in divine pocket dimensions or alternate realities. Maybe that was where Nat had lost Christmas, in the desert with the Western Well—or in Spring's Country, before her mother threw her out.

The memories should have been terrifying, but so much else had happened they caused barely a ripple.

"The fuck I can't," Dima snarled. The bright happy music faltered for a moment, the great crystal chandelier tinkling dangerously.

"You want to try the swamp, *mal'chik*?" The woman's accent on the last word wasn't bad at all; she sounded like Mama cursing in the old country's tongue. "Because that's where you end up, causing trouble in *my* house."

"Dmitri." Nat shook her head and shoved her untasted glass at him. He moved as if to take it, stopped before his hand closed, and its fall flowered into breakage on highly polished parquet. "Oh, shi—I mean, I'm sorry."

Mama would have told her to *clean it up, silly stupid girl.* Bending down, or getting on her knees, to mop up the mess was probably just asking to be kicked.

Or something worse.

But the woman just shook her head, dreadlocks moving with fluid grace. Maybe a broken glass was no big deal, here.

So Nat slipped her backpack from her shoulder, and pushed it at the gangster as well. "Here. Hold this. It'll mean I have to come back, right?"

The crowd around them stilled. Now the woman in indigo

did cross her arms, cocking her head and watching with bright interest.

Dmitri's fingers curled around the top of her backpack; his arm tensed as if it was far heavier than it looked. "You give me this?" His dark eyes narrowed, deadly serious, and his other hand tightened on the glass tumbler.

"You *hold* it," Nat corrected. The arcana were in there, and while he might try to steal them . . . well, she'd solve that problem once she'd solved all the bigger ones. "Like layaway." No, that was the wrong word. "Insurance. So you know I'm coming back."

"Unless you die," the woman added, not quite helpfully though her tone was very sweet indeed.

"I never thought I'd get out of this alive." As soon as she said it, Nat's lips tingled, and she realized it was true.

Oh, she did *want* to live. Who didn't? But in the little yellow house on South Aurora, you learned from birth what you wanted and what you got were two very different things.

"Maybe I peek inside. See what Drozdova hides." Dmitri's snarl wasn't pleasant at all. It wasn't any surprise, either.

The longer this impossible divine bullshit went on, the less astonishing it became.

"If you want to get a faceful of my dirty laundry, go ahead and be a pervert." Nat stepped away, so he had to grab the backpack or drop it. The champagne spreading on the floor lifted into bubbling curls of sweetish smoke, and the glass melted, sank into wood like heavy liquid met by a thirsty towel. The parquet was pristine again.

It was a helluva trick. Far better than blotting, sweeping, and gently working any stain free with an almost-dry cloth. Divinities made great housecleaners—why had Mom been so determined to use mortal methods? Had her daughter's bare existence robbed her of the power to do otherwise?

Nat found that for once, to her everlasting relief, she didn't care. "I'm ready," she informed the woman, lifting her chin and hoping like hell she looked even a little prepared.

"Nobody's ever ready." But the other divinity held out one slim, strong hand. Her nails glittered, her necklace twinkled, and her expression was closed, almost neutral. "Marie."

The handshake was short, brief, to the point; warm skin against hers felt human indeed. "Nat."

"Technically, Marie Catherine Laveaux." She paused for a moment, as if waiting for Nat to recognize the name.

Figures. She did recognize it, in fact, but asking questions would get her nowhere at this point. "Technically, Nat Drozdova."

Dmitri snorted, but Marie ignored him. "This way, then." She turned on one heel—the Cubans, like tap dancers', had metal plating under the toes and tiny iron caps on the heel-bottoms. The crowd, now silent, parted. The bubble of hush moved with Marie, intensifying until the music pouring from other rooms was lost in dark water.

Nat followed. She did not look back.

A PAINTED TARGET

Dmitri Konets stalked through the crowd, his boot-toes spitting colorless sparks and his eyes burning. It was Laveaux's house, of course, holy ground, but if even a single motherfucker laughed, or so much as *breathed* in his direction . . .

The backpack dangled from his left hand, heavy with power. He could break open its zippered mouth and root around—at least one part of her arcana was in it, probably all three.

The stupid little *zaika*. "Insurance," she said. As if she couldn't manifest another flint knife, or another item glowing with numinous force, just by existing long enough. Once she learned how, she could even select a mortal item of the proper shape and keep it close; will, time, and divinity would do the rest.

Did she know that trick yet? She was certainly learning fast. Discarded arcana could wreak terrible havoc among mortals, but their charge was finite when separated from their generator.

They were, after all, only tools.

A pale flicker at the edge of Dima's peripheral vision was Calhoun in his accustomed eggshell linen suit with perpetual faint sweat-rings under meaty arms along with the shoulder-holster on the left side, placing his custom leather wingtips with prissy care and drifting just close enough to make his presence known. He wouldn't dare start anything here—the Midwife of Metairie generally let her guests settle their scores without interference, but she made an exception when it came to cops.

Besides, like all of Friendly's faces, he was a coward.

But no doubt he was salivating over the bag Dima was carrying. His *zaika* might as well have painted a target on Dima's back.

The house didn't quite want to let him go, but one of his kind always knew where—and when—to leave. The front door tried to hide; he slipped through like a shiv between ribs and his lip lifted at the line of carriages swarming for entry. A piercing whistle split the Louisiana night, and an ice-freighted wind ruffled the surface of Lake Pontchartrain behind Laveaux's domicile. No few of the gaunt carriage-thestrals sidled, the steady clockwork stream of visitors broken for a single endless moment.

The whistle turned into a metallic screech before dropping into the growl of an angry engine. Two headlights bloomed, bright vicious white, and the black car finished its lunge into existence on a cloud of burning rubber, stopping at the end of a long black smear. It snarled like he did, and Dima didn't bother slowing, tossing the backpack through the open window. He dropped into the driver's seat, the door slammed, and he caught sight of Calhoun on the steps, the good ol' boy's fat thumbs tucked in his braces and his florid face turning brick-red as he realized he was once again too slow.

Dmitri even gave him the finger through the open window, and his laugh melded into the engine's steady roar.

He had an errand to run anyway. A loose end to tie up, a little insurance of his own to indulge in. Three mortal days was more than enough.

Dima showed his teeth, spun the wheel, and stamped on the accelerator. The thiefways folded around him, and with a sound like the last tubercular cough of a dying bandit married to the feedback-laced scream of a stooping hawk on summer tundra, Dmitri Konets and his chariot vanished from Metairie.

THE
TREE

SWEET-TALK

Down a slope of velvety grass from the bright-lit wedding cake of Marie Laveaux's home, a vast greenhouse of frosted glass soundlessly opened a massive side door at their approach. Spiderweb strands of white-painted iron held the panes, and the building's exhalation was full of damp earth and growing things. Faint silvery light bloomed under the greenhouse's roof, which was welcome since the night was a wet bandage pressed against the eyes.

Water lapped close by; Nat followed Marie's moving shadow over a wooden threshold and onto a floor of pale, river-smoothed gravel. The warmth would have been welcome except for the absolutely soaking humidity; Nat was glad her peacoat was left safely in Baby.

She felt curiously naked without her backpack, but it had been the right move. Or so she hoped. "I'm looking for the salt-black tree," she began.

"Did I ask?" Marie's dreadlocks swayed, a river of segmented ink. Her metal-sheathed heels didn't dare sink into deep, shifting gravel. "Yours isn't the only story tonight, Drozdova. It's not even the most interesting one. You pay for passage, I provide it, and we're done."

It might not interest you, but I'm still the one living it. Nat buttoned her lip, though, glad she was wearing boots. A faint susurration went through crowded greenery as she passed, like her mother's houseplants or Koschei the Deathless's indoor garden.

Funny, the memory of the sorcerer wasn't terrifying anymore. Just faintly unpleasant, a half-forgotten childhood nightmare. The silvery light came from a flock of bright dots overhead, pale fireflies moving like the will o' wisps in a clearing before a giant cedar on the other side of the continent.

A central aisle held long wooden tables; Marie's collection of alembics, burners, grinders, and drying racks was far more extensive than Koschei's too. Glass and polished metal reflected tiny shimmers; something bubbled in a black cauldron over a low flame, its faint nasty steam dissipating as it slid heavily down the rounded sides.

Had this woman once been mortal? It probably wasn't wise to ask.

"Funny," Laveaux said, halting and swinging to face Nat, the whites of her eyes and her teeth gleaming in the indistinct illumination, a faint gloss on her perfect lips. "You're not running your mouth too badly. That thief you came with, he's always bitching about something."

The urge to defend Dima died in Nat's throat. Making excuses for a man who was clear about wanting to kill her was the height of idiocy, just like making excuses for Mom.

But the reflex was so strong. Instead, she laced her fingers together, denying the urge to touch anything on the table, or any of the rustling, curious plants. "So I've noticed."

Marie's laugh was warm and rich, but with a chill undertow, a frozen current sliding past a swimmer's thrashing legs. "Well, come on over here, girl." She performed another turn, military-precise, and strode down a side aisle. "Ah, yes. Right where I left you."

Nat's eyes adapted to the gloom. A square, squat wooden planter sat in the middle of a cleared space, the egg-pale stones around it reflecting firefly glow. A tuberous brown root almost overflowed its confines, rearing out of dry, exhausted brown dust.

Her mother might have identified it with a glance. Nat stood still, her hands knotted together and her head cocked, examining this new strangeness.

What the fuck?

"Do your thing." Laveaux made an impatient movement. "Then I'll do mine. I don't have all night."

I don't even know what my thing is. It burned on the tip of Nat's tongue, her mother's brusque irritation fighting for release. But that wasn't quite right, was it?

When she wasn't busy listening to Maria Drozdova's voice inside her head, Nat did all right. If nothing else, this little scavenger hunt had taught her *that*.

So she approached the wooden planter carefully, examining the gnarled root. It looked charred, as if someone had taken a blowtorch to it in cruel slashing patterns. "Look at you," she said softly. "Oh, honey. What happened?"

"Don't sweet-talk it." Laveaux's tone turned baleful. "He knows what he did."

"This will go a lot quicker without your commentary." Nat was amazed at her own daring. But really, you couldn't rush a plant.

Everything bloomed in its own time. That was one lesson she hadn't minded learning from her mother.

Marie's sigh was the sound of a woman with no time for anyone's bullshit; the entire greenhouse hushed.

Nat's knees bent. She sank down as carefully as she ever had in ballet class before Mom decided it was too expensive.

We can sell the shoes, Natchenka, they are still worth money. Go clean your room.

A bad memory, but there were good ones, too. Looking over a weeded row and feeling the relief of green leaves with enough space to breathe, or walking slowly with an old aluminum watering can, careful not to flood or parch but measuring out artificial rain in precise, proper proportion. Bracing a top-heavy sunflower or dahlia with a stake and scavenged string, just the right amount of support balanced against leeway for the stem to swell with wet nutrition brought from spreading roots.

Nat had learned so much, really. You couldn't help it, living with the Drozdova.

Her fingertips ached. The big, gnarled, dust-choked tuber quivered as she stroked its scarred skin. Its pain rasped up her arm—so thirsty, broken glass slice-burning, mute screams filling her own throat.

Animals could howl. Plants were forced to other measures— the lovely smell of cut grass was, after all, a yell of chemical distress. Roots in soil cooperated with mycelium, entire networks passing along food, moisture, information—and power.

"Mandrake," she murmured. "That's what you are."

Oh, it was so simple—they positively ached to talk, to flood a sympathetic listener with information, wisdom, friendship. They *recognized* her, as much as her mother's roses or lettuce or datura knew and obeyed Maria Drozdova. It wasn't any great effort to coax a plant into whatever she wanted.

That was true power. Or at least, one form of it. Her eyelids fell halfway; she didn't need to see. Or, rather, she did see, just not externally.

The greenhouse's rustling silence filled with warm wind, a patter of rain just this side of cold. Dry dust in the planter turned dark and rich; scars shrank, replaced with smooth brown. The root dove, snuggling into fresh dirt like a tired puppy into a pillow. Tiny creaking noises heralded leaves rising hairlike from its crown, unrolling in fast-forward. Even in the indistinct quarterlight their rich glossy green glowed. Stems rose too, buds swelling at their tips, but Nat halted them before they reached apogee.

The root needed rest.

"A little deeper," she whispered. Tendrils dove—she *felt* them, sensed the blind questing tentacles as they slithered through the planter's bottom, pushing aside wood that remembered its own time of quiet growing before axe and saw turned it to dead usage. "There."

It felt right to stop. So she did, and opened her eyes, drawing her fingers free of thick, loamy soil. Another deep, singing rustle passed through the greenhouse, every living leaf and bole, every root and flower, every insect or burrowing thing aware their mistress had spoken.

Summer could shower them with abundance, and Harvest reap their maturity. Winter, of course, scythed and cleared for the next year's burgeoning.

None of them could do what Spring could, though. They could not *awaken*. Nat let out a wondering sigh, the exhale shifting into a soft, disbelieving laugh.

I could get used to this. Did her mother feel it, Nat performing a miracle? Things grew when Maria told them to, of course—they wouldn't dare otherwise.

But during all the years in the little yellow house, she'd never seen her mother do anything like this. The houseplants needed their special songs and rituals, the garden hours of labor under scorching sun or summer rain, pruning and tidying in fall, the compost heap required turning by hand at precise intervals.

Had Mom hidden this magic, knowing it would cause questions from a little girl the cats talked to, knowing it was proof that the world was not dead, prosaic, *normal*?

A new idea tiptoed into Nat's head, shy as the first pussywillows daring to breach winter's wall. Maybe, just possibly, there was something her mother couldn't do.

Until she eats me, she thought, and braced herself for a shudder that never happened. It was weird, of course—how could you get used to the idea that your own mother wanted to consume you, maybe even sucking the marrow from your bones just like from a roasted chicken?

Both Leo and Mom did that, claiming it was the best part.

"Well." Marie Laveaux stepped close, gazing at the result. Leaves quivered at her nearness, the flowers keeping themselves tightly furled. "Not bad."

I don't need your approval, Mom would snap. Nat, however, simply rubbed her fingertips against her jeans and rose. It felt good to have done something right for a change. The darkness didn't press quite so closely now, and she met Marie's gaze squarely.

"Consider your passage paid." Laveaux turned again, setting off over shifting, clicking stones. "Let's get you on your way."

Tiny waves lapped at a curve of grassy lakeshore while the house rollicked with jazz behind them, everyone still apparently having a good time. A chorus of shouts rose with a particularly hot drumroll under a horn solo, melding with the hum of something that had to be cicadas despite the season. Lake Pontchartrain was a black mirror, breathing faint white mist upwards; Marie halted on the slope and whistled a long, crystal-piercing note.

It was nice to not be freezing at the end of December. Still, Nat wasn't too crazy about the humidity. It was like breathing through a tepid-soaked washcloth, even if the grass and scrub at the lake's rim were suddenly aware of her presence and rustling with anticipation.

A faint splash in the distance gave birth to more ripples. "Rules," Marie said, brisk and businesslike. "Be respectful. Keep your arms and legs inside the ride at all times. If you misbehave, the ride reserves the right to swallow you whole. Last but not least, no refunds."

That covers everything, I'm sure. Nat nodded, then cleared her throat when the tall woman glanced at her. "Yes, ma'am."

The mist moved uneasily. A long trailing vee pointed shoreward, moving steadily closer. A shadow reared, and Nat didn't move only because her feet flat-out refused.

Holy hell, it's the Loch Ness Monster?

But it wasn't. The vast, gleaming-wet wedge-shaped head was a few shades away from black, like Marie's indigo suit but in another direction—probably green, Nat guessed. *Swallow you whole* wasn't a euphemism—the serpent looked like it could probably unhinge its jaw and fit Baby, not to mention Nat herself, in its gullet before slinking deep in impassable bayou to digest the whole cargo.

The head lifted on a scaled, dripping, muscular column. Its tongue flicked, and the sheer size of the thing, or even its utter unreality, couldn't take away from how beautiful it was. The beast looked *right*, in the deep-burning way of other divinities. More foxfire glimmers gathered in its eyes, moving in slow, hypnotic swirls answered by a wave of twinkles passing through Marie's necklaces, echoed by her fingernails.

"State your destination." Laveaux was businesslike and crisp, but she gazed fondly at the serpent, and it dipped its head slightly, a graceful approximation of a bow. "Speak clearly."

Oh, my . . . Nat couldn't even finish the thought. "The, uh." *Wow.* "The salt-black tree, please."

The massive head lowered further, approached. A ropy, muscular, forked tongue flickered silent-swift, tasting the air; its gaze was unnervingly steady. No gleam of fangs showed, but that didn't mean they weren't there. The thing's eye was a huge glassy orb, pearly nictating membrane flicking as well. Finally, the serpent nodded again, and the soft slippage of lake against shore took on a deeper echo as more of a vast, shining length pressed against sodden grass and thick scrub, scales retaining their gleam as thorns broke useless against their armor. The head lowered yet more, flattening on thick clipped lawn between her and Laveaux until it was only knee-high; Nat realized what the creature intended and a deep atavistic shiver slid from her scalp to her toes.

No. No thank you. But this was what she had to do.

"Climb aboard," the woman said. "And remember, *be respect-ful*. The bayou can hold any number of bodies, Drozdova."

So can the East River. It took all Nat's courage to raise her foot, setting it gingerly on the giant snake's head. Its chin pressed deep into soft soaked earth; could smaller ones flatten themselves like this? "I hope I'm not too heavy." The words held a definite squeak.

This time, Laveaux's laugh was warm caramel. Underlit by gleaming necklace beads, her eyes were dark hollows and her high cheekbones knife-sharp. "He's carried mountains, little girl. I don't say this often, but good luck."

"Thank you." Nat shifted her weight, and in a few moments was balanced precariously on a giant snake's head. It rose, the motion smooth as silk; at least it didn't sway or rock like the carriages. It wasn't even like surfing, or so Nat imagined.

Instead, the head remained curiously still, the world sliding around them like the revolving rooftop restaurant they talked about in Midtown. Marie's white-columned house retreated, music Doppler-vanishing into the distance. A soft satiny sound was lake-water against undulating, scaled sides, but again, the snake's head was the stationary point and all else simply slithered away on every side.

The thought—that this beast was long enough to circle the entire globe and just had to shift a bit to take a rider from one point to the next on that circuit—rested somewhere between exhilarating and creepifying, fine hairs raising all over Nat's body and deep wonder alloyed with dread pouring cold water through every vein. The snake's tongue flicked as it moved, the lake twisting a few degrees off-center and realigning. Citylight receded under a misty chill, a membrane matching the beast's inner lid drawn across the horizon.

Dark shoreline loomed, cypress, tupelo, swamp oak, and other trees swelling under long gray-moss capes. A breeze ruffled the cloaks, and the movement—very much like *those who eat*—was only half as scary as the head underneath her trembling boots. She didn't even dare to glance over her shoulder, simply froze, quivering like a hypnotized bird, as the serpent plunged into the bayous.

All sense of speed or direction vanished. Water silk-lapped scaled sides; branches crackled as a long fluid weight crept over bars of drier land. Tiny plops and rasps surrounded them—many things here hunted at night. Alligators, probably, and cottonmouths. She didn't know what else lurked in this part of the country, except for catfish and very large rats, and while she was as familiar with rodents and their high piping voices as any New York girl could be, snakes were an entirely different proposition.

As for the gators, all she knew was that they drowned you before they ate. Was it, she wondered, better or worse than the flint knife?

Maybe that's how Mom would do it. The Knife, and then . . .

It grew warmer.

Round blue lights bobbed amid the trees, ghostly reflections hanging on flat black water. Salt-smell mixed with mud and vegetable rot; a few times another, much fouler odor made her entire midriff cramp before the reek blew away on a short, faint breeze that never managed to move her hair or cool the pinpricks of sweat blooming on her forehead.

Warmer yet, and the darkness was no longer winter-chilly but moist-warm. The heat was like the inside of a giant mouth, perpetual bacteria-laden exhalation from a huge digestive tract.

The bluish lights weren't fireflies. They were much bigger, and a few approached curiously before turning away, distracted, small skull-faces with rolling, searching dark eye-holes and small scream-hinged mouths. A scientist might call them swamp gas, but Nat heard tiny forlorn cries when they drifted close enough, and it seemed quite likely they had pissed Marie off in some fashion, or disrespected the ride.

Who knew what other dangers lurked out here? A body rotting in all this muck might never be found, and a soul could wander forever this maze of tree-corridors, glassy water choked with moss or algae, and hanging shifting moss-curtains.

Time is a river, too. As the snake-head slipped easily for another shore, gray light filtered through mist rising from the water. It wasn't daylight; Nat looked up. Another short soft sigh of wonder escaped her parted lips.

A pendulous cheese-rotten moon now hung above the bayou, peeping through the imperfect cover of moss-hung branches. The trees pulled back, taking fluttering veils with them, and it was just the mist, the snake's head, and ripples in dark, unseen water.

And on the far bank, a massive twisted trunk gleamed as wet as the serpent's sides.

SALT-BLACK TREE

It was impossible to tell what kind of tree it had been. No leaf, needle, or blossom clung to its spreading, begging branches. None of the lush, teeming growth dared approach this silent sentinel; it stood upon a dark, blasted rise empty as its arms. A salt-mineral tang reached Nat's nose—this bayou was brackish, the sea creeping stealthily inward.

Like a thief.

The snake's steady motion slowed. Its tongue flicked unceasingly now, and its head curved from side to side, testing. Finally, it chose an angle of approach, and eased closer.

Apparently the giant creature didn't like this place, and Nat didn't blame him. The cloying warmth had intensified, and under a flood of overripe yellowish moonlight the trunk and painfully contorted limbs were crusted with leprous damp. Salt, Nat realized—the dead wood was caked with it. More wet, grinding crystals oozed from the bark's channels, collected in clefts, and fell with tiny plops when it became too heavy to cling.

Oh. So that's what Mom meant. Nat shivered. The Well under its perpetually blooming cherry tree felt uncanny and the big cedar in Coyote's clearing was simply uninterested, but this tree was somehow *aware*. It watched Nat draw closer on the head of a giant viridian snake.

And she could swear it recognized her.

Tiny shudders raced down her back. The cloying heat intensified, and that slight breeze just made it worse. Sweat gathered every place it could—her neck, her temples, behind her ears, her armpits, the small of her back, the fold where her thighs met her hips, under the curve of her buttocks, behind her knees. Even her ankles, safely in her boots, were damp. Her toes were about to wrinkle. How did people even *breathe* in this part of the country?

The snake's head reached the shore. It edged gingerly forward, flattened itself, and now was the moment of truth. Nat had to dismount.

"Thank you," she whispered, faintly. All the divinities seemed to find her manners hilarious, useless, or some combination of the above, but what the hell else could you do in a situation like this?

Sliding from the noggin of a giant mountain-carrying water snake couldn't really be accomplished gracefully. Nat bent her knees, slipped, and let out a miserable little cry cut in half as she jolt-landed on powder-dry beach, tiny talcum-puffs rising around her faithful boots. A distant splash broke the hush, and a soft coughing sound as something feathered burst into flight followed before stillness folded over the world again. The moonlight, pitiless now that it had a clear avenue, poured over the shoreline, black water giving up curls of white fogbreath. The moon limned moss and foliage cringing from the tree's environs, and edged every snake-scale with silver.

The snake eyed her sidelong, its tongue flickering madly. It clearly didn't like this spot. Nat didn't like it either, but she could see why Mom would hide the Heart here.

Nobody would just drop by this particular vacation destination.

Knock, and you will be answered. Well, that was pretty simple, even if none of the rest of this was. Maybe she should even be glad Dmitri wasn't here with his nasty comments and murderous grin.

Still . . . it might be nice to just hand someone, *anyone* the damn gem and close her eyes, waiting for whatever would happen afterward. The heat was enervating, and she'd just crisscrossed all of America in varying states of terror and despair, not to mention aching grief.

She was, Nat Drozdova realized, so fucking tired of all this bullshit.

"Thanks for the ride," she repeated. Cotton-muffling silence ate the words. "I suppose I'd better get it over with, right?"

The snake withdrew, a long resigned sine-wave of muscle, scales, and fluid motion. It lingered offshore, though, a slithering silver-dappled shadow in tepid brackish water.

Nat turned her back on the shore, trudging slowly up the rise. The sand was full of cinders; they crunched disconcertingly, like tiny bones. More bitter gray puffs rose. No wonder nothing grew here. Had some malignant divinity blasted this place, or did certain locations just end up like this, poisoned with power? The sense of vibrating force, of *there*-ness, was undeniable; maybe a location could be a divinity as well.

Were all the myths true, or did the truth make the myth?

The hush was as cloying as the heat. The moon's face turned a deeper sickly yellow, and its crater-shadows formed a leering, decayed grin.

I don't like this. But there was no choice.

The tree loomed above her. It stank of salt, and of rotting flesh. Nat's stomach cramped. A thin soundless rustle in the branches like the pressure of her pulse in her ears, the ash-heap giving way slightly underfoot. Her calves ached as she slipped, regained her balance, and stepped into corkscrewed, tortured branch-shadows.

Up close, the saline-weeping trunk sent up tiny curls of steam. The tree shimmered with heat, and Nat's face felt tight and shiny. How anything could burn in this humidity was beyond her. She wanted to take a deep breath, but the reek of this infected bayou-pocket clawed at her throat, her stomach rolling over and over.

Nat Drozdova coughed, choked, and lifted her right hand. One small fist, flesh shining-frail, reached through shimmering, simmering shadow.

She knocked on the trunk. It gave resiliently, like an overripe fruit's splitting flesh, and if there was anything remaining in her mortal stomach she would have lost it right there. Her knuckles tapped a second time.

Oh, ugh. It's awful, it smells bad, I hate this, Mama I hate this, why did you—

She didn't have time to finish the thought. The branches, released from torpor, swarmed downward with eerie silence. Her hand sank into the bark on the third tentative tap and bark crawled up her arm, warm and rasping as a feverish cat tongue. Roots exploded from the pile of cinders, her boots submerged and ankles clasped in sticky, irresistible fingers.

The world turned over with a sickening crunch and Nat was dragged upward, her head slammed against the trunk's yielding hard enough to daze. It dangled her upside down as a viridian snake hissed, water foaming as the huge creature thrashed too far away to render aid—or take a mouthful.

She didn't even have time to scream before saline-weeping bark crusted over her.

The salt-black tree swallowed her whole.

PROMISE FULFILLED

Maria Drozdova sucked in a tortured breath as the intubation, slick with mucus and traces of bright mortal red, was drawn free of her esophagus. Baba's long, skinny fingers attended to the task with a certain amount of facility and efficiency, but no excess gentleness.

Once it was done, she laid the medical detritus aside. The machines quieted; even they knew Winter was not in a mood to forgive interruption at the moment. Mortal doctors and nurses went about their business in the rest of the Laurelgrove, apparently forgetting this room with its window—charging more for daylight was an ancient practice—even existed.

For now.

The window, though it had been sealed for safety and to keep air-conditioning or heating costs lowered, also understood it was better not to test the beldame's patience. It stood wide open, letting in a harsh refrigerator glare and frigid breath from the ice holding New York trapped in a pale, bony palm.

Down the hall the elevator dinged; cat-soft footsteps prowled from its jaws. They didn't click or clank, but it was obvious they were a pair of black boots with shining silver toe-caps. Taking his time, the thief strolled past rubes who ignored his presence, and he hummed a lullaby of the old country as he approached.

Maria's papery eyelids lingered at half-mast over faded, bloodshot blue eyes, their pupils merely, humanly black. Baba smiled down at her, smoothing the hospital pillow. Next to the window, standing in the freezing wind but not shivering, stood an old man with a full head of gray hair.

Leo lit a hand-rolled *makhorka* cigarette. Maria's gaze flickered balefully to him at the snap of the cylindrical silver lighter, but for once he ignored the glare. A striped scarf wrapped several times around his throat; he had kept the several layers of flannel button-up and chunky knitted jumper since his woolen peacoat was elsewhere. He smoked in silence as the harsh rasp-crooning lullaby drew near.

Maria's hand, scrawny as Baba's own, lifted, fingers flutter-waving.

"Hm?" Baba leaned down. Her lips were unpainted today, corpse-bluish. They curved in a gentle, predatory lynx-grin. "What's that, little Maschka?"

"Salt . . . black," the old Drozdova husked. "The tree. She . . . will . . ."

"Oh, your little girl might surprise you yet." Baba touched the sheet folded neatly over a blanket-top. It wasn't as snowy as *her* linens, but there was no Vasilisa the Beautiful to launder here, no Dascha the Green to frown at stains until they cringed in shame. "You raised her to welcome the Knife, didn't you. Sent her to *Catholic* school, of all things. All that guilt." The beldame paused, and her whisper was harsh. "But hope is a weed, and so is love. Someone loved that girl, I think. At least, enough to matter."

Maria's gaze stuttered back to Leo. Hatred burned in her blue irises; her thin wrinkled lip lifted.

"*Not enough,*" Leo murmured in the language of the old country. "*There is dirt in my mouth, Grandmother.*"

"*As if it's the words that matter.*" Baba spoke in the same tongue, her accent thick and countrified, before she snorted. "*Silly manchild.*"

The humming paused at the half-open door. A soft knock, as

if he visited a beloved invalid, a grandmother or elderly aunt. A shadow slid through the iron-gray light of deep winter—*weather event*, the ecstatic newscasters were calling it, *once in a century*.

Baba could have told them differently, that these things happened whenever she damn well pleased. But what would be the point?

Dmitri Konets stepped into the room. His dark hair was slicked back, his suit was brushed, pressed, and sharp-creased; the tattoos were visible on the backs of his hands, some slipping down his fingers to the last knuckle. Others peeped from under the neckline of his snowy shirt, the top button undone and the collar crisp but not overly formal. The only new addition was a black backpack clinging to his right shoulder, humming with unhappy force. His tie was extremely loose, black as a night-hunting shark, and he carried a clutch of ragged winter-dead weeds ripped from under the snow in Princo Park.

A little girl with honey hair had often spoken to the cats there, though her mother told her it was all imagination.

Dead thistles also lurked in the bouquet, added from the yard of an abandoned lot on South Aurora where a haunted house listed and leered. Dmitri spared a quick flicker of a glance at the old man near the window, looked again—it took less than a heartbeat—before his attention turned to Maria's bed. His grin sparkled, wide and white, lacking any kindness or amusement at all.

Despite that, a great deal of pleasure lurked in the expression. "Mascha, Maschka, my darling Maschenka. It's been *too* long." He hitched the bag higher on his shoulder.

"I have it," Maria croaked. A momentary flush crept into her gaunt, wrinkled cheeks. "Baba, I have it." A croupy, rheumy cough spattered bright crimson, yellow sludge, and traces of golden ichor onto her sharp chin, a sore at its bottom point glaring angrily. "I will give it to you. She's *in the Tree*, you can . . . you can do what . . ."

"A merry chase, gathering old arcana." Baba shook her head, her wild cloud of iron-hued hair fringing into white at the tips. The heavy wrapped lace of her black dress whispered as she straightened. "Very smart, Maschenka. A good plan."

The sky didn't change color, but the sunlight thinned. The fluorescents overhead buzzed, their song thickening as shadows acquired greater weight. Every shade-edge became sharp, and where the light was blocked by a solid body a faint boiling stirred, like oily ink dropped into fresh water.

"Only thing I can't figure out is why you didn't send her with a car, Mascha." Dmitri laid the crackling brown bouquet at the foot of the bed. Maria's feet were indistinct hillocks; she was skeleton-thin by now, held to existence only by the beldame's gracious refusal to descend. "Still be chasing her if you did, I think."

Maria's gaze flew to Leo again, and the old man rocked back on his heels. Her vengefulness lacked its former strength, however, so he recovered almost instantly, and rummaged in a pocket. "*Sigareta?*" he said, with only a token quaver at the end of the word.

"*Nyet, dyad'da, spasibo.*" Dima studied him closely now—mere politeness, since he already knew or guessed this man's relation to his *devotchka*. "Not yet. Let me guess. Papa?"

"Uncle," Maria rasped, but Leo nodded.

"*Da,*" he said. "My beautiful girl."

"Does you proud." Dima patted his chest with a flat hand, twice. "Dmitri Alexevich Konets, *dos'vedanya.*"

"Lev Nikoleyevich Myshkin." Perhaps this old man was where Nat gained her politeness from. "Once I was a prince, too. But that was the old country."

"Shut up," Maria husked. Leo dropped his gaze, and returned to smoking in silence.

"I'd shake hands, but . . ." Dima shook his dark head, turned back to gaze at the woman on the bed. "I made a promise, my hungry Maschenka. You must know."

"Baba." Maria stirred, her sticklike arms raising, her wasted legs puffing the coverlet. "Baba, I have it, *you can have it back!*"

The window gave a burst of freezing wind, and the shadows thickened. The beldame and the thief burned with vitality, bright in the face of that consuming, and the old man by the fluttering pinkish curtains was by no means as real, as *there*. But he was more solid than the furniture, and not nearly as washed-out as his great love, whose face was a skull and whose hair, once rich gold, was now only thin whitish hanks clinging to a yellowing, drawn-tight scalp.

"Did you think *I* coveted the damn thing?" The beldame clicked her tongue, a harsh wooden sound. "Dear me, Mascha. You imagine everyone's like you; that's the downfall of greed." She straightened, stepping away from the bed. One of the machines gave a slight squeal, cringing as her rough silken skirt brushed its plastic casing. Its display, tracking Maria Drozdova's slow, stuttering heartbeat, disappeared under a burst of static. "Whatever you're going to do, Konets, the time is now."

Dima bore down on the bed. Maria let out a whispery cricket-scream; she was too weak to struggle much. Leo studied the floor.

The thief's fingertips brushed Maria's bed jacket. A slight tingle raced up his arms—a dark-eyed girl had touched its buttons, her aching unanswered love brimming free and slopping over black silken stuff embroidered with cheerful red roses. One of the blossoms lingered over a skinny shoulder; Dima bent closer, closer, grinning as the old Drozdova tried desperately to fend him off. The backpack slid, arrested by his hand secure around the strap, barring it—and everything inside—from any reunion, however temporary.

He bit, teeth shearing effortlessly through fabric and flesh, even sinking into the ball of the humerus underneath. There wasn't much blood, but he drew like a mosquito until he had a mouthful of bitter, brackish fluid. In her former strength, it would be rich golden ichor; fading into mortality as her daughter waxed, it degraded into scarlet blood. Now it was practically dust, but there was enough for a mouthful.

And that, indeed, was all he needed. Dima Konets straightened, making a soft humming sound of satisfaction and stepping away; his dark head turned and he spat the sludge.

He had promised to fill his mouth with the thief's blood, and the oath was fulfilled. His tongue flickered, cleaning sharp white. Working the jacket's threads free was another job, and he set about it, like a cat surprised by a lemon peel.

Maria's screaming was barely audible. Baba glanced at Leo. "Anything to say?" The beldame was rigid, her hands knotted bone-white fists under a mass of fraying black threads. Her skirt moved again, as if something other than legs writhed under the material.

Leo took a long last drag from his cigarette. "My little one . . ." he whispered. "What will you tell her?"

"Don't got to tell her shit," Dima said. He picked at his teeth with a thumbnail, his mouth a sour, distorted smile.

"She knows," Baba said, and perhaps it was kindness in her dry, businesslike voice.

Perhaps.

Leo closed his eyes. His shoulders slumped wearily. Maria stiffened, her back arching. The wound on her shoulder blackened; there would be bruise-deep finger-marks spreading from it—the brand of a divinity whose time was done, Baba's prerogative to grant or withhold.

Winter's scythe had descended, and the cut was irrevocable.

The shadows swarmed, their clawed hands begging; their mouthless faces pressed against prey. It could be painless, true. The Cold Lady often granted narcotic ease at the very end, when she judged it warranted or necessary; Baba and her other faces could do as much.

But sometimes, they did not.

Regardless, it didn't take long. The shadows crawled *inside*, consuming. The whistling cricketscreams were mercifully short. Leo's breathing grew labored; the divinity who had brought him across an ocean was gone. His fate was not *those who eat;* simple transparency thinned him until there was nothing but a faint scent of harsh black burning *makhorka* where he had stood.

The mass on the bed—the husk of a divinity—crumbled inward. A sharp, red-tinged glitter dappled the walls with white, and the mouthless shadows cringed.

Dima Konets turned away, striding for the door. The backpack stopped struggling; there was nothing left in this room to call to its contents, however faintly.

"Sure you want to leave?" Baba called after him.

"Got what I came for." He paused at the threshold, his head slightly turned. "In a tree, eh?"

"My next stop, so don't get any ideas." Baba leaned over the bed. Dry golden dust—the only remainder or reminder of Maria Drozdova—finished its ruin with a faint sibilant noise. Lodged just below where her ribcage had been, snuggling into her unmade vitals, was a nest of black twigs with a fierce bloody glitter caught in its throat. "Are you sure this is the game you want to play, Dima?"

"Went across the country twice." He didn't move just yet. "Be a shame to disappoint her, *neh*?"

A scratching, a sigh as golden dust faded on an icy breeze. A black bird large as a vulture, something like a raven, with bright crimson gleams in its intelligent eyes, hopped onto the windowsill. Dima finally looked back as it took flight into the freeze outside, a thunderclap of feathers and a soft, husky laugh.

The bed was empty. If something he wanted had been there, well, it was gone now.

So the thief ambled away, still picking with luxurious patience at black strands caught in his sharp, sharp teeth. There was business to attend to in town, his uncles and nephews needing direction, reminders, luck granted or withheld.

Plenty of time, now.

"*Zaika moya, khoroshen'kaya devotchka,*" he murmured as he walked unseen down the hall. "Come home soon."

INCARNATION

T hree days, the Midwife of Metairie said, for all who find the salt-black tree spend that long clasped in its arms.

The first passed slowly, amid hushed and steaming bayou. The heat never altered, no matter who ruled the season—Summer, Harvest, Winter, or Spring herself. A dry slithering like scales against the cinderfall rustled at odd intervals, the tree's crusted trunk bulging uneasily as something inside it stirred.

There was rest in its embrace, certainly. As the first day wore to a close, the bulges and creaks subsided. Nothing struggled for long; hanging upside down inside the tree filled the head with rushing vision, pressure mounting behind the eyes, lungs heaving against gravity as the hanged body moved inward towards the tree's core. Wooden rings creaked, parted, reformed as they absorbed something foreign.

The first night was black and bleak. Some few times a mortal had chanced across this place, driven by ambition or desire so great as to grant almost-divine strength. The crusted branches yearned, twisted by an awful pressure, begging for release.

None was granted.

A soft, lipless voice whispered in the ancient tongue every infant understands before birth. You could trade, you know.

The second day held the same breathless heat, but as dawn rose tiny crackles raced over rough, crusted bark. Moisture dripped. A scarlet tinge bloomed through salt, receded. Among the roots, tiny dabs of crimson rose.

Far to the north, in a city grasped by winter, the last rattling breath of a foreign divinity passed. A hush even deeper than usual fell over the cinder-mound and the salt-black tree. Carmine spatters touched its roots; its branches gleamed, charcoal full of evaporated ocean blooming with bright blood.

Deep inside the rings, a frantic pulse calmed. The struggling stopped. A woman who had once been a honey-haired girl went still, sensing . . . what?

Yes, ambition could bring you to the tree. Still, what was a plan, a scheme, a hunger to surpass but need? Necessity was the great driver.

All who came here had a wish.

Life is life. You could trade. Is that your desire? *The language of the unborn was forgotten with an infant's first breath, yet it was spoken here.*

And understood.

Some, like a one-eyed child of the coldest north, wanted rune-knowledge. Some, like a deathless, paper-dry sorcerer, required power. Some, like a man with skin like midnight and a horrified gaze, sought freedom. Some, like a limping child with burn scars swallowing most of her skin, demanded vengeance. Some, like a midwife even divinities respected, simply tested themselves against mortality's constraint.

Even a perishable human could pay what the tree demanded.

Hanging in blood-warm darkness, the querent heard a pulse. Occasionally a red glow reached through the rings, backlighting visions too excruciatingly personal to be described—determination, horrific memory, guilt.

And deep, endless shame.

The second night was full of half-heard motion. Unseen things swirled about the cinder-hill and its throbbing, crowning spike. Feathers brushed thick humid air, water rippled, a dry tearing slithered past before becoming the faint creak of wet scales drying, choke-distant screams, the soft panting of creatures pushed past suffering into simple mute endurance, the slight groaning exhalation of vegetation using the hours of darkness to grow.

The third dawn rose sanguinary instead of gray, and the wet womblike heat was nothing short of brutal. A shimmer roped about the tree's gnarl-knotted roots, the spent gleaming skin of some unimaginably large, legless reptile. The salt-black tree burned unconsumed, and smoke rose from the cinder-hill, mixing with the water's misty exhalation.

It is time. *Though the tongueless voice held no impatience, its command could not be denied.* Speak your choice.

But no, the burning was not wholly flame. Scarlet anemones bloomed from the black, crusted trunk, fragile petals refusing to flutter free.

Even the mortal, the perishable, the weak could choose here. This last refuge stripped the powerful and granted to the powerless, humbled the proud and comforted the broken. Surcease could be found here, a trade for a beloved, revenge for a wrong too large to be righted even by Justice's long, sharp, blindly moving arc.

But in return, the salt-black tree demanded truth.

Another voice spoke. It would be familiar to a dark-haired thief or a mute father who was once a prince, known since birth by a golden-haired divinity who hated its every syllable. It was familiar to the black bird circling above the tree, waiting and casting a vulture-shadow upon the cringing mist.

"I want . . ." *A long, hitching breath. The anemones stirred, petals rippling under a hurricane that did not touch the fog or smoke.*

When a storm is purely internal, not a single leaf stirs. And yet, the change is there. It exists.

"I want . . . to . . ."

Blood-colored flowers waved in agony. The tree bore down ruthlessly, squeezing the very deepest truth from its inhabitant. The great cardinal-dipped secret known to magician, divinity, and fool: KNOW THYSELF.

"I want to live!" *Nat Drozdova howled, and the anemones exploded. Petals shifted, transformed as they were torn free.*

Butterflies. Hundreds, thousands of gem-bright motes whirled free, their quick-drying wings the color of fresh arterial spray. They cut through rising smoke and skimmed the water, ruffling the mist, each tiny creature liable to crushing by any passing predator.

But together, in a suffocating cloud, they were deadly in their own right. Wicked proboscises, needle-sharp, could puncture even the thickest skin; the flock could drain what it wished in bare moments.

They whirled in a cloud, then spread, winking out one by one. A faint scent of jasmine lingered, cutting through smoke. The salt-black tree bulged, a long moist rip opening in its side.

Headfirst, the Drozdova tumbled free. She landed on the cinder-shore, slick-wet, naked, and vomited a gout of golden ichor. Curled around herself, her ribs expanding, the divinity—for such she was now, incarnated and sealed, Spring in all her glory from her tumbled curls to her flexing rosy-nailed toes—sucked in the first breath of her new existence.

And she screamed as the newly born must, while a shadow swelled over her and a black bird, somewhere between a crow and a vulture but too large for either, dove.

CONSOLATION, NOT YET

"S teady," a dry, half-familiar voice said. "It's a bit of a shock, I know. Take your time."

Torn from floating, amniotic warmth, Nat bent over and retched again. Baba de Winter's hand on her arm was strong but didn't bite; the grasp was strangely comforting. The fact of Nat's own nakedness wasn't, but after . . . what she'd just done, it didn't seem very important.

At all.

A dry, translucent snake-shed curled around the tree's roots; Nat heard the brush of a million tiny wings. Power flooded her, as natural as the lung-filling she was struggling to accomplish. Baba's free hand struck a pale back between winged shoulder blades, a pitilessly accurate slap shocking a newborn into the duty it would perform until it could lay down the burden of existence.

Breathing. And with the exhale came a long cheated howl.

"*It's noooooot heeeeeeeere!*" the Drozdova screamed, the salt-black tree rocking from the force of the cry. She bent over, gold-tinged damp drying on flawless skin. "*Not here not here nooooooot heeeeeeere!*" Then, a long final scream.

"*Moooooooooooooommmmmmmmyyyyyyyyyyyyyy!*"

Baba, her unpainted mouth tight, simply held the other woman's arm. There was no solace for this grief; it could have been eased through in stages as a native divinity slowly learned what she would supplant, and how lonely it would be.

Instead, the slice was swift and absolute, cutting to the quick. A sobbing child mourned what she should have had, knowing full well what she had been granted instead.

There was power in knowledge; eventually there would even be consolation. But not quite yet.

Sobs wracked a divinity's divine daughter; Baba de Winter's slim, iron-strong arms eventually enfolded her. The beldame stroked the young woman's wildly curling honey hair, gold highlights deepening as birthfluid was brushed free. Baba even hummed a soft tune incongruous to her angular black-wrapped frame, a lullaby brought to these shores by immigrants packed in stinking holds. They fled for many reasons, from fear to the bright desire for something better, and they brought so much with them.

Yet they ached with loss, just as all expelled from the familiar do.

Elsewhere in the bayou wind whipped water both fresh and salt to a froth, bent trees before its fury, loosed gouts of cold, stinging rain. Lightning stabbed, and the ozone smell of rage accompanied deep wallowing thunder. It was the type of storm which usually appeared as winter faded, and old folks watched the sky balefully while the younger, less wise, were caught in the downpour.

Eventually the tempest passed. Baba stroked Nat's back, patted her shoulder. Her humming became words as the Drozdova quieted.

"It was never here, little one." Winter spoke softly, with none of her usual brisk displeasure. Very few would hear this tone from her, and rarely more than once. "She kept it under her own ribs; must've been uncomfortable. She planned to have you bring the arcana to the Tree and trade yourself, and I was supposed to take the damned bauble and let it happen."

A last, terrible, almost-painless shudder passed down Nat's entire body. "You knew."

"Maybe I did. Or maybe I'm just not shocked." Baba's sigh was heavy, and all the weariness in the world filled its sinuous length. "Not much surprises me anymore, at least."

"I didn't want to die." The tree was supposed to remove the shame, but Nat still *felt* it. Why?

"Of course not. You haven't even lived yet—though that's no insurance. Worse happens all the time, somewhere in the world." Clearly finished with any coddling, Baba loosened her arms. She held Nat at a distance, examining her granddaughter, and even being buck-naked on a gritty cinder-warm shore under a creepy-ass black tree, scrutinized by that dark, ruthless gaze, didn't seem half as daunting as it would have before Christmas.

Now *there* was a question. "What day is it?"

"According to the mortals here? January first, *S' Novym Godom.*" Baba nodded sharply, let go of Nat, and turned on her heel. She was back in her business suit and heels; stringy muscle moved under the flour-dry skin of her calves as she strode to the Tree. It rustled menacingly, but she paid no attention, merely bending to snatch the dry snakeskin cloaking its roots. In her hands it shrank, thickened, turned opaque; by the time she stalked back to Nat it was a fall of shimmering pale-green cloth with golden edges.

She cast it over Nat's bare shoulders and clicked her tongue, an impatient noise Coco in her atelier would have found familiar. Nat obediently lifted her arms.

The dress swarmed over her, soft material draping, hugging her curves and seamlessly sealing. Long sleeves brushed the backs of her hands; the hem hovered above Nat's ankles and the waist came to a deep point in the front. It looked like Baba's party dress, but without the fraying.

"Call it a present." Baba stepped back, rubbing her dry palms together briskly. A ruddy gleam flashed; the steely twigs holding her mass of gray hair twitched as strands sought to escape.

Then she opened her hands, and cupped in them . . .

Looks like a bloody diamond, Nurse Candy had said, and she was right. The gem glimmered, pulsing softly with its own inner rhythm; though it burned with white brilliance the light turned rubescent at its edges. Faint tinges of blue showed too, veins returning to their source; its glow spread in questing tendrils.

It was beautiful, but it was also trapped. A thorn-nest of blackened iron branches curled around the gem, and it cringed mutely from the sharp points just as any casual brush from out-side would draw blood.

"I'll teach you how to carry it." Yet again and for once, Baba de Winter's tone held no razor edge. "That's the last gift. After that, you have to go and learn."

"Okay." But Nat looked away from the thing she'd crossed the continent twice to find. *I'm barefoot in the swamp.* "How the *hell* am I getting home?"

She hadn't meant to say it aloud, but inside the Tree there was no difference between thought and speech and she hadn't quite readjusted. She looked back to catch the very last of a rueful smile disappearing from Winter's thin, corpse-livid lips.

"You have a car, Natchenka," Baba said, and lifted the bright-gleaming gem in its thorny setting. "Now listen closely; I'm only going to say this once."

WINTER NEVER LASTS

The green hills of Spring's Country now held no furious black spiderweb, no diamond lightning in the distance, no dozing sense of dread and threat. Still, Nat took mortal roads most of the way.

It was how the journey had started, after all.

There was an entrance to Elysium in Atlanta, but Nat passed through like a ghost on the artery of I-85, wending steadily northward. Charlotte grew on the horizon, approached at a steady lope, swallowed a blue car built from curves very like a '68 Mustang's, and finally receded like a wave on a shore—lake or ocean, it didn't matter. At Petersburg, with the sun falling just past its winter-day apex, Baby swung briefly off the freeway, pausing to idle in a space outside a 7-Eleven.

The mortal clerk—Harry Chastain, fifty, heavy, balding, engrossed in a car magazine—didn't even glance up when a barefoot woman in a long pale-green dress shading into gold at sleeves and hem stepped through the sliding glass doors, the electronic *someone's here* beep as familiar as his own breathing.

He did, however, shiver a minute later as the sound repeated while Nat stood in the chips aisle and looked at rows of bright packaging. An edge of sudden chill far deeper than even Baba's displeasure touched her skirt and the backs of her hands, ruffling her mass of unbound curls.

The Cold Lady looked just the same—a teased black mane

too dark for nature or dye, her generous mouth as corpse-livid as Baba's unpainted smile, the same black tank top and skinny, cord-muscled greenish shoulders. Her silver belt buckle gleamed under sickly fluorescents.

She was barefoot, too.

Linoleum was pleasantly chilly against Nat's soles. She could have opened Marisol's suitcases and found some footwear, but it seemed unimportant when you'd been vomited out of a salt-black tree. Sealed, renewed, reborn, and a complete, total failure at the one thing you'd set out to do.

Even if you'd been set up to fail—by your own damn mother, too—it stung.

"Here for me?" She stared at the corn chips. So many different flavors. Was there a god of snacks? Maybe she'd find out some-day. "Or him?" She glanced past the Cold Lady; the clerk was still engrossed in his magazine, his head bowed and the bald spot on the crown glowing.

"Just passing through." The Cold Lady examined the shelf of offerings too, tapping an unpainted finger against her pallid cheek. "Thought I'd grab a Yoo-hoo. I love that stuff."

Go figure. "My mother?" Nat had to ask. "And my . . . Leo? My father?"

Baba had already told her they were both gone, of course. *Your mother and her consort.* The soft inner sense of certainty returned the same answer.

Still, Nat couldn't quite believe it. What child could; what child ever does? The parent is the first Eternal mortals ever brush.

"On to whatever awaits." The other divinity bent nearly dou-ble, studying the shelf as if to compare prices. Maybe she was just being polite. "But you knew that."

"So there's something else? After you?" Standing in a 7-Eleven inquiring about the afterlife was probably something every di-vinity did as a matter of course. Maybe she'd even get used to it, after a while.

"That would be telling." The Cold Lady's smile didn't alter. It was, all things considered, rather gentle. "Your season's approaching. Winter never lasts."

Neither does anything else. "I'm getting used to cryptic conversations and weird occurrences." Nat glanced, almost guiltily, at the counter, but the mortal ignored them both, probably in self-defense. A cluster of broken veins showed on his nose, and he coughed slightly into a cupped, hairy fist.

"Mortal lives are just as weird, dearest." The other woman finally selected a medium-sized pack of Cool Ranch, bright plastic crinkle-cringing under her touch. "Fish don't really think about water."

"Yeah." Nat couldn't decide what she wanted. There was no nausea, no emptiness—the tree had done its job, and she might not ever feel hungry or thirsty again. How long would it be before even cravings vanished—was food just window dressing now? "Pretty sure I'll see you again soon. Someone wants to kill me." *And he's late. Three days was the agreement.*

Dmitri could find her if he wanted to. What was he waiting for?

"Is that my only reason for visiting? It seems a pity." The Cold Lady dangled the blue bag from one slim greenish-ivory hand and straightened, regarding Spring with bright, benign interest.

"Yeah, well." Nat's gaze happened on a red cylinder. She discovered she liked the thought of Pringles after all; she took the one standing just on the brink of the shelf, automatically moving its replacement soldier forward to the jump-off point. It made things easier on the stockers. "Do we ever change? Divinities, I mean."

The Cold Lady threw her head back and laughed, a merry ice-tinkle. Behind the counter the clerk shivered again as he turned a magazine page, but he didn't look up. Maybe he thought a goose had walked over his grave, or something.

Maybe one had, since *she* was here.

"Oh, Drozdova." The lady wiped at her eyes with the fingertips of her free hand. "What do you think I *am*? Or you, for that matter? Come on, let's get you something to drink, those are full of sodium. You want lemonade? Sodapop?" A good-natured grin fanned wrinkles at the corners of her dark depthless eyes; she didn't have dimples, but it was close. "Vodka?"

Booze sounded good, but Nat was driving. Did divinities get DUIs—did Friendly hand them out? It was the kind of question Dima might have answered. "Yoo-hoo sounds good. Haven't had it since I was a kid."

"Two Yoo-hoos it is." The Cold Lady brushed past, heading for the glass beverage cases in back. "Nice car, by the way."

"It was a present." The Léon-Bollée might be rotting in the yellow house's falling-apart garage. It was painful to think about; Leo had worked on it so much. All that effort wasted. "Can I ask you something?"

"I'm here, you might as well." The other woman found what she wanted, opening the case and leaning into a burst of refrigeration. Did it feel warm, to her?

"Do you have a mother?"

"I have all the mothers, Drozdova." The skinny, barefoot woman turned somber, selecting two plastic bottles. It was a wonder they didn't shatter in her icy hand. "And all the fathers. Daughters, sons, sisters, brothers, aunts, uncles, cousins—you name it."

In other words, that's a silly question. Or maybe you weren't born, but somehow made. Coalesced. Were there different Cold Ladies on different continents? Nat's own feet, resting on indifferently mopped linoleum, weren't chilled at all. She could probably run over broken glass and not feel a single scratch, though she wasn't about to test that theory yet. "I just wondered."

"I like questions. Shows you've got an open mind." Two familiar plastic bottles of oversweetened chocolate milk in her strong left hand, the bag of chips in her right, she let the cold-case door swing shut with a sharp, definite sound. "I think you'll be curious for a very long time. Let's get these paid for."

We're not going to shoplift? "Funny." Nat's cheeks felt strange;
she was smiling as well. Divine or not, at a certain point you
just had to throw up your hands and go with the absurdity of
survival. "I used to think money was the hardest thing in the
world."

"For some it is. We've got other problems." The other divinity
paused. "But I've got a minute or two more. We can stop in the
candy aisle, if you want? The little pleasures really count, and I
suspect you won't want to stop again until you get home."

"Yeah." Nat followed. "What kind of candy do you like?"

"I don't discriminate." The Cold Lady laughed again, a soft
numbing chuckle. "But right now I think we could both use
some chocolate."

✕

Winter dusk swallowed Baby's steady motion; Nat kept her
speed just above mortal, flickering through ice-cautious traffic
as if she'd been doing it all her life. The Pringles didn't last past
Chester, but she saved the Yoo-hoo. Cities clustered thicker on
this coast than amid the west's wide sprawl; Richmond came
and went, and the tingle in the air around DC told her more
than one divinity was aware of her passage.

The ferment of mortal power probably made divinities bubble
up, active as a sourdough starter. Mom had taught Nat how to
keep one alive for loaves of tangy, chewy white, but she preferred
proper black bread. It really was the only thing for soup.

Were there still servings of Leo's borscht frozen in margarine
tubs, hiding in the ancient Frigidaire? Those would last as long
as winter did, no matter what else fell down or rotted in the little
yellow house. The entire city was probably a giant freezer.

Dawn bloomed rosy over the Atlantic near Wilmington. She
was making good time; Nat cracked the bottle of chocolate milk.

It went down easy; plowed snow glistened, piled on either side of sanded, salted freeway. The top layers were melting, unseasonable sudden warmth bringing a treacherous coating of slush over deeper ice. A tiny thaw in January wasn't entirely unknown, even with the polar flow dipping southward.

Driving all night didn't make her tired. The vast soft sense of physical well-being was even deeper and eerier; mortal aches and pains had utterly vanished. She might not even have the chance to get emotionally fatigued, depending on what happened when Konets found her.

Flicking Baby between cars, dodging ahead of semis, bypassing thickened traffic with a slight mental flexing—easy, and natural as breathing. She was even taking it for granted now.

Maryland passed, a brief shot of Delaware like a tiny glass of celebratory birthday or got-a-job vodka, then over the bridge into New Jersey with the turnpike throbbing under Baby's tires. Avoiding the clot of Philadelphia to her left, she arrowed north, her bare toes pressing the accelerator and Baby's engine perking up like a migrating bird sensing the end of a long flight.

Before her mistress was quite ready, Baby took cloverleaf curves, circling to finally settle onto 440. Anticipation thrummed under Nat's breastbone, answered by the car's steady excited thrum.

She was almost home.

THE
RETURN

THE BUCK, STOPPED

To go through Staten Island without worrying about mortal traffic was a luxury she might never get used to; Nat caught herself fretting about where to park Baby and had to laugh, gripping the steering wheel so hard her knuckles were bloodless.

New York looked different when you were driving. Winter sunshine glittered sharply on ice-scalloped buildings, glowed on snow tainted with car exhaust and a million mortal exhalations, limned the puff-breaths of hurrying pedestrians with gold. Horns blared, buses heaved past, trucks rumbled. The city greeted her with a *fuck ya how ya doin, won't ask where ya been*, and Nat's eyes blurred with unshed saltwater as street corners and vistas became more and more familiar.

Finally, a few blocks from Fort Greene Park, Baby jolted aside like a leaping fish, a silvery scalegleam running down her painted sides. It wasn't quite a parking space—for one thing, her hindquarters were blocking an alley with just enough clearance for a sanitation truck to heave itself into—but she wasn't a mortal vehicle, and in any case wouldn't be there long.

Friendly might come by to write out a parking ticket. If he did, Nat might teach him a lesson or two.

She pushed the gear lever into park and stretched—rolling her head from side to side, arching her spine, pointing her toes on either side of the brake pedal. A yawn caught her by surprise.

Even a divinity could get mild stiffness from a long drive. Maybe it was merely psychological, but the end result was the same.

She could, she supposed, open up the trunk and get a pair of shoes out of Marisol's suitcases—no, Nat's suitcases now. That would mean getting out barefoot, and even a new-minted incarnation of a season might not want to waltz around Big Apple sidewalks without at least a pair of sneakers.

It wouldn't matter to the Cold Lady, and Nat had driven all this way with her toes al fresco. But she closed her eyes, concentrating, and asked politely.

The world, after all, *wanted* to obey.

When her lids drifted back up, a pair of brand-new green espadrilles sat neatly in the passenger seat. She slipped them on, watching people hurry past on the sidewalk. They didn't even glance at Baby; a meter maid happening by wouldn't see the blue car.

It was nice to be ignored, but only if you wanted to be.

She wasn't going to feel the cold, but she reached into the back seat anyway. Leo's old peacoat was there, heavy and comfortable; she patted Baby's dash and glanced habitually over her shoulder, checking traffic before opening the door.

The wind wasn't as knife-sharp as she expected. A radio blared from a bodega's open cigarette window; women hurried by with their heads down and their purses tucked hard against their sides. A man in a beret walking an Afghan hound glanced incuriously past Nat; his dog's great sad eyes lingered longer.

"I suppose you'll find somewhere to wait." She patted Baby's door, and the car purred in response. "I'll call when I need you. Keep the suitcases safe for me."

By the time she reached the end of the block, Baby was gone. Nat took a right, her stride lengthening, hands deep in the peacoat's pockets. One fingertip touched plastic; she drew the tortoiseshell sunglasses free.

Funny, she didn't remember sticking them in there. She

opened their arms, and settled the shades like a headband again. They felt right, nestled in her hair.

No mortal glanced at her; Nat's reflection in passing windows was no more or less odd than anyone else's. Brooklyn throbbed just like an engine; she crossed against the light, her heart giving a familiar, fearful, entirely mortal leap when a wine-red Buick whooshed past, its passage ruffling her skirt.

Nat thrust her hands deeper into familiar woolen warmth, a pill of shed fabric under one fingertip. Midblock, she turned hard right again, and the tiny courtyard before the Laurelgrove swallowed her.

The Christmas tree was gone from the foyer. A janitor balanced on a step stool was taking down foil letters shouting *Happy New Year,* and Nat realized the faint sour smell wasn't just hospital disinfectant but a collective citywide hangover swirling down the drains.

This city partied hard for any renewal at all. You had to admire the dedication, the belief in not just any future but the most shining version of it. Maybe that's what Jay lived on, and green-clad Daisy too.

Nat didn't have to sign in, show ID—not that she had any, Dmitri still held her backpack—or make self-deprecating jokes, gauge the expression of every nurse hurrying by in sensible shoes. She didn't have to smile apologetically at white-coated doctors, or step aside for even the lowliest orderly. The mortal world simply flowed around her, a river barely rippling past a smooth rock.

She half expected another patient to be in the familiar room. Maybe it was a gift or, more likely, a simple coincidence that it was empty. The bed was neatly made, waiting for the next inhabitant; the sealed window panted a bright sunshine square on the pink-cushioned bench underneath. The bathroom door was slightly open, white tile bleached and glowing as usual.

The only thing missing was Maria Drozdova in her silken bed

jacket, her hair neatly braided under a bright kerchief. *Have you gone yet? Have you seen Baba?*

There wasn't even the faintest hint of her mother's perfume, or the rosewater she dabbed beneath her eyes. *To keep them bright, Natchenka.* Just bleach, floor wax, the persistent reek of mortal illness, and a brassy edge of finality.

Of death.

All the times she'd been in here, Nat had never done more than glance out the window. Now she stepped close, resting the fingertips of her right hand on the sill.

The glass panes in their heavily repainted frame gazed onto what had been a mansion's garden back in the Gilded Age; in summer the nurses might wheel a patient or two out to get some sun. Now it was a forlorn, half-frozen star of wheelchair ramps set amid winter-dead shrubs in concrete containers, a leafless oak too sleepy even to shiver stretching its bare arms skyward in the southern corner.

Nat turned away, stuffing both hands back into safe pockets. They turned into fists, clenched aching-hard. She stared at the empty bed, sunshine on her shoulders granting no warmth.

I want to live.

"Mama." It was ridiculous to talk to yourself in an empty hospice room, but who cared? Maria couldn't hear her daughter now; Nat could say whatever she wanted.

Of course, had her mother ever really heard her? Nat had just been an impediment, a tool.

"*God,*" she breathed, reflexively. It was silly, even if she'd still been mortal. Who did divinities pray to? There didn't seem to be anybody; the buck stopped right at your own front door.

What was she doing here? Nat closed her eyes, but only for a moment; the sudden velvety blackness was a reminder of the crusted tree's squeezing, amniotic dark.

If you'd loved me, Mom, I might have traded myself without

*hesitating. But if you'd loved me, would you have asked me to? Would
you have done this?*

There was a step in the hallway, cat-soft with a slight metallic
tinge at the forefoot like a sharp, bright silver toe-cap on a black
leather boot. Nat ghosted to the door on slipper-soft espadrilles.
Peering out into the familiar, dingy mortal passageway, she bit
her lower lip.

Nurses at the station, their scrubs in cheerful cotton colors. A
balding male orderly pushing a cleaning cart; in the next room,
muffled voices—a doctor's tone of forced cheerfulness, a patient's hesitant replies.

The Drozdova let out a shaky breath. She glanced back at the
pristine, much-bleached bed, waiting uncomplaining for its next
occupant.

Things did change after all. Even divinities.

A few moments later, the room was empty. Not even a lingering thread of jasmine remained.

HOME AGAIN

S he could have made the bus come early, but Nat waited at the familiar stop amid a collection of oblivious mortals. The morning warmed as noon approached, slush trickling under icy carapaces. Tires grinding over sand-gritty slush made sounds like salt-crust dropping from black branches into a cinder crust; when the bus finally snort-heaved its massive bulk to temporary stasis she climbed aboard, tapping her finger once on the fare-reader. It beeped pleasantly, and the driver—a woman in a black knit cap with frost-reddened cheeks—didn't even blink, staring at traffic to gauge its flow before piloting her battleship into the stream.

Sniffles and coughs ran down the bus's length; a business-man cradled a leather attaché and half-dozed, swaying as the vehicle jolted into motion. A young curly-headed man gave his seat to a heavily pregnant Filipina woman in a flowered blue scarf, a patterned, padded plaid raincoat straining at her mid-dle. A schoolkid with a red backpack sat next to a brown-haired woman whose chin and protective closeness both suggested they were related; he stared at Nat from under his thick blond bangs, his mouth slightly open.

Nat smiled. He grinned back, one of his front teeth gone. It felt like he had a doctor's appointment. A faint golden sparkle swirled over him and his adult companion—mother, aunt? A pang went through Nat's chest.

So she could bless them, the . . . the human beings, the mortals. It was a nice surprise.

She held on to the upright, her legs remembering how to ride a bus's sway with no trouble at all. The rolling of Marie Laveaux's carriages was far more unsettling; so was the steady rhythm of Ranger's big black horse. She even preferred this to the floating speed of Dima's black car.

The familiar, no matter how painful, was often preferable to anything else.

Each stop was a port on a bumpy, heaving sea. Nat worked her way closer to the door; already, they were only two scheduled halts away from South Aurora and Harney. Which was a few blocks from her destination, sure, but she wanted to walk.

Besides, there was a faint grinding at the edge of her awareness. A heavy growl under a shining black hood, its snarling silver ornament a shape somewhere between wolf and bear.

She hopped down from the bus steps and set off at an amble, hands back in her pockets and her head down. A mortal girl would hurry, her mind already home and planning cleaning chores, watering houseplants, making sure an elderly uncle had eaten, worrying about the bills, considering want ads for sublets or roommates, wondering if she could pick up a few more hours at her first or second job.

Someone shouted. A car horn blared in reply, the song repeated *ad infinitum* over the city all day, and all night as well. Under that music lurked the carnivorous engine-sound, a gleaming black car moving shark-lazy. A dark gaze behind a clean windshield—no ice or slush-spatter daring to collect on its lens, no snow falling to clump on wipers—rested upon her back. Incense-heavy cigarette smoke floated lazily through a slightly lowered window.

No mortal car would honk at *that* black beast. It stayed hidden behind the packed mountains of snow solidifying after being scraped aside by plows; the drains underneath ran with stealthy trickles as a midday thaw worked at the edge of winter's bony grasp. Scattered salt frayed the freeze as well. After a last violent hurrah, the season of cold rest and dormancy was taking a breather. Maybe there would be another storm or two, but some invisible balance had tipped.

The days were lengthening, a globe-wobble drawing the sun closer.

Nat paused at the corner, considering the snowy waste of a half-vacant lot. The haunted house was a lot smaller than she remembered. Its boarded-up windows were no longer as baleful, and though she remembered what it was like to run past with her heart pounding and her breath whistling, she felt nothing but a strange piercing nostalgia.

The engine behind her revved slightly, a silvered boot-toe feathering the gas pedal. *I like this game,* the sound said, *but hurry up.*

She paused just long enough to make it clear she wasn't going to be rushed, then set off again. Brownstones on either side held echoes—the slap of a snowball against her back, running feet, children's voices.

Crazy Natty! Witch-girl! Freak!

And Leo's hand, huge and warm, holding hers. *Little shits,* he often muttered, balefully. *Pay no attention, Natchenka.*

Nat tasted garden dirt, mineral water from the ancient green hoses that didn't dare to leak when Maria handled them. She watched the sidewalk's familiar veins through a slop of melt and scattered rock salt, deicer pellets mixing in at intervals.

Finally, she halted. Exhaled sharply, and looked up.

The white picket fence was no longer white but rotting cream. Uprights listed crazily, gaps like punched-out teeth along its brokenback length. The gate hung listless on rusted hinges; they gave a scream as she pushed, stepping over the invisible boundary into a cold bath of yet more memory.

Don't lie, Natchenka. None of your temper. Go clean your room.

You call that finished? Don't spoil her, Leo. Don't look at me like that, little girl. Cats don't speak here.

The yellow house was indeed a ruin. The roof had caved, its sides bulged shapeless, and the garage—normally hidden around the side along with the small gate leading to the back alley lined with garbage cans—squatted like a tumor, paint scab-peeling on its sides. The fallen stone chimney was a snow-covered cairn; the front door sagged inward. She didn't even want to think about what had happened to the houseplants, and nothing in the cupboards would be usable or edible now. The frozen borscht in its margarine tubs would be safe until spring, but digging to get to it was a chancy proposition at best.

Mom's jewelry was probably in the wreckage of the upstairs, gold rings and gold hoops, but Nat felt no urge to go inside and look for it. Nor did she want to find her teddy bear, or even her ancient duct-taped laptop.

The mortal Nat Drozdova was gone. She was home, at last.

"Fuck," Nat said, softly. "I hate this place."

A sharp lighter-click, a harsh inhale. "Eh, *zaika*."

Nat turned.

Dmitri Konets stood on the other side of the ramshackle, quivering gate. His hair was freshly combed, his suit just a few shades away from the truest possible black, and his boot-toes gleamed. He pinched a cigarette filter between his right first finger and thumb, taking a short drag; his left hand held her old school backpack.

"Welcome back," he said.

ALL PAID UP

"You're late." The ground here remembered her; Nat was fairly sure that if he stepped over the gate's threshold she'd have an advantage.

Exactly what good it would do was up for debate, though.

Dima shrugged. Behind him, South Aurora went about its quiet residential midday business, taking no notice of a glossy black muscle car parked in front of what had been a little yellow house standing in proud defiance of stodgy fudge-brown neighbors. Technically, the car was across the sidewalk and a hedge of packed snow, but no mortal would notice or complain.

"Thieves, men," the gangster said. "Both unreliable. You a big girl, should know that."

Oh, she did. "Everything's unreliable."

"Some things, not so much." Of course he was contrary. It was in his nature. He stuck the cigarette into the side of his mouth and continued, squinting through rising, heavy smoke. "You could fix it, you know. Easiest thing in the world. Your ground, your power. Nice and safe."

I suppose I could. Nat shrugged. Her dress-hem moved on a warm breeze, and the fence rippled, creaking like dead dry branches under a heavy wind.

Dima lifted his left hand. He extended his arm over the gate, wincing only slightly. His suit-sleeve rippled against invisible resistance, and Nat tensed. Her backpack hung, a large ripe fruit, and when he opened his hand it landed with more of a thump than a squelch on cracked, slush-drenched flagstones.

The gangster almost-flinched once more, but he slowly pulled his hand back, his dark gaze locked with hers. The faint crimson pinpricks in his pupils swelled once, dangerously, and when he had finished the motion and shook his left arm, flicking his fingers, snow hissed into melt, a long branching lightning-line up the sidewalk.

"There," he said. "Insurance. All paid up."

Nat took a step. Another. The espadrille soles clung like they had spikes; she was in no danger of slipping. "Not quite."

"Well, you could visit Baba." He nodded, blinking against the smoke. It probably stung.

No doubt he liked it that way.

"I told her I'd find it for her." Even though she hadn't, Nat had given it the old college try. Now there was a thought—would she be able to take classes? A divinity could probably cheat on exams with ease, but it seemed counterproductive. Like Leo said, there was no substitute for hard work. "And you promised to kill me."

"Did I?" He plucked the cigarette free, flicking it aside, and his lips peeled back. His teeth snapped together twice. The heavy sound, like billiard balls on a nice clean break, sent a shiver down Nat's spine. "Better stay on that side, then, Drozdova."

Nat approached the gate, slowly, brushing past her backpack. The hum of mortal traffic in the distance faded. She halted just at the edge of safety—but that was misleading, since he could obviously reach over rotting wood and rusted hinges. He'd just made a point of doing so.

She rubbed her hands together, her palms making soft sweet sounds. *I'm only going to say this once,* Baba whispered.

It was so easy, once you knew how. A bloody star bloomed as Nat cupped her hands, iron lightly claw-pricking her skin. Nat's throat was dry—even a divinity could feel fear.

If he wanted to kill her, she'd be seeing the Cold Lady in her mother's shattered, rotting garden. No more Yoo-hoo for Nat Drozdova, and maybe another Spring would find this forlorn ruin, remake it into a snug little den.

Dmitri Konets stood stock-still. He looked down at the Dead God's Heart.

The gem responded, sensing its home even though the nasty inward-curving teeth prevented its flying free. Nat *concentrated*, closing her eyes. For once the darkness was kind; the jewel's setting gave a creaking thrill, iron singing a low distressed song as the spikes retreated one by one with aching slowness.

"Take it," Nat said, and her arms straightened. "It's yours, after all."

The gem itself sang too, a trailing, excited note.

ON HER WAY

For what seemed like forever, the thief of thieves stared at his own heart. It was just as ruddy, as brilliant, and as throbbing as he remembered; the honey-haired girl, her eyes closed, also raised her chin a little.

It would be easy for a bright, bone-handled straight razor to leave its home in his pocket, cleaving air and flesh both. She'd once seen the result of its bright deadly work, a deathless sorcerer gasp-gurgling.

Gold highlights crowned her; the tortoiseshell sunglasses nestled in a soft wavy cloud like they belonged there. The shapeless wool coat was well-loved, catkin-soft, and did its best to protect what lay underneath; her pale green, gold-edged dress flowed over shy curves. Green shoes peeked from under the hem, and only Spring would ramble in such frail footwear.

His fingers, stone-hard and feverish-hot, closed. They covered her hands, folding the gem and its barbaric setting out of sight—a shell protecting tender inner meat, a glowing seed inside fragrant pulp.

He could still squeeze, impaling her fingers on clawed iron. Golden ichor would burst free. She might even scream, changing her mind about trusting a thief.

It was very well within Dmitri's power. He had bought his freedom; he had chosen to stay in this alien country. He could choose again.

As many times as he wanted, as many times as he wished.

Tiny dots of sweat touched his forehead. His snarl was an old steppe wolf's, eyeing a dish set in the snow—tender tasty viands, to be sure, and the hand offering them just as succulent.

Iron quivered. Metal melted without heat, slithering between the touch of two divinities. Dima's fingers tightened once, and though the Drozdova did not flinch tension invaded the slim column of her neck, her graceful shoulders. She swallowed, her throat moving, and he watched the fans of her dark, golden-tipped eyelashes against her cheekbones, her lips drawing in slightly like a lost, forlorn child expecting a vicious slap.

"I told you," the thief said softly. "I make exception for you, too." His teeth glinted, and the Heart trembled like a small animal between them. Quivering invaded his pretty *devotchka*; the Drozdova's skirt made a soft sound as it moved. "Keep this for me."

Gently, *exquisitely* gently—because he did not have to be so careful, and he wanted that very clear—he pushed her hands away, back to her side of the gate.

Nat's dark eyes flew open. She stared at him; oh, he'd surprised his *kotenoka* once more. "But it's your—"

"Pfft." Dima snatched his fingers away, shaking them back into suppleness. "What am I going to do, put thing back in my chest again? Would be stupid, and I am not stupid man."

Her gaze dropped to the gem. It still pulsed, just as brilliant, just as blood-tinged. The setting, though, had changed.

Silver scales rasped; a fluid snakelike length cradled the Heart. A supple chain pooled underneath, ready for clasping lightly around a lovely throat; it would nestle against another heartbeat, hiding under a shirt or a modest dress's neckline. For all the gem's size, it now seemed lighter, ready to be worn instead of locked in a thorn-nest.

"It's beautiful." As if she'd expected it to stay ugly.

"I take it to Baba, someone just steal it again. I keep it, perhaps same thing." Dima waved away any objection she might think of. "Steal from a thief, who will care? But you, Natchenka L'vovna—if someone steal from you, *I* have a word with him, *neh*? Much better this way." Dmitri stopped, his mouth hardening. He dug in his suit jacket's breast pocket and produced the battered pack of cigarettes; this time it was blue, the writing on its back old-fashioned formal French.

"I haven't been called Natchenka in a while." Those brimming dark eyes held another question, but Dmitri Konets stepped back from the gate. He'd answered all he would today, and the inquiry died on her lips. But, because she was a woman, another objection took its place. "You could . . ."

Nat bit her lip, swallowing the rest of the sentence—*you could just take it, and be done*—when he snarled.

Dima smoothed his expression; it took more effort than he liked. "I said keep it for me, *devotchka moya*. In English, even." He tapped up a fresh cigarette. "Put it on, so I see pretty thing before I go. I drive you all the way across country, I keep *those who eat* away. You owe me that much."

She tilted her hands, letting the chain slip underneath, playing with the light caught in the gem. "I will," she said quietly. "But not because I owe anything."

"Now you talking like thief, *zaika*." There was a click; flame popped into life. Smoke burned down into his empty chest, yet another pleasant sting. "Hope for you yet."

She smiled, a soft secret curve. The chain slid around her neck. It didn't need a clasp—it melded together painlessly, and the bright gleam vanished under her dress's draped neckline. The Heart's steady throb was almost a stranger now, but that was what happened when you found a different home.

The old one receded, and you were left right where you needed to be.

"So." A god of thieves took another step back, cocked his dark head. "You repair house, make it nice and snug? Maybe I come back, have tea."

"I'm going to travel for a while." Half-surprised, as if she'd just realized it. Her fingertips tapped against scaled iron polished to silver brightness, then brushed at the lump under silken green. "But when I do come back, I'll pour you some vodka. Very cold."

He nodded, and stood for a few moments, smoking in silence. The wind was soft, a moment of deeper thaw, and tinged with jasmine. "So," he repeated. "See you."

Dima didn't wait for a farewell. He merely turned on one heel, stalked away. Plowed snow creaked and shifted; he stepped through the newly made aperture and the engine of his black car roused.

He didn't look back, for he always had business elsewhere. A heavy door slammed, his chariot dropped into gear, and tires bit the slush-heavy roadway.

※

Nat Drozdova watched a pair of angry red brake lights vanish up South Aurora, listening to the hiss of steaming snow melding with the fitful return of mortal traffic. Behind her, the ruin of the little yellow house creaked as it settled deeper, losing any last purchase on wholeness. After a short while she bent, scooping up her backpack. It settled on her shoulder, a welcome weight.

Another engine-sound approached. This one had a much sweeter purr; Nat didn't look back at the dead garden or fallen walls. Still, as she closed the resisting, groaning garden gate her hand shook just a little. The necklace, warm against her breast-bone, pulsed with a slow even rhythm.

Maybe even thieves were reliable, in their own way.

Nat whistled, a low melodious note. It had barely left her lips before a slew of slush pushed to either side from Baby's gleaming tires. The blue car halted, settled into an idle, and Nat used Dima's passage burned through the snowplow mountains, her sandals balancing on soggy slickness. She dropped onto the now-familiar leather of the driver's seat with a sigh, her backpack curling up on the passenger side like a tired dog.

The Drozdova resisted the urge to look at the wrecked house again. Maybe when the real thaw came she'd want to return, but she doubted it. Instead, she reached for the radio knob, turned it with a click. Joe Cocker was singing bye-bye to a blackbird. Both Mama and Leo had liked that song.

Natchenka L'vovna. So Dima knew, too. Maybe one day she'd ask him how.

Nat curled her hands around the steering wheel. She'd wondered, for almost all her mortal life, what it would be like to really, truly leave.

It was time to find out. Baby's gearshift clicked, the orange bar settling over a capital *D*, and she pulled away from the curb. Slush made a low sweet sound; a place no longer home receded. At the end of the block, Baby turned left, and even the rearview was clear of the past.

A deeper gold crept into sunshine; the days were lengthening even though nights still froze solid. No, winter wasn't over, not yet.

)(

But Spring was on her way.

ACKNOWLEDGMENTS

Thanks are due first and foremost to Devi Pillai and Lucienne Diver, without whom these books would literally not be; much gratitude is likewise due to Claire Eddy and Sanaa Ali-Virani for their heroic patience and diligence through a worldwide pandemic and other assorted nonsense. Writing is a lonely job, but it's made easier when there are good people standing guard at the cave mouth.

A resounding thank you goes to my children, to my beloved Bailey, and to Mel Sanders and Skyla Dawn Cameron, fellow miners at the word-veins. A portion must also be measured out to Nikolai Petrovich, who always answers my disturbing, outlandish questions with calm good temper.

Last but never, ever least, I thank you, my dear Reader. Let me repay your kindness in the way we both like best, by telling you yet another story. . . .

ABOUT THE AUTHOR

LILITH SAINTCROW was born in New Mexico, fell in love with writing during second grade, and has continued obsessively ever since. She currently resides in the rainy Pacific Northwest with her children, dogs, cat, and a library for wayward texts.

lilithsaintcrow.com
Twitter: @lilithsaintcrow